FALSELY BRANDED A THIEF, CASH TURNS RENEGADE TO HELP THE CHEYENNES

A fugitive from pioneer "justice," Cash sides with the Indians, who test him time and again in battles against his own people. For the Cheyennes are never quite sure that Cash, a white man, can be trusted.

Then the day comes when Cash has an opportunity to prove himself to the Indians once and for all—by offering his life for that of Broken Arrow, the greatest Cheyenne warrior of all time. Will Cash risk death to regain his honor?

THE RESCUE OF BROKEN ARROW

by Max Brand

writing as Evan Evans

WARNER

®

PAPERBACK LIBRARY
NEW YORK

WARNER PAPERBACK LIBRARY EDITION

First Printing: May, 1967
Second Printing: April, 1969
Third Printing: March, 1973

This Warner Paperback Library Edition is published by arrangement with Harper & Row, Publishers, Inc.

Cover illustration by Charles White

Warner Paperback Library is a division of Warner Books, Inc., 315 Park Avenue South, New York, N.Y. 10010.

CHAPTER I

WHEN the council of the caravan was called around the central campfire, it was like a meeting of barbarians. Unshaven faces like these must have filled the hordes that pushed from Russia and the North through the German forests, and fought the Romans along the Rhine and the Danube; and the same brown skins and the same bright eyes must have moved in those armies. Like them, too, these people moved with cattle and horses, and had their children with them, often, in their covered wagons.

They had finished their cookery over the fire that evening, and now they stood around, or sat, with children fringing the inside of the group, very keen to enjoy the trouble, as children always are. There were fifty men in the party, and except for a few professional scouts, the rest were on the whole well-to-do adventurers starting for California to find gold, or men with families determined to make a new start in a new land. Although the deerskins of the scouts and the hairy faces of the men gave a wild look to the party, there was nothing cheap or ragged about them. They were well clothed. Their bodies were plumped with good food. And they showed all the effects of a well-organized leadership.

Their leader now occupied the attention of all eyes. The others eased back a little from him on both sides, as though they did not wish to rub shoulders with his eminence. He was a little more careful in his dress than the others, looking very much like a rich Louisiana planter about to take a ride. That effect was heightened by the fact that he carried a riding whip in his hand, and that the beautiful head of his horse, Clonmel, rose behind him, and made a very fine background for a very fine man.

He wore a short beard, neatly trimmed, and instead of shaving, he habitually clipped his face very close, leaving the sideburns long, and trimmed the mustaches so that they jutted out to stiff little points on either side of his mouth. A good brown leather belt around his hips supported one of the Colt's revolvers, army style, in a handsome holster, and gave a military touch to his appearance. This was natural, for Fitzroy Melville was not only the elected "captain" of the caravan, but he had also been a full-fledged captain in the regular Army of the United States. To those who did not know, he seemed a little bit of a dude; but in truth he was an experienced and practical Indian fighter and plains' campaigner who already had guided three parties across the green or brown sea of the prairies. He knew both the central and the southern routes, which doubled his value. For the rest, he was a big fellow, with heavy shoulders and the look of one who could trust himself in any emergency.

He began to speak with care, a little heavily, like a man who wishes to show that he has been well educated and has not forgotten good English.

He said: "Ladies and gentlemen of our party," which politely distinguished them from two or three robed forms that stood on the outskirts, Indian hangers-on or spies upon the caravan who were tolerated because of their enormous value in bringing in fresh meat every day, "—and because we have been on the trail so long, I think I may add, friends! —we have covered several hundred miles, now, without any serious misadventure, and without, I hope, too much fatigue. . . ."

He made a little pause on a rising note which was so irresistible that there was a general murmur of agreement, and several fairly loud voices could be heard to say, "Better than we ever expected it to be!" and "Thanks to you, captain!" and "We've been well led, that's the answer!"

The captain had cleared his throat softly to allow time for these remarks, which caused a general warmth of good feeling and mutual trust and belief in him to spread through the circle.

Without taking any particular notice of the applause, Melville allowed his eyes to touch lightly and brightly on the faces of those who had applauded him most vigorously, and then he went on:

"But in every company of this size there is sure to be some disagreeable adventure, or encounter, or faulty member who falls below the average!"

He paused again, then went on solemnly: "We are met here this evening for the purpose of considering one of these unlucky elements in our own organization, a man I have repeatedly warned to take better care of his time and the manner in which he spends it, a man who repeatedly has broken the laws of our band, which were first voted upon and signed by every male member of the caravan. Cashel, stand up!"

As he said this, there was a little rustle as people turned, and all eyes dropped with a sudden force and fixity upon Cashel, who sat on the opposite rim of the fire-lit circle.

He was young—not more than twenty-one, certainly. And now as he lifted his head, his red hair flamed like a toss of fire, and his Irish blue eyes gleamed also. He did not shrink from the steady regard of the company, hostile though it

6

was. His short nose wrinkled with scorn of them, and his broad chin jutted out a little to meet their enmity.

"I'm easier sitting," said Cashel.

"Stand up!" commanded the captain again, striking his riding breeches lightly with his whip.

"I heard you," said Cashel, "but it's warmer sitting."

It upset Melville to be withstood in the very beginning like this. But he was too wise to start with violence, so he merely made a sufficient pause to allow everyone to observe the rank insubordination of this youth, and then he went on, in a different tone, with his heavy bantering.

"When we were gathered together and about to set out," said the captain, "we just lacked one member to make up what I considered a full complement and a perfect size for such an expedition—that is, fifty men capable of bearing arms, and well furnished for the trip. At this juncture, a young man came to me and said that he had about completed his preparations and that he would like to travel with us. He showed me, in the dusk of the day, a wagon with six mules, and the interior of the wagon seemed to carry a good many boxes and represented a considerable weight. I even cautioned him not to carry more than two thousand pounds, because over rough going that would tax the strength of his animals badly enough. I want to point out to you that although he was admitted to our party through my negligence at the last moment, a thing for which I can never severely enough blame myself . . ."

Here he cleared his throat again, and the stoppage was naturally used for a heavy chorus to declare that the captain was quite free from blame, while a volley of gloomy glances of condemnation were fired at young Cashel.

"Although it was due to my negligence," continued the captain, "still I did put him through some sort of an examination. I particularly tried him with both revolver and rifle, and, as you all have learned from the experience of your own eyes, I found him to be an expert with both. There are shooting galleries in New York," he added in explanation, "and the gangsters there have made the streets of the city more dangerous than the prairies, infested as these are by wild Indians!"

He frowned, but felt that he had made a good point, and was willing to let the others contemplate it.

"This young man gave me an odd name, which he said was his own."

It seemed that the name of Cashel had been a thorn in the boy's side before this, for now he lifted his head with a little alert cant to one side, very like that of a dog, inquiring, and inquiring for trouble.

"His name," said the captain, letting a malicious smile glitter in his eyes, "is something that I'm still not sure of. But it is something like 'Band-on-Sure-Cash,' and it has since appeared that sure cash is what he actually is looking for!"

Cashel stood up. He was rather under than over the average size, and he was not at all extraordinary in any way; yet something about the bright red of his hair, or the blue, vivid eyes, or perhaps a peculiar energy that shone out from him made him seem to be stepping away from the people about him, like a figure in the lighted foreground of a painting.

"My name's better," said he, "than any horse-stealing Melville ever owned!"

The captain scorned to notice this personal attack and continued. "Mr. Sure Cash assured me that his outfit was complete, or nearly so, and that he would finish it in every detail by buying the extras of others in the caravan, and after I had seen him hit the bull's eye six times in six shots, I was willing . . ."

"Cash is not my name!" shouted Cashel, "and you well know it! There's not a man here has a better name than I have, or one that's half as good. The Bandon and the Suir are two of the finest rivers that ever ran, and where's the fool in the world who never heard of Cashel Rock, and the tower and the chapel, and the church on the top of it? Bandon Suir Cashel is the name that I gave you, and every blessed name of the three is pure Irish, I thank God, and no Melville had anything to do with the . . ."

He was not stopped, but drowned out by a general voice of rebuke that continued until he had finished speaking. It was true that though he spoke of Ireland, his accent was not Irish; but nevertheless he appeared to speak as a foreigner, and those were days of violent nationalism.

The captain, waiting for the interruption to pass over, now continued: "The outfit of Cashel was incomplete, as I've mentioned, and I foolishly took his word for his performances. He was admitted, had the articles read to him, and he duly signed them with the name of B. S. Cashel, or Cash-all."

Even this feeble joke brought a loud laugh from the listeners, and turned the boy crimson with anger again.

The captain continued: "The first awakening came the next morning, when I saw that the six mules, which had appeared fair enough in the dusk of the day, were by sunlight a miserable collection of scarecrows. They looked old, broken down, and crippled. But the boy assured me that with such care as he knew how to give them, they soon would be fat and strong again. They were too recently in from the trail,

8

and that was the only trouble with them! To me, they looked more like gifts than mules, but it was the beginning of the journey, and I was so well pleased with the rest of the party that I hated to send back the youngster. I trusted too much to his word.

"And he actually kept those poor, dying creatures going for a week, and then one dropped in its harness, and a second went totally lame, all in a single day. Shortly afterward, another broke down and had to be abandoned, and a fourth sickened and likewise fell in the harness. Two mules remained out of the six, but both were incapable of pulling their own weight, and they were traded off to an Indian the next day.

"It was then our duty, according to the terms of the agreement, to shift the goods of our unlucky companion into our other wagons, and pull them through for him, no matter at what inconvenience to ourselves.

"Rather than do this, I consulted with some of the members of the party, and they pointed out several things to me: That it was true that Cashel now had a full equipment, from shirts and socks and boots to medicine chest and soap and thread, and that by slow degrees he had acquired extra coats and hats, and all that a man needed for the journey, but that a good many of these things were hardly suited to his size, and that although he declared that he had bought these articles, no man was ready to say that he had received a penny of cash from Cash-all, and that nearly everyone in the caravan had missed a good many articles. It looked as though the clever Mr. Cash-all had 'borrowed' a little from everyone in turn, and then had put the heap together. In view of these considerations, I talked to him, and told him that we offered him a riding horse and some compensation for his goods, though the wagon was so broken down and crazy that it would have been foolish to offer a price for it, even to a man named after two rivers and a rock in dear old Ireland!"

There was another laugh.

Cashel, enduring the recital of his supposed misdoings, bore every eye with wonderful effrontery.

"We offered the horse and some money to Cashel on consideration that he would leave us and return to the starting point, or go wherever he pleased, so long as we were freed of his company. He refused, and claimed the privilege of the articles which we all had signed.

"We therefore gave way to him. We put up with grievances which we could not actually prove, such as the suspected thefts, and we continued with him in our company until this evening when, as I think most of you know, he won so regularly at a dice game with young Mr. Chisholm, yonder, that Chisholm came to me and told me he thought there was something wrong with the dice that Cashel used."

"The cur!" said Cashel. "He wouldn't say it to my face!"

Young Chisholm, losing a good deal of color, drew back into the rim of the circle away from the furious eye of the Irish boy.

"I went to Cashel and proposed a few passes with the dice. He agreed, hungrily. And when the dice came into my hands, I examined them and was certain that they were weighted. I split one of them up, and actually found the lead inside! This evidence I laid before a number of our leading members, and they agreed with me that we must hold this meeting to-night and that I should pass such a sentence on the offender as I saw fit. I am going to ask you to vote on this proposal. Those in favor of vesting me with authority to punish Mr. Cashel as I see fit will raise their hands."

Upward flashed hands all around.

"Those contrary minded?" said the captain, with a politely inquisitive smile.

Not a hand was raised, and young Cashel ran his bright eye slowly around the circle, noting down faces with a patient malignity as though he would forget none of these.

The captain now turned back to the culprit, and there was an undoubtable satisfaction in his face.

"Cashel," said he, "it becomes my duty to pronounce a judgment on you, according to my position in this caravan, and also by the explicit vote of the party, which has just been taken. Taking into consideration everything that has passed, I feel convinced that you are not a worthy member of the company, that you are a sneak thief now, and might be a highway robber under better circumstances; that your skill with weapons was patiently acquired not to shoot game or to defend yourself, but to hunt down your fellow men like beasts, as proved by your attitude in every quarrel, when you snatch out a gun. Furthermore, I believe that you began this expedition unprepared with necessities, and that you have equipped yourself with them by theft along the way—and certainly there is nothing more detestable than to steal from one's companions on the march! You have fought with the young men and insulted your elders, always relying on your efficiency with weapons and never willingly meeting another man in honest fight, with bare fists. Altogether, Mr. Cashel, you are the least agreeable and valuable man I have ever had joined to me in such an expedition, and I can freely say, one of the lowest and most unworthy men I have ever encountered."

He paused. The severity of his denunciation made the others stare, but they nodded in gloomy assent to everything that had been said. The guilty man, glaring about him, said not a word in reply, but his upper lip twisted back from his teeth in an expression of animal-like hatred and fury.

"Still," went on the captain, "I don't wish to be too harsh. I therefore give you a choice of punishments. One is to leave this company on the back of a saddle animal, that will be provided for you, together with food, weapons, and ammunition. The other is to allow yourself to be tied to a wagon wheel and have a whip stroke laid on your back by every man in the company!"

CHAPTER II

IN THOSE days, there still were public floggings in many of the states, and the discipline of Negro slaves kept the whip in practice everywhere through the South, and in mind through the North as well.

Still, it was a bitter choice for a proud man to make. There seemed less pride in Cashel, however, than a sort of foxlike cunning. He made one last survey of the faces about him, and then he said, wisely without attempting to appeal from the judgment:

"I'll take tonight to think the thing over, captain."

The captain frowned, but though he suspected something wrong, he was not able to say what it might be.

"That's a fair proposal," said he. "But in that case, we'll have to secure you, Cashel, until you've endured the punishment. Let me give you one bit of advice. It might be for the comfort of the party to be rid of you; but I hardly advise you to take the alternative of riding out alone into this empty country. Tucker and Crockett, will you get the irons out of my lead wagon and put them in Cashel's?"

It was done, accordingly.

They brought the clumsy, heavy handcuffs and fastened them over Cashel's wrists. A chain ran from these to other manacles about his ankles, and he was fastened to the huge rear wheel of the captain's wagon. The other wagons stood in a wide circle, ready for defense, with the cattle and the draft animals, however, permitted to graze outside the little fort, since sign of Indians had not been seen for several days. Two herdsmen watched the livestock, nevertheless, keeping them close at hand, and three others stood guard, to be relieved by two other watches during the night, while the caravaners turned in to sleep.

Other than the guards, the last man up was the captain, who went the rounds and saw that everything was in good

11

order. Coming back, he paused with his horse—which was too valuable to be allowed outside the girdle of the wagons—beside the prisoner fastened to his wagon wheel. A blanket had been put on the ground, and Cashel lay on it in seeming comfort, with his face turned up to the stars.

As far as the captain could make out, his eyes were closed, and for a time Melville watched him curiously, with an odd mixture of emotions. Every mess in the caravan had been cleared up by the accurate rifle of this natural young hunter, but aside from that talent, he had been the source of more trouble than any one man who ever journeyed in a Melville march, in the army or out of it. He had been a man apart from the beginning. And his attitude when hunting for game on the prairie was exactly like his attitude when mixing with his fellows in the camp. He had been, from the first, a beast of prey, taking where he could, and never held back by any sense of fellowship. Eager for spoils and greedily retaining them all, sharp-tongued, inviting no confidences and giving none, he had been hated with a growing passion all the days of the march, and there was not a man in the company that would not gladly have thrust Cashel out into the wilderness, or else laid on the whiplash with a heavy hand.

Then, as Melville was about to move on, Cashel's voice spoke to him from the ground:

"A good night for stars, captain," said he.

"Ay," said Melville, surprised by this greeting, which was totally impersonal in tone, untouched by venom or by pleading. "A good night for stars, Cashel."

"I was thinking, just now, captain, how they'd prove that anything I have was stolen from them."

"Proofs are hard," said the captain. "When one man thinks that your coat is at least first cousin to a coat that used to belong to him, he might be mistaken, but when another thinks that he recognizes a lariat that you're using, and a third man believes he bought the boots which are obviously too big for you, and a fourth feels certain that he once owned a certain red flannel shirt because of an ink spot on the cuff, then it begins to be very hard on you, Cashel."

"No proofs!" insisted Cashel.

"You can't expect the shirt and the boots to hear the voice of the master and come to him, though," said the captain mildly, amused by the working of the boy's mind.

"You'd believe them if they did?" asked Cashel.

The captain laughed, softly, because he did not wish to rouse any of the sleepers nearby.

"Well," said Cashel, "I asked because there's one good thing about you, and that's the horse you ride. A good Irish horse with a good Irish name."

"Yes," said the captain. "He's an Irish thoroughbred, and Clonmel is an Irish name, as well."

"Now, you own that horse, don't you?"

"I do," said the captain.

"Will he come when you call him?"

"Usually, yes!"

"Try him now!"

The captain stepped back.

"Come here, Clonmel," said he. "Come here, old fellow!"

The stallion had been grazing the shortened grass near by, but now he lifted his fine head and came straight for Melville, until Cashel whistled, soft and short, like the single note of a bird. At that, the dark chestnut swerved, and started toward the boy. In vain, the captain called again and again, but the stallion came straight on, and sniffed affectionately at the face of the prisoner.

"I guess it's my horse?" asked Cashel.

Melville drew the stallion back, as though it had been contaminated.

"What have you been doing to him?" he asked. "Feeding him?"

"Not enough to keep a cat," said Cashel. "I've been talking to him, and he liked the sound of an Irish voice. Goodnight, Melville!"

He turned a little on his side, presenting his back to the captain, and the latter, after hesitating for a moment, tied up the stallion, threw down a feed of dried grass mixed with grain for him, unsaddled him, and climbed up into his lead wagon to go to bed.

Bandon Suir Cashel lay still; he even snored in the profundity of sleep until the moon walked over the rim of the wagon top and shone in his face.

Then he wakened.

Folding his thumbs into the palms of his hands, he drew them easily out of the manacles, and then sitting up, he took a flat bit of watch spring from his packet and worked it into the keyslot of the leg irons. They gave way; he pulled their stiff jaws open and stood up a free man in the shade of the moon, close to the wagon.

Next he pulled off his boots and glided in over the tailboard of the captain's wagon.

It was very dark inside, but he knew exactly what he wanted, and where it could be found. There was hardly a wagon interior in that entire caravan that he did not know by heart, and this one above all, for the captain loved good equipment, from boots to guns, and always had the best. What Cashel wanted above all was a fine new Colt's repeating rifle, a weapon hardly yet known on the plains, and dearer

13

to the boy's heart than a model of it made of one entire diamond. He found the gun hanging in a soft chamois case —so was it prized and cared for by the captain! And as he took it down, he heard the captain stir, and then sit up.

Noiselessly Cashel drew his knife, and slunk back against the side of the wagon. He could make out the very dim outline of Captain Melville through the shadows, but the captain, with a little muttering of impatience at his own folly, immediately lay down again and sighed as he composed himself for sleep.

The necessity of murder taken off his hands, Cashel remained where he was, crouching there with a wonderful patience until his ear assured him that the captain was really sound asleep.

Then he continued his explorations.

He got a case of three fine hunting knifes, two good Colt's army revolvers, and a heavy bag of ammunition for these weapons.

He could have taken much more, but for his purposes he did not want a heavy pack.

Then he crouched again in the darkness and considered, but already he had taken long forethought in considering his needs, as he lay in the irons beside the wagon wheel. No, there was nothing in the world that he particularly wanted, other than those weapons and the ammunition for the guns, together with as fine a horse as he could get.

So he climbed down from the wagon and turned his attention toward the stallion, Clonmel.

CHAPTER III

CLONMEL, like a good horse, had finished his food quickly and now he was flat on the ground, sleeping as soundly as any tired man. Cashel took the captain's own saddle over his arm, but before rousing the horse, he looked about the compound.

The silence of the place was wonderful. It was deathlike, and Cashel would not have cared greatly if death did come down on every living soul in that place, before the morning. He would have been glad if an Indian rush had swallowed it, once he had the sleek, deep barrel of Clonmel between his legs. Yet there was a wonderful peace and beauty about the scene.

He told himself that it was the swinging line of the humpbacked wagons against the moon-brightened sky, but he knew in his heart that this was not true, but that the peace here was that thing which he had seen and wondered at in others, and never had found in himself. He was, as the captain had suggested, a gangster. And though New York was large and his own gang was powerful, the stench of the boy's life had been too great for the gang to conceal or the city to leave unnoticed. The best his friends could do for him was to send him away with money in his wallet and a pair of good guns for emergencies. So he had traveled light and fast, but hardly fast enough.

He had started north, and they almost caught him in Burlington. He dodged south and barely twisted out of their fingertips in Baltimore. He fled west, and they hunted him in Pittsburg, and almost had him again on a river steamer going down the Ohio. He could not swim a stroke, but he feared the river less than the law, and he was right.

He dived overboard through a porthole, and after nearly drowning, he got his hands on a bit of driftwood, sufficiently buoyant to keep his chin above the water. So he had paddled to the shore.

That was the last escape, but still the fear of the law was in him. Or, rather, hardly the fear of the law so much as the fear of man.

In his own Manhattan, he could find his own kind, and there alone. Among the thugs and the cardsharpers, the gunmen and the gangsters, the counterfeiters, drug peddlers, and all the list of night lovers, he could find convenient associates, and people he understood.

They were not friends, of course, but they were amusing associates. They talked well, speaking of other people's exploits, but making themselves the heroes, and smiling coldly as they talked of broken banks, and dead men, and such small deer. They were not friends, but they were kin. Their interests were his interests. Their pride was his pride, and it was the interest and the pride of the jungle beast.

He had had one great day in his life, and that was when the great Forrest Morgan himself called for him, and the boy went to him over the tops of roofs, and stood on Forrest Morgan's softest rug in Forrest Morgan's most private office and heard himself called the most valuable man in the whole outfit. The outfit was the "gang," in which Cashel and his kind banded together, not in love but for mutual support in crime.

But so very great had grown the deeds of Cashel that even Forrest Morgan could not protect him, nor could the wide mantle of the gang be thrown over his shoulders. So many compliments had been paid to him—and he had been foisted out into the wilderness like a beast. This was the only point on which he was blind. He could only think of New York as a great and desirable kingdom for which he yearned in his heart, and he would have given blood out of his body to return to it and move once more among its shadows. That was the goal toward which he moved, though he had sense enough to know that he could not attempt such a return until a good deal of time had flowed backward beneath his feet.

New York was his country, because in it were all the things that he prized. There he had a value, while in the rest of the world he must pass as a counterfeit coin. In New York he could make demands. In New York he was so prized that twenty men, yes, or fifty, would be set in motion for his sake! And he knew as much of his city as a jungle beast knows of his jungle—he knew the recesses that were most dark, the bogs, the marshes of society, the coverts that were most deep and the ways that were most entangled—but never the tops of things, where the sun shone freely and the world was open to the day.

Yet for all his knowledge of the great city and his love of it, he was amazed to find that he never had found there the thing that this prairie caravan offered to him. The subdued throb of life had never been out of his ears, or the steady pulse of action. But now time went past his face on viewless feet, and it became worth while to wonder where it flowed. Doubts now entered his mind for the first time. For the first time he was half convinced that there might exist honor, decency, faith, love, and truth among men, because here this circle of life was sleeping, and two or three tired men kept their eyes vigilantly open to guard against dangers.

This made on the boy such an impression that he was on the verge of returning to the wagon, waking the captain, restoring the stolen things to him, and confessing all that he had intended to do. He grew hot with the generous resolution. It was like a great sacrifice, and sacrifices always are temptations to truly saintly or boyish spirits. And, beginning in this manner, submitting to the shame and the sorrow of the lashes the next day, enduring the martyrdom of continuing with the travelers after his disgrace, perhaps he would find a way to do some great thing that would strike the hearts of his companions and make them suddenly look up to him almost as they looked up to Captain Melville.

So that way to honor among his fellows opened before young Cashel as one last gleam of sunset parts the horizon mist and gives to the sailor the loom of an unknown land.

The light faded from his mind at once, and in an instant the purpose he had touched in his thoughts became utterly abhorrent to him as though it had been an impulse of madness.

He saddled Clonmel with the captain's own saddle, and

fitted the bridle deliberately over his head, feeling an odd pleasure in the touch of his hand upon the soft muzzle; for now Clonmel was his own! With the easy assurance of the dyed-in-the-wool thief, he felt a full sense of ownership and possession, as much as a bill of sale could have given an honest man. He was delighted to see the great horse part his teeth readily to receive the bit, and still he lingered in peril to pull out carefully the forelock beneath the brow band.

He knew the whole story of Clonmel, of the races he had run, of the horses he had beaten, of his wisdom in paddock and field, of the imperial line of his ancestors, and of the golden dream of Captain Melville to go far west with this king among horses and there establish a breed without a peer. For all of these reasons Clonmel was precious to the thief, and doubly dear because in stealing him he would be breaking the captain's heart.

With this he now swung himself lightly up into the saddle, and for the first time felt the horse beneath him.

"Who's there?" called an abrupt, and yet lowered voice. "Is that you, captain? I could tell Clonmel in a dark room, I think!"

The thief waved his hand, and the guard, who had stepped inside the wagon circle, moved straight on across it. That left the way open, and Cashel rode unhailed and untroubled out from the compound and into the level dusk of the prairie.

CHAPTER IV

HE DID not make haste because he had a sublime confidence that Clonmel could outrun the buzzards in the sky in case of need. But being willing to put a good distance between himself and the compound, he kept Clonmel at a steady jog that ate up the distance faster than the lope of a wolf.

For two or three hours he maintained a pace that was fairly steady, not the easiest pace in the world, but one that he had heard the experienced riders say a horse could maintain longer than a gallop by far, simply because two feet were always on the ground. He was by no means at home in the saddle but after being racked for the many days of the march by the cheapest saddle mules to be had in the entire train, to sit on the back of Clonmel was like stepping into a boat and flowing down a river.

He estimated that he had put ten miles between himself and the caravan when at last he decided to stop and camp for the night. So he dismounted, unsaddled, and hobbled the stallion, and rolled himself in a blanket for sleep.

He waited for that sleep quietly, contentedly, knowing that it would come, since he had the virtuous sense of a man who has done his duty. He had slipped his bonds, crushed Captain Melville, the cool and impeccable, and escaped from the hands of the honest fools who formed the caravan. He was content. All hands were still against him, but this was as it should be until at last he should return to his own country and walk again in the dark alleys of the land he loved.

He was not afraid. Only the sweep of the great horizon startled him a little. It always did, and made him feel as though he were being held up on the palm of a great, dark hand to be quietly looked into by the arching stars. But he was not afraid.

There was a logical power in the mind of the boy that made him free from the usual terrors of lonely men. Most people think of starvation, lingering death, or the swifter horrors of a death by thirst when they are cut off from their fellows and dropped alone in an unknown wilderness, but these fears did not trouble Cashel. To be freed from the presence of his peers was a relief to him, as a wolf is relieved when it is no longer surrounded by dogs. And as for dread of starvation, he never had had that as a boy, walking hungry in the streets of New York. For he could tell himself that all the houses around him were filled with people who ate and drank and had money in their pockets. Therefore, he had only to find a way of opening doors or windows in order to come at their stores. In this way he had learned young to supply his wants. And now as he sipped from the saddle canteen, which the careful captain always kept filled, he told himself that deer, antelope, buffaloes must be grazing on the rich and tender grass of the plains; they were his food. They must not only eat but also drink, and where they drank he would drink also. So he felt at home, and presently his eyes closed and he slept.

When he wakened it was not yet day, but the verge of day was on him. It did not make the heavens brighter, but the earth appeared more black, and he saw the horizon line as a dark, soft undulation far away. It was not the coming of the day that had made him rouse, but a peculiar sound; hardly a sound either, but rather like a deep vibration of the earth the pulse of which had disturbed him.

With the dizzy brain of one hardly yet recovered from sleep, he wondered what this quivering could be. An earthquake, he thought, or perhaps a wind far away—for there was just such a suggestion of moaning about this noise as the wind might have made. He had heard of tornadoes and other freaks of the storm in this part of the world.

His first care, in any case, was for the stallion. But he

18

could not see Clonmel in the half-light. It was only after he had stood up that he made out the horse.

Clonmel was two hillocks away—that far he had industriously traveled with his hobbles in his effort to find the tenderest grass. Now he was coming back as fast as he could, and the boy could see the pitching of the stallion's head as he labored with a short and hitching gallop to get on.

If Clonmel was frightened, then he could be sure that there was a real cause for fear, and it happened that he now saw something moving to the north. He saw it with some difficulty, for it was more or less like the mere spreading of a cloud shadow, sliding out thicker and closer over the ground. Almost at the same time the failing wind sprang up, sweeping strongly toward him out of the north.

Instantly the deep and vibrating murmur came to him as a roar, as though that spreading shadow were actually the breaking front of a huge tidal wave.

Young Cashel gripped his Colt's rifle with amazement and with a rare fear. He turned to run toward his horse, but then he saw that the black flood was bearing down with such uncanny speed that it would surely overwhelm him before he could reach the wings of Clonmel to carry him safely away.

And now he began to be able to see the onrushing mass by its own light, as it were, and make out in it the rise and fall of bulky forms, a boom, and a clattering of sound, and then the gleam of eyes—or was it the tossing of a myriad of short horns? For he saw them clearly, at last—a vast, living wall, a tidal wave indeed, and composed of the uncounted bodies of stampeding buffaloes.

Young Cashel knew that he was not better than a dead man, but even then he could not help turning a little to glance over his shoulder toward his latest theft.

The stallion no longer tried to accomplish the impossible and get to his new master, but turning his back on the rush of the bison, he was trying to plunge away, but was held down and back by the restraint of the hobbles.

That portion of the great herd that was advancing toward Clonmel seemed to be the center, at least it was thrusting forward with greater speed than the wing that extended toward the position of Cashel, and a wild shout burst from the lips of the thief as he saw the tossing horns of the cattle sweep up on Clonmel's haunches.

A similar battle front was rolling down on himself, but he could not withdraw his fascinated eyes from the horse, and he could not help feeling the passage of the ten thousand stamping hoofs over the tender body of the thoroughbred. So all the history and the greatness of Clonmel would be stamped in crimson into the prairie grass and he would be forgotten. . . .

No, in a mightier effort than he had made before, the great horse snapped the hobbles, and instantly he was away before the buffaloes like a bird from a leash. They could no more overtake him than they could a hawk loosed into the air.

So young Cashel turned back to face his own death.

The buffaloes had lurched nearer than he had guessed they could in such a small instant of time, for they ran up out of the dark of the plain like combers of the Horn that give their shoulder to the ship almost before they are seen washing out the stars overhead.

He hardly saw them, so great was the roaring noise they made. It was filled with squealing and with booming bellowing, and with the rattle of horns and the clicking of huge divided hoofs as they snapped back together when feet were lifted from the earth. But most of all, it was the sheer weight of hoofs that made the sound, turning the earth into a hollow drum by their might. He felt his senses stunned more than they would have been by the sea roar of storm waves against steep rocks. It would have been easy to surrender passively then, and let death go trampling over him, numb as he was by this prodigy. For still he could hardly believe that these were animals and not an earth wave thrown against him.

Then that faint light which he had thought he saw along the front of the advancing army grew more palpable. It consisted of the gleaming of wet nostrils, the faint shine of a hundred thousand polished horns, the flashing of bright eyes. It was undoubtedly mirror enough to give back some of the light of the dawn, and enough to show Cashel that death was rolling into his face.

He gave one thought backward, toward the stallion, wondering with the lightning apprehension of the mind if the great horse would wander off to become a king in a wild herd, and if his chestnut sons and daughters might not found a new and glorious herd upon the plains.

That was his last thought except for himself. They were now so close that it seemed to Cashel he could see individual pairs of eyes fixed on him, and that he could pick out a vengeful shake in the horns just before him.

He had not tried to fire at any distance because he knew that if he had the slightest chance of splitting the herd, it would only be by dropping them close at hand with the most accurate shots. He knew enough of plains hunting already to be sure that a buffalo head-on is the most difficult of targets to hit in the bulls eye. But that was his one chance.

He found himself deciding on it, and taking it with perfect

calm. And his thought went back to a certain blind alley in Baltimore where he had almost been trapped, and how he had set his back against it and turned to face the rush of three men.

They had charged home on him, but out of the fighting tangle he had been able to writhe away unhurt and take to his heels again, leaving two hospital cases behind him. He thought of that same desperate moment as he faced the herd, and wished again for merely human enemies.

He picked the tallest hump in the surging bulls straight before him, and fired. Straight on came the monster, though there was something strange about its gait, and Cashel saw that it was actually sweeping toward him without taking a stride. The pressure of the mass on either side was great enough to hold it up for an instant, but then it slipped down to the ground. Two or three others hitting the dead bull at high speed tossed in the air as if they had been thrown up by the force of a great explosion. One of those bulky forms landed at the very feet of Cashel, and the weight of the fall crushed the air from its lungs with a peculiar, deep moan.

He gave not the flicker of an eye to this, but straight into the hole that his first shot had made in that battle front he kept firing.

He knew that his second shot had failed. He knew it by the singular instinct of the good marksman, as surely as though he had been able to follow the bullet's flight with a touch of his hand. But the third sent down another tossing pair of horns and widened the breach.

Great, shaggy forms were lunging by him on either side, giving him no more heed than split water gives to the rock that has shunted it aside; he heard their deep grunting of effort, for the herd had run far that night. But still he fired, and now he saw the bison turning as they reached the first fallen dead. And still they turned, as though a great invisible hand were there parting the current and making it roar helplessly past. It was as if he stood in the heat of a hurricane and heard cities going down with a roar, while he remained untouched.

Then, suddenly, there was nothing before him but the gray, quiet line of the northern horizon.

CHAPTER V

HE HARDLY gave a look or a thought to the dead, trampled bodies before him, or to the marvelous nearness with which the beating hoofs had come to him before they sheered away, or the quickness with which the buffaloes had lurched in behind him, leaving him standing in a little perilous strip of untrodden turf. What interested the thief was his latest prize, so he turned and looked with yearning, straining eyes in the direction in which he last had seen the great horse flying.

But all the southern horizon was blocked with the mist of dust that rose with the buffaloes, and by glimpses of their bulks breaking through that mist. The stallion was gone, but a fond hope grew up in the boy's mind that Clonmel would not desert him, but would circle freely and swiftly back to find him again. What gave him a touch of doubt was the vast roar of that army, stretching shadowy across the undulation of the prairie. Moving with such an incalculable swathe, it might be that they would herd Clonmel wildly before them for a day's march, and beat out of the earth any trail or scent or sense of direction by which he could return to his master.

Cashel's breast swelled as he thought of this loss, but he would not admit that Clonmel was gone until he saw the stallion dead or in the hands of another man.

He could not understand why the horse was above value to him, though he might have guessed if he had remembered that no man or woman ever had been anything to him except at a definite price, whereas the stallion had come to him with instant love. In fact, Cashel did not care to understand. He wished to leave Clonmel a mystery, for this made him greater and the horse greater likewise. It was a thing to be kept inside his own breast. It was the first accomplishment of his life about which he had no desire to boast even to the innermost members of the gang.

Now he took from his mind even this sorrow and preoccupation. There were other things than the fate of Clonmel to occupy him. And as if to point the conclusion, he saw three or four buffalo wolves loping steadily along the prairie, looking big as horses against the dawn line on the horizon. He snatched up the rifle with a sudden fury, and a quick shot.

A big wolf pitched into the air; he fell, and was on the ground before the short, broken howl rang against Cashel's ear.

"I can't miss," said Cashel to himself. "I'm a dead shot, now. I can't miss a life; I don't dare," he concluded.

But here, instantly on the heels of his sorrow for the horse, he was feeling a peculiar grave pleasure such as he had known before. His one hand against many was the old course of his life.

Day grew up around him. He examined the dead buffaloes. There were five, that had either dropped by his bullets, or

22

had tripped on the fallen and been battered to a finish by the hoofs of the charging animals behind. The air was still rank with the smell of the trampled grass, and tainted by the strong odor of the herd, and Cashel decided that he would camp on this spot for a time, in the hope that the chestnut might return to him as a dog returns to its home, even from a great distance.

First he had to have water. He found in a small hollow, a mile away, a small pool standing, through which a wing of the buffaloes had charged, leaving the water little better than a sort of liquid mud. He knew how to deal with this, however. He had been shown this and many other things by some of the wiser heads among those hunters who had ridden out from the caravan with him during the long march.

He dug a shallow hole three feet from the margin of the pool, and then went back to the dead bison to butcher enough meat to last him for some time. He knew enough to take none of the bulls, but to take a cow whose neck had been broken by a fall, and whose head was trampled almost to a pulp. From the bulls he took the tongues, and the cow he cut up with what skill he had.

After that, he returned parched with thirst and found his trench filled with a clear water, cold, but strangely bitter to his taste. It could hardly be poisonous, however, so he drank of it, filled the canteen, and went to his camping grounds.

There, with buffalo chips, he made a low fire, and with that smokeless heat and the help of the burning sun, he dried the buffalo meat, slicing it in long strips about a half-inch square—another art that he had learned on the march. It dried to the core in a wonderfully short time on his jerking rack, constructed of the horns of the fallen bulls.

This work pleased him. He remained there for two whole days and nights, keeping up the fires and tending the meat, but always aware of an increasing sense of depression.

In part, that was because it seemed to him that the horizon was creeping in upon him and contracting; and in part it was because the stallion had not returned. He gave up hope on the evening of the second day. Clonmel, bent on a return, could cover a hundred miles a day without real effort; he had not come back, and it was impossible that he should return now. His failure, together with the boy's increasing sense of peril if he remained here, decided him to begin a march.

He had a blanket, the case of knives, the rifle, the two revolvers, and a heavy burden of ammunition; but the saddle itself had been battered to a heap under the hoofs of a thousand bison. This he left behind and went on with his march at daybreak.

23

He had no direction, except that south and west the stallion had last been seen on his flight, and in that course Cashel set his mental compass. For still, blindly, he kept some hope that the great chestnut would once more run beneath him, and hear his voice, and lift his fine head, and make Cashel feel like a bird on the wing.

He had covered a good half-day's course when a puff of southern wind sickened him with a dreadful stench, and almost immediately he saw the cause of it. There was a dry, shallow, steep-banked draw cutting across the face of the prairie, and this ditch had been struck by the ocean of buffaloes, filled with the bodies of the forward ranks, and then crossed over by the rest of the stampede. It made Cashel veer away to the west to avoid the horrible smell, and then lean his step until it was well behind him.

He was no philosopher, and yet he could not help wondering that such a sea of life should have been used so blindly, and so much valuable energy and such a treasure of hide and horn and flesh poured away to fill up a ditch in the wilderness! That thought did not trouble him long. There remained in his mind only two things: the longing for Clonmel, a great and ceaseless ache, and the increasing dread of the horizon.

Out of that horizon he saw the wolves drift now and then; and over it the carrion-eating buzzards floating high in the heavens hunting for death on the plains; and out of it he heard by day and night faint wailings and cries like the lamenting of lost souls.

Perhaps those were wolves yelling, or cougars crying, or the coyote giving a shriller tongue, but always it was the unseen life that encircled Cashel, and traveled with him behind a veil. He could find its footprints in the grass now and then, but usually there was no sight or trace of it.

So the fear grew up in him stronger and stronger, until it became almost a desire for companionship, unknown to him heretofore. It never approached a panic, but it kept him tense, even in his sleep, and began to draw a thin shadow down his forehead between the eyes.

For a good week he marched southwest, keeping to the general direction the horse had taken when last seen, doing so because he had no other course to attract him. During that time he saw not a single game animal! It amazed him, considering how many myriads swarmed upon the great plains; but this way of his was swept clean of life. He had looked upon a great pool of it when the stampede went past, and now he was in a vacuum.

Then, one day, he saw something moving on the plain far behind him. From the first hummock he reached, he sighted the object, using the little field telescope which the captain had always carried in his saddlebags.

The round circle of vision floated here and there, and finally into it rode a horseman, with the sun blinking on his naked shoulders, and his back bent in a bow.

An Indian!

Cashel went to the next clump of tall grass, and entering this he lay down on the southern face of the rise and prepared to spy. By the time he looked back, however, the Indian rider had disappeared into some hollow that could not be seen on the green face of the plain.

For an hour Cashel waited, peering this way and that with the glass, but still he had no view or sound of the red man.

Then, with a start, he understood the explanation.

It was impossible that the other could have disappeared so rapidly; it was very unlikely that he had stopped in any hollow to cook food, for there was not a trace of vapor rising into the sunlight. The red man had disappeared for the good and simple reason that he was a hunter of men as well as beasts, and the white traveler was a fair prey.

A fair prey?

Cashel looked with a faint grin at his Colt's rifle—a treasure even to a white frontiersman, to say nothing of its incalculable value in the eye of a wild red man. He touched the butts of his revolvers, whose heavy weight had tempted him to throw at least one of them away. And there were the knives, and the glass itself, and the watch that ticked in his pocket.

Any one of these items was enough to buy his scalp six times over.

He was being hunted, and perhaps the hunter was even now close at hand!

The old thrill rose up into Cashel's heart, the tremor of excitement, and then the cold, sweet wine of danger pouring through his brain.

He began to move in order to survey the ground behind him and on each side, but now he stirred with the caution of a hunting cat. It might well be that the red man had his eye on the grass of that low hummock, watching for the least stir that the wind could not account for. So the thief stirred slower than time, softer than the movements of a snake in the tall blades, and gradually lifted his head until he saw behind him the loom of a living, moving thing- -the shadowy outline of a man rising to his feet and jerking a rifle to his shoulder. This he saw from the tail end of his eye, made clearer by the two brilliant high lights struck out by the sun, the rifle barrel and the sweat-polished shoulder of the brave.

Young Cashel rolled over on his back like a puppy at play and sent a snap shot squarely at the heart of the stranger.

CHAPTER VI

HE HEARD that bullet crunch like a broken tooth on a bone. It shivered the stock of the Indian's rifle, numbed his hands with the weight of a blow heavy enough to knock down most men, and caused the broken gun to topple into the grass.

Cashel, swift as a ferret on the trail of blood, was on his knees as the Indian caught a knife from his girdle and swayed for the charge.

Yet he did not leap.

He had left his robe behind him and was dressed in a loinstrap only, so that Cashel could see the long muscles of the legs flex, stiffen, and then relax as the red man straightened and tilted back upon his heels again. The hard-gripped hand of the hunter who so nearly had dropped on Cashel like a hawk from the sky was still on the hilt of his knife, but the wild battle light was passing out of his eyes, and his savagely contorted features now gradually relaxed.

Cashel watched and studied these changes with the utmost relish. He was about to kill this red man with no more compunction than he would have slaughtered a calf, and with infinitely more enjoyment. For, in the distance somewhere was the man's horse, and Cashel was footsore. Reason enough for a killing! And all the cruel heart of Cashel rejoiced as he regarded the other down the barrel of his Colt.

He watched the most minute details, the great arch of the chest of the warrior, and how the outer muscles strained and slid as the big man breathed, and the knots of the stomach muscles, the last of his contracted strength to relax; and he saw the glistening of the black war paint, like oil on his face, and the trembling of two red-tipped eagle feathers upon his head.

This was no common man, Cashel knew, and therefore the slaughter was the more pleasing.

But a vague understanding also rushed in upon him as he knelt there, covering the heart and then the head of his enemy—a knowledge of that peril of the horizon from which he had felt himself shrinking in the last few days. It gave up wolves from time to time, but it also gave up wolflike men.

The brave was now composed in body and feature; even his nostrils no longer flared.

"How!" said he quietly.

26

"How will you have it?" answered Cashel snarling. "Head or heart, my beauty?"

To his amazement, the son of the prairie answered in good enough English: "Favor my horse for half a day and he will then be able to go. Now he is tender in his right fore-leg."

Cashel blinked, then steadied his gun with a hard grip.

"Where is your horse?" he asked.

"He is lying in the tall grass behind the second low hill on your left, friend."

"Does he lie down when you speak?"

"Yes, if you strike him behind the knee and press on his withers he will lie down and stay down until you come for him again, even if you are away for a day."

There was no relenting in the heart of Cashel, but he felt a greater interest. He had been about to slaughter a wild beast, and was amused to learn that the creature was a man. So much the gift of language had accomplished for the chief —for that must be the meaning of the feathers on his head.

"How," said Cashel, "did you know that I would stay here for you?"

"By the blink of your glass," said the other instantly, "when you looked at me. The sun caught on it and warned me that you had seen me."

"So you came to cut me off?"

"Yes," said the brave frankly.

"Why?" asked Cashel.

"You are," said the other as calmly as before, "a scalp, a coup, and a gun for me."

Cashel moistened his lips, and then he could not help smiling, for the frankness of this savage was so much to his own taste that he felt he was speaking for the first time to a man he could understand He had seen Indians before, and in the caravan he had been at a good deal of pains to pick up a rather extensive Cheyenne vocabulary, since that was the tribe and the tongue of the best of the Indian hunters who had attached themselves to the train. But he never before had seen an Indian stripped of the stiff dignity with which he so often dresses his natural simplicity when he is in the presence of strangers.

"Friend," said Cashel, "you are going to die in about half a minute, or a little less."

"That is true," said the brave with composure.

"Then why," asked Cashel, "didn't you throw yourself at me with your knife in the first instant, before I got my bead on you?"

"You had your gun on my heart, and after the first shot, I knew that you would not miss."

27

"It is easier to die," said Cashel, "fighting than standing still."

"That is true," said the Indian, "but you see that I am not yet dead."

"You will be in ten seconds, my friend."

"That may be. But white men often stop to think, and that makes them change their minds, very often."

"Tell me," said Cashel, "why I should change my mind about you."

"I can give you only one good reason," said the other, after a little pause. "I can tell you where the next good water hole lies in your march, and you are now bearing away from it, your canteen is empty, and you would give a great deal to know where you will get the next drink."

"From your own water pouch," said Cashel.

"I have not tasted water for a sun and a half," answered the other calmly.

It made Cashel forget his own aching thirst to think of what the red man must be enduring at this instant.

"How do you tell, friend," said Cashel, "that I am so thirsty?"

"Your eyes are big," said the red man, "and your lips are cracking."

Cashel smiled. This mingled simplicity and observation pleased him more and more. He never had met a man so near his heart, he decided again.

"Do you think," said Cashel, "that for the sake of a water hole I will let you go?"

"You haven't much to gain by killing me," said the other.

"And why not?"

"My rifle is broken, and yours is already a much better gun. My horse is already yours and the place where it lies is pointed out to you. My knife is worn out to the backbone of it, and you do not take scalps."

"Are you a medicine man?" asked Cashel. "Do you read minds?"

"I am not a medicine man," said the Indian. "The medicine that I made before I rode out from my tepee promised me a great good fortune. I asked for a great thing, and the medicine said that I should have it. However, I imagine that you don't take scalps because your nose is red, your hair is short, and your feet are in stiff shoes."

"In other words, because I haven't been in this country long enough to pick up its customs?"

"That is true."

"Friend," said Cashel, "unless you are tired of talking, tell me what you started on the warpath to find—scalps and guns, as you said before?"

28

"I am not tired of talking," said the Indian, with his first smile, "because I am not tired of life. I started on the war-path to get the medicine horses of the Pawnees."

"And what are they?"

"They are two white mares, friend, that are swifter than the wind, that can run on the clouds, and that keep their riders from wounds."

"Bah!" said Cashel. "Do you believe this rot?"

"Not a bit," said the other.

"No?" cried Cashel, more and more pleased with this strange man.

"No," said the red man. "because I know they can't run on clouds, or turn bullets in the air. But their riders believe in them, and so do the Cheyennes. That is why I took the trail."

"Their riders—and also the Cheyennes—but what has that to do with you?"

"A great deal. I am a war chief, my friend, and twice I have fought against the Pawnees, and seen their two young chiefs on the white mares ride straight at my young men, and my best warriors have fired, and missed their shots be-cause they expected to miss, and then turned and ridden away from sure death! I have been beaten twice and I have had to run away with the rest of my men. The young braves no longer will follow me. The Pawnees laugh at me; and my favorite wife has run away with a young brave who never took a scalp or counted a coup!"

Cashel laughed, but softly, for fear the vibration might disturb his aim. His arm was growing tired, and he slowly lowered the weapon to his side.

"You're still dead if you move," said Cashel, "because I can send my snap shots home."

"My rifle already knows that," said the other, "and I cer-tainly shall not try to die while the talk is still better than water in my mouth."

Cashel laughed more openly, and saw a sympathetic smile on the lips of the other.

It was not hard to tell that this Indian was as brave as a lion even if he were as wily as a snake.

He was, for one thing, the finest naked specimen of man-hood that Cashel ever had seen, well upwards of six feet, and made strong and lean in every limb. It was a wonder that the gaunt belly could give nourishment to those wide branch-ing shoulders, and the deep chest, and the entanglement of muscle that covered his body.

"Friend," said Cashel, taking up the Indian's word, "I ought to brain you with the bullet that's now under my trigger, but the fact is that I've laughed at you, which makes my finger a little slow, and the second thing is that I'm also on the trail of a horse, which makes us poor devils in one boat."

"A horse?" said the Indian, expressing not the slightest surprise or joy in this implied promise of mercy.

"A red stallion," said Cashel, pain coming over him as he spoke, "a red stallion, so much faster than your two milk-white mares, and so much more full of medicine, that if you saw him running over a hill you'd think that he *was* in the sky."

"Good," said the chief. "Let me help you to find him. I walk fast, and your sore feet can rest on the back of my horse!"

CHAPTER VII

WHENEVER I think of the march across the prairie of that Cheyenne chief and the white thief, I cannot help laughing. You would have had to comb twenty great cities of white men to find a more venomous scoundrel than Bandon Suir Cashel, the American-Irish gunman, sneak thief, and yegg. You would have had to comb twenty Indian tribes to find a nobler red man than Walking Dove.

He had taken nine scalps and counted fourteen coups. The scalps were a matter of personal vanity and decoration, but the coups were a national ornament; they were the poetry of the race, as you might say. He wore red-dipped eagle feathers in his hair, which meant something. He had the look of a king, and the manners of a man so great that he did not have to bother with petty pride. Walking Dove was so celebrated that his fame even had escaped from the width of the plains and had come to the newspapers in the eastern part of the country. Editors had spoken of such leaders of the Indians as Spotted Deer, Two Horned Buck, Walking Dove, etc., though perhaps at the time they had congratulated themselves a little upon their intimate knowledge of the wild men of the plains. But Cashel was only famous with a gang in New York, and certain numbers of the police of the metropolitan district. You might say that he was great enough to be hunted, but not great enough for the public prints.

However, when the pair were journeying across the plains, the Indian treated the white man as a brother, or even looked up to him. This condition was due partly to the fact that the white man had spared his life, and partly to the equipment of Cashel. That this was stolen made not the slightest difference to the red man; or rather, it was an added reason for admiration. Cashel discovered this very early on the march, after a day when he had been busily improving his vocabulary in Cheyenne.

Said the chief. "How many horses, brother, did you pay for the rifle that shoots many times without reloading?"

Cashel replied simply, because it was a relief to him to be frank, and there was no reason why he should prize the opinion of the Indian, "I paid nothing. I stole all my guns."

"Ha!" said the Cheyenne. "From an enemy, brother?"

"Yes," said the thief. "From an enemy."

He could say that safely. All men were his enemies, in a sense. For the first time in his life he heard stealing praised and reduced to a moral philosophy.

"What is better," said Walking Dove, "then to take your own comfort at the cost of the foe? Whatever is stolen from an enemy makes him weaker and your own tribe greater."

That was a philosophy which passed very well on the plains, where the people were always fighting with their neighbors, and where a brave had to ride two hundred miles, say, to steal from his foe. It was a different matter when it was done as Cashel had done it, but though he appreciated the difference, in a way, the important thing was that he had found a man who had appreciated his talent.

"I myself," said the Cheyenne, "have stolen three horses from the Pawnees, and two from the Sioux. This I did in the course of three war parties, and my success made the young men willing to follow me."

It never had occurred even to Cashel to boast about his thefts, but he could say honestly: "Brother, some of the white chiefs among my people have called me the greatest thief between the two oceans."

He said this in Cheyenne, for he had been picking up the tongue rapidly in the past few days of constant conversation with his companion.

This remark of his the Indian considered for a time, and then he said: "That is a great deal, my friend. And to be great among many is of course better than to be great among a few. I have heard that among the white men there are villages so great that into one of them two times all the population of the red men could walk, and still there would be room."

The thief thought of the greatness of New York, with more than a million inhabitants. then a freak and monster among the cities of the New World and really greater than anything except London among the places of the world.

"Yes," said he. "If all the white people of that city were turned into buffaloes, they would fill this plain from one horizon to the other."

The chief considered this remark in silence.

31

They had made their camp for the evening now, and sat cross-legged on opposite sides of the remains of the fire glow from the buffalo chips over which they had cooked their food.

"There is that one great city," said the chief, "out of which all the white men come?"

"No, no," said the boy. "There are others. One of them is almost as great, and there are many others. The white men gather into cities like the rivers into lakes."

Again the Indian considered.

"The red men," said he, "are the chosen people of Tirawa. He is far the greatest of the Sky People. He looked over the earth and saw that this place was very good. He put the Indians here. He made the great rivers to go through the level plains. First he gave us dogs to pull our travois. Then he made horses and sent them to us. He filled the country with buffaloes so that we should have plenty to eat. Still the red men have a hard time when long and cold winters come, and often they are hungry. How, then, can the white people live in such multitudes?"

"In their cities," said the thief, "they make many things, which they sell to other white men who live in the country and raise grain."

"Like the cursed Pawnees?" asked the Cheyenne carefully.

"In the same way, except that they raise a thousand times more."

"What do they make?"

"Well, they make repeating rifles like this, and revolvers. And there is this watch."

He pulled it out.

The Indian looked at it with a smile that he made disappear at once. It was plain that he could not believe what he heard.

"Listen!" said the boy, and held out the watch.

The Cheyenne gravely received it, looked at it, and turned it from one side to another, interested by the brightness of the metal and the glass. Suddenly his mouth opened and he placed his hand over it. Above the rim of his hand, his eyes stared wildly, for he had noticed the movement of the second hand. A little later he raised the watch to his ear and listened, his eyes enchanted.

He had heard the ticking.

"This animal," he said, at last returning the watch cautiously, "is continually talking. What does it eat, brother, and how does it walk?"

"It neither eats nor walks," said the thief, enjoying the sensation he had produced.

"How long will it live, then?"

"For ten times the life of a man."

"And what is it saying?"

"It is telling me how long it will be before the morning comes. In the morning it will tell me how long before the sun goes down." The Cheyenne nodded and blinked. It was plain that this was beyond his comprehension, but he asked no more questions.

He merely said: "I have heard such things as you tell me from other white men. It is a good thing when all of a tribe agrees in what it will say of its home village. But suppose that a poor red man should go as far as the great salt lake of which the white men talk—what would he find?"

"These cities of which I speak," said Cashel, "and then if he took a big canoe and went to the other side of the salt lake, he would find other white men speaking different languages, and very great in numbers."

"So!" said the Cheyenne, and grew silent.

He could not have indicated more clearly that he considered his companion a gigantic liar.

"And," said Cashel, "if he went to the western salt lake, there where the sun is setting, he would have to go a greater distance, but at last he would come to people of yellow skins, and there are twice as many of those as of all the other people in the world."

"Good!" said the chief tersely. "Then when they care to, they ride out and take many scalps?"

"No. They haven't as many fire canoes and guns, big or little, and they shoot crooked."

"The red men," said the Cheyenne, "are only a very small people, then, and they live in a little corner of the world?"

"That's true enough."

The Cheyenne nodded, as one who had come to the conclusion of long thoughts.

"A great lie is the best," said he. "I am going to sleep, brother."

He wrapped himself up in his blankets and was instantly asleep, while Cashel, a little chagrined now that he found all his statements doubted, arranged the guns under his head, and the knives beside them; for the only security he enjoyed was his wakefulness, and the hope that if the Indian stirred during the night, his eyes would open. He had tied the Cheyenne carefully on the first night, but afterward gave up this precaution. So far as he knew, Walking Dove made no effort to take advantage of him. He did not know whether to attribute this to the respect that the Indian might well have for his skill with a revolver and his accuracy in snap shots, or whether Walking Dove was biding a secure time when he might take the white man's scalp and all of the weapons which he so much admired. At any rate, the nerves of the

33

thief were strong enough to endure the strain. He fell asleep on this night as securely as he had ever fallen asleep since the days of his childhood. That is to say, every hour or so his eyes snapped wide open. It might be only that the wind touched his face more strongly, or that some sound quavered out from the wide horizon, or that a shadow had crossed the face of the moon. Any of these things were sufficient to rouse him. The only suspicious circumstance he had ever noticed, was that night he saw his companion raised on one elbow and steadily regarding him. Otherwise there was nothing.

Now he fell asleep, and several times wakened, to see the clouds in motion, and the stars and the moon sweeping grandly through a troubled sea overhead.

At last, something touched his arm.

Young Cashel turned as a wildcat turns out of slumber, and laid the muzzle of a Colt's revolver none too gently into the ribs of the Cheyenne. The big chief merely smiled.

Then, stretching out his finger, he pointed across the dimness of the morning plains and there, against the rim of the coming day, Cashel saw a dark troop of silhouettes moving, horses, and humpbacked riders. But two of those horses were not black. They were milk white, and the thief realized, suddenly, that these were the white medicine mares for which his companion was hunting.

CHAPTER VIII

THE PAWNEES halted their march.

"They have seen us," said Cashel. "They will come sweeping down on us, Walking Dove."

The Cheyenne shook his head. He pointed out that there was rising ground behind them, which made so dark a background that even the Pawnee wolves would not be able to see them. He suggested that there was probably water, yonder, and that the troop had stopped for that reason. And Cashel listened with a new respect and faith, for the Indian's truth had just been exemplified. The hand which touched Cashel's arm might as easily have crushed out the brains of the white man; and Cashel was depressed to think of it. However, he felt that he now could trust the red man to a certain degree, and that all of their relations one to the other were wonderfully improved.

They lay prone. The daylight was increasing. Then, leaving the white man behind him, the Cheyenne crawled over to

34

his horse and made it lie down. And now, as the sunrise drew nearer, and clouds of cupreous red hung in a great burl on the edge of the sky, the Pawnees recommenced their march.

They went across the sky line as they mounted and descended a small hummock, and they were readily counted as they stretched along in single file. Thirty-two men were in the party, and behind them came three or four boys driving a herd of the remounts. From a walk the warriors hit out in a steady lope, and so they streamed away, with the two white mares still running in the center of the procession, apparently led by neighboring braves, but with neither saddle nor rider on their backs.

When they were gone, Walking Dove came back from the place where he had allowed his pony to stand up again, and his face was a study of vigorous emotion.

"Look, brother," said he. "There go the horses of the Pawnees. There goes their luck in war, and their faith in themselves. If we steal away their medicine, we steal away their hearts and souls. They will be weaker than children. Do you believe me, brother?"

"There are thirty-two," said thet white man dryly.

"Not enough," answered Walking Dove, "to make an army, and more than enough to make them careless. Shall we ride behind them, friend?"

"To steal the white mares, Walking Dove?"

"To steal the mares, brother!"

"They are riding southwest," argued the boy with himself, "and that's my course, also. They're riding southwest—and besides, it might be a grand game!"

No honorable motive could have inspired him so much as this. To follow the Pawnees and to steal!

It reminded him of the time when the great Forrest, chief of his gang, himself had pointed out the house of the police commissioner and said, "Under his pillow he has the chart and the signed confession and the whole story of my brother, Bandon!"

And it was not to please the chief that he ventured on that occasion. It was the sheer drunken excess of terror and delight that had led him through the third-story window, and then to slide shadow-like through the house to the actual bedroom of the commissioner. He remembered how the great man of the law, hearing something, had heaved himself up on one elbow and glared about him, looking a wild figure of a man in the moonlight. But half an hour later, the needed things were slipped out from beneath the pillow of that same head, and Cashel was gone with them.

"The greatest job that ever was done!" said the chief.

But Cashel did not need this praise. The adventure had been its own reward.

"We'll travel behind them," said the boy. "But how'll we keep up with them, Walking Dove?"

"A weak man," answered the chief, "can walk as far as a strong horse will run. We shall have to go slow before the sunset."

He was right.

As they marched south and west on this day, they came into view of distant mountains, cloudlike on the horizon, and growing until, by the midafternoon, one lofty peak could be seen distinctly, looking wonderfully near, with smaller companions about its knees, and a thin pencil of fluttering mist standing out from its lee side. Sunset turned the mountain and its pennon red, as the two came into a badlands where they had difficulty in picking out traversable ridges; but almost immediately the ground dropped away, and they saw the golden face of a stream that ran through the hollow, and the soft glow of willows on both sides of the stream. There, where the bank stepped back into a broad meadow, the Pawnees had pitched their camp, and the instant Walking Dove saw them, he hurried down into a gulch near by and motioned his companion after him.

The descent was so steep that the boy dismounted and led the tough pony along. He had ridden all that day, for the Cheyenne disdained to rest himself by taking a turn in the saddle, and continued all those hours to stride relentlessly ahead.

In the bottom of the gulch the two crouched side by side, with the pony stretched at their feet, and the hand of its master ever ready to grasp its nostrils and shut off a whinny.

What the meaning of this procedure was, young Cashel could not imagine, until he saw the up-pointing finger of his companion, and then saw just above them—pendant in the sky, he almost thought at first—a rider on a horse with a shaggy mane, and the long, slender shadow of a war lance stretched across its neck. It was a Pawnee, to judge by his cropped head.

He sat there apparently looking down at them securely, and then disappeared.

"He's gone for help, and we'll be bagged!" suggested Cashel anxiously.

"He would have tried one shot on his own acount," said the Cheyenne confidently. "Listen!"

A rifle shot sounded not far away, drifting to them over the gulches of the badlands, and then two or three more in rapid succession.

"They have missed their deer at the first shot. I hope they

36

have killed it with the others," said the Cheyenne. "Otherwise they may hunt for game until they find something more than meat!"

He said this with the utmost composure, and then glanced suddenly away from the face of the white man. And Cashel knew why. For his scalp was prickling, and he knew that some of his fear must be showing plainly in his eyes. With more than a white man's courtesy, the Indian avoided staring at his companion.

The red of the sunset was out of the sky and the dim twilight commencing before the Cheyenne permitted a move.

Then he led the way up the slope.

He had left behind him his robe, and was dressed now in moccasins and loinstrap alone. He had squatted on his heels, carefully streaking his face into the hideous pattern of the war paint, and repluming his eagle feathers. If he died, he was to die as a chief and a man of renown.

His weapons were an old-fashioned pistol stuffed inside his belt, a knife hanging from the opposite side, and in his hand, as he crawled, he pushed before him a short throwing spear, also an excellent hand-to-hand weapon for a close fight.

But the white man carried the repeating-rifle, and the two revolvers.

So they crawled up to the ridge, and went along the sawback until they were almost hanging over the camp in the meadow beneath them.

By this time, the carcass of the slaughtered deer—for Walking Dove had been right—had been cut up and roasted around a low-built fire. The band had eaten. And now two or three dogs which were followers of the party were gnawing bones on the edge of the circle of the dying firelight.

Stretched on their bellies, and sheltered completely behind a ragged rim of rocks, the two looked down on the camp. The Pawnees were already asleep, in large part, and the last of them rolled in their blankets shortly after the two reached their lookout. Only one remained on guard, not walking on the outer edge of the little encampment where the horses wandered in the meadow, but keeping close to a spot in the center where the white bodies of the two mares now were growing dim in the twilight. Then the white man was able to make out the nature of the novel fence which enclosed the pair. Spears had been thrust into the ground and raw-hide lariats stretched around a space sufficiently large to afford a bit of pasture for the mares.

"They have no care at all for their own scalps or for the horses that have been carrying them. Now, brother," said Walking Dove, "we could stampede their whole herd, but what would that gain for us and for my whole people? The luck lies in the white mares. They are the brain and the heart of those thirty-two men."

He nodded to himself, and it seemed clear to Cashel that his companion was far more superstitious about the powers of the strange white horses than he cared to admit.

They waited there on the ridge, with the Cheyenne muttering a prayer which Cashel made out in part, and which was an eloquent appeal to Tirawa to draw a thick veil of clouds over the bright face of the moon.

That moon, which seemed no brighter than a cloud at first, was now pouring down a terribly strong flood of light, but the prayer of Walking Dove hardly had ended before the face of the river began to be tarnished, and then ran black. The camp fell away in distance as if a mist had covered it, and staring up at the moon, Cashel barely could distinguish it behind a dense, rising wall of clouds.

The wind had changed, and the clouds rose steadily in a great, thick wall, putting out the stars, making the moon itself a presence rather to be guessed at than seen.

"Now," said the Cheyenne chief, "It is time for us to go down together, brother."

"To go down?" said the thief. "What shall we do there, Walking Dove? There are thirty-two men and one of them is not asleep!"

"I have prayed to Tirawa to make his eyes dim until I have my knife in his throat," said the chief calmly, "and you see for yourself that Tirawa hears me tonight!"

He pointed in the direction of the moon as he spoke, and all of Cashel's disbelief was unable to save him from a little giddy thrust of pleasure and fear.

He touched the shoulder of Walking Dove.

"If we have to fight," said he, "we'll need something more than guns that fire one shot. Take this."

And he put into the hand of the chief one of Captain Melville's beautiful new revolvers.

CHAPTER IX

THE TARNISHED face of the river seemed to attract the attention of Walking Dove even more than the camp of his enemies at their feet, and he led the way covertly down to it, keeping behind the top of the ridge, and so getting down to the water's edge. All of this he did without speaking to his companion to explain the purpose before them, and Cashel asked no questions. He was content to skirmish about the edges of this danger, feeling fairly confident that, in spite of his bold bearing, Walking Dove would never venture into the camp of the Pawnees.

On the bank of the stream, the Indian cast about until he found a fallen tree trunk, half devoured by rot. This he signaled to Cashel to assist him in launching, and when they had pushed it well out into the water, it rode high, and Walking Dove nodded his head in consent.

He led the way again, stepping into the water and holding his weapons high, so that the water would not get at them.

Cashel hesitated. He could see that the plan of the Cheyenne was to walk down in the water, letting the log act as a shield behind which they could move unspied by any watchers from the camp; but it seemed a foolish exploit to him.

What could be gained when they arrived, no matter how close, at a spot where thirty-one warriors slept, hair-trigger fighting machines ready to spring into action at a whisper?

Yet he followed.

Every moment he was on the point of saying that he would go no farther, and that it was high time for them to go back, and each time some sight or thought or memory held him back, and sometimes he told himself that he who had conquered the Indian brave in fair fight would not now be shamed by holding back in the crisis; and again it was merely the sight of the broad, muscular shoulders of Walking Dove, and the little curling wake that formed behind his back as he pushed the log downstream that kept him going. And still again, a curious feeling of fate possessed Cashel, stirring all his Irish blood and making him feel that the issue and the action here were outside of his control, no matter what he wished to do.

So he walked into the water, keeping guns and ammunition above the surface, and laboring down the stream, heartily wishing that Walking Dove lay dead and scalped on the prairie where they first encountered. But he was still unable to draw back, although his feet slipped on the slime and the rocks at the bottom, and although every moment he was in danger of submerging the guns which his arms ached in holding up. Bitterly he wished, too, that his slender body were made and muscled after the fashion of the Cheyenne!

They went on with the utmost slowness, keeping where the water was hip deep, and twice stopping altogether when the brave peered over the upper edge of the log and reconnoitered the enemy. Cashel ventured one glance in a similar manner and saw that the whole encampment was now in plain view. For the shore shelved gradually down to the water from the meadow above, and they could see some of the sleepers huddled in their blankets, and the figure of the motionless sentry from the blanketed hips to the head.

How could they expect to avoid the vigilance of that eye? Nevertheless, the Cheyenne guided the log slowly and steadily, and when it came to a stop with a slight jar in shallower water, the white man knew that it was grounded against the water line under the Pawnees' sleeping place.

The whole thing now appeared to him totally incredible. He half expected to see Walking Dove leap out from the water and rush up the bank shouting a war cry, and striking down a few of his enemies before they cut him to pieces. Somewhere along the march of the caravan he had heard tales of redskins running amok.

In that case, Walking Dove could run to his death while he, Bandon Suir Cashel, went back up the stream, wrung the water from his clothes, and stole away with the Cheyenne's pony. Walking Dove would have the satisfaction of wiping out his two defeats at the hands of this same war party. He, Cashel, would have the satisfaction of a horse to himself.

And, with cold, narrowed eyes, he looked toward the wide shoulders and the ugly face of the warrior, and noted the faint bronze of his shadow, floating and running in the water, but never flowing away.

In this manner they remained motionless for some minutes. The Cheyenne did not speak, and though cold was penetrating to his marrow, the white thief was sufficiently stiffened with pride tot refrain from making any objection.

Then he saw Walking Dove raise a finger and point over the edge of the log. Cashel, peering cautiously over, saw that all things remained as before in the camp, with one exception. The moon was still buried in cloud, the white mares glimmered faintly in their narrow pasture, still moving slowly as they grazed, the sleepers were obscure mounds of shadow, but one of these mounds had risen, shaken off its buffalo robe, and now took the place of the former watcher, who immediately stretched himself among the others.

The new guard seemed younger; at least, he was certainly more active than his predecessor, for he began to walk up and down just outside of the corral, with a quick, nervous step, now and again pausing to look carefully all about him.

"Good!" said the Cheyenne, moving closer to the thief. "Now we can go!"

"Go where?" asked Cashel in a whisper.

But Walking Dove did not answer, as though his mind were filled with his thoughts and plans and his hearing dimmed. He passed around the lower end of the log, which now began to thrust its upstream end farther out into the current and sway downward with the force of the stream. This pushed Cashel forward like a hand.

Twice he hesitated. Then he saw Walking Dove turn and look back toward him. He could not resist. He was more frightened than he had ever been in his life, but he could not remain in the river when his companion went on toward danger, particularly since Walking Dove seemed far from being a madman about to rush out in order to kill and to be killed.

He went forward behind the Cheyenne, therefore, saw Walking Dove hesitate an instant at the end of the log, and then they both stepped out into clear view of the camp!

The dull light of the moon, which sifted down through the thick clouds, had seemed a mere candle the moment before; but now it was like a searching sunshine as they came out into the face of the danger.

But the camp did not stir. The huddled forms lay still. The guard was walking away from them down the side of the horse corral. And the white mares gleamed nearer, but still like half-seen ghosts.

Straight on toward the shore went the chief, not hastening his strides, but merely making them longer, as though he feared to make a noise of rippling water as he moved. And duly behind him came the white man, determined at the first disturbance in the camp to drop into the water, abandon his guns, and float downstream. He crouched low and thanked fortune for the big shoulders of the brave.

The sentinel turned. And at once Walking Dove shrank down low in the meager shadow cast by the shore. A small covering that was, and yet Cashel discovered that the camp was now blotted out from his eyes. Only the head of the guard walked back and forth against the sky.

From this position they worked in still closer, until their knees were on the edge of the water, and the weight of his wet clothes hung like lead on the shoulders of the thief. He was trembling, with fear and excitement, and with the cold. But though he looked narrowly at the glistening, naked body beside him, he could not detect a tremor.

And then from the edge of the darkness above them a form of a dog started out—a big wolfish creature which was apparently trotting down to the river's edge for a drink. It saw the men no sooner than they saw it, and a snarl formed in its throat as it dodged.

Cashel, paralyzed, could neither move nor speak, but the Cheyenne reached with the speed of a fighting snake and caught the throat of the big animal. And Cashel saw the quick gleam of fangs that sliced the forearm of the warrior open. Then the bright knife of the Cheyenne wet home in the throat of the dog.

It dropped without a sound and lay head downward on the bank, with its long tongue lolling out and its head flung back at an impossible angle, as though the knife stroke had severed the vertebrae.

Cashel moistened his dry lips and looked with horror and admiration at the Cheyenne, but the latter was still kneeling on the bank. He held his hands out, palms down, and his head was bent.

His voice as he spoke was the softest of murmurs, but Cashel knew enough of the language by this time to make out that the words ran something as follows:

"Under-water people, you have covered me with your hands, and you have carried me in your arms safely to this place. You have been kind to me, and I shall not forget. If I come safely home to my tepee, I shall give you my gray mare with the sway-back, and my second-best deerskin shirt, the one which is worked with the red and blue porcupine quills."

He raised his head and his hands and continued this singular prayer—it would have been mere bargaining, except for something vital and reverent in the manner and the voice of the chief:

"Sky people, you have pulled a robe over the face of the moon for me. Therefore I know that you are hearing me. And if you will give me and my companion the two white mares and a safe home-coming, then I promise you my red stallion and my yellow one, and six mares which are the best in my herd, and I shall give you the iron pot which I bought from the trader last year. It is new and strong and good. I will give you my best rifle, and both the new hatchet and the one with the broken edge. I will give you my beaded moccasins, and make a feast in your honor and tell all my tribe of your great goodness to me, so that other braves will be encouraged to make sacrifices to you, far richer than I can afford to make."

When he had finished speaking, he remained for a little while on his knees, with his head thrown back, and his arms outstretched very much as though he had been overcome by the profundity of his own emotion, his soul following his words upward.

The sand under the hand of Cashel grew hot, and he knew it was the blood of the dog, so that he jerked his hand away in a horror.

Suddenly he heard the Cheyenne speaking to him quietly. "Are you ready, brother?"

Cashel said nothing. He was a good distance past speech,

and still seeing with the mind's eye that snake leap of the Indian's long arm, and the knife stroke that ended the dog. Would not a man's life have gone out like that of the dog, if the knife's blade went home in the tender hollow of his throat?

"The blood of a Pawnee dog is the foretaste," said the Indian. "We shall have the blood of a Pawnee wolf before we finish the night. Come, brother!"

He went instantly up the bank, crawling.

CHAPTER X

THE MOMENT they were over the edge of the bank, Cashel felt that he was transported into the midst of the encampment. They could hear the breathing, stertorous and harsh, of one or two of the braves, and at that moment a dog stood up, looking as large as a man to Cashel.

It lay down again instantly, however, turning around a couple of times after the manner of its kind when striving to find a soft place. But dogs were not the chief thing to be feared. There was the sentinel who still walked up and down the side of the corral by the slender war spears, and the long, sagging lines of the lariats which formed the enclosure.

He had just turned away from the river, however, and they were among the first of the sleepers when the guard reached the end of his beat.

At that, Walking Dove flattened himself against the ground, and so did Cashel; and only as the boy lay prone, colder at heart than his body was chill with the soaking clothes that clad him, did he see the hand of the sleeping Pawnee flung out before him—a big hand, gnarled with battle efforts, he judged, and big at the angle of the wrist, so that it was not hard to guess that there was enough power in the hand to take him by the throat as the Cheyenne had taken the dog!

He began to tremble so strongly that he was sure he would waken the men on either side of him, and he knew that when the Cheyenne began to move forward again on his fool's errand, he would not be able to follow.

He was right. He saw the body of his companion sway up on hands and knees, and he himself was weak as water in every joint and could not follow. Shame gave him enough warmth to rise the next instant, however, and he went forward until the stir of an Indian near by among the sleepers made him flatten down again.

The man had been lying wrapped in a pair of good blankets,

43

it seemed. One of these he was casting aside, and the other robe he retained huddled over his head and shoulders and most of his body, while he moved around to find, like the dog, a softer place. And, finding it, he sank down again in the same manner and was instantly asleep and snoring with the utter relaxation of a very tired man.

Walking Dove was up again and trekking forward, as usual, on hands and knees, but this time Cashel did not follow. He lay prone, again weak as a child, but it was a new fear that held him this time, and that was terror of the new idea that had formed in his mind, the rise of an impulse which he instantly knew was too strong to be resisted.

Once in a theater such as impulse had come to him. He had seen a cheap necklace of pearls around the fat throat of the woman in front of him and he had wondered if he could possess such skill and lightness of finger as to detach it without alarming her. To fail meant instant capture—and the scorn of the gang! But the moment that the idea occurred to him, he was helpless.

He had gone from the place out to the street, but there the vision of the fat folded neck returned to him, gleaming in the gaslight, and back went Cashel to his seat, to take the little clasp delicately in his fingertips, find the lock, and work it, then raise the one end so that the other might fall freely through the air without flicking the bare skin. So, by a miracle, he had succeeded, and got for his pains no more than a twenty-dollar imitation—that and the devout prayer that such an impulse never would master him again!

It was with him now, and so distinctly did the old scene come back upon him that he felt he could smell again the taint of gas in the air, and the thick summer's heat of that Manhattan night, and how the fat woman's head was canted a trifle to the left in the intensity of her interest in the play. He could remember the play, too, and the quartet of farm hands who grouped themselves around the pump at the end of their day's work, in the first act, and sang plantation melodies.

He told himself that, now, he would be no such fool, but still he knew that the temptation was pulling him more than ever the mountain climber is drawn by the lure of heights to hurl himself from the rim of the cliff.

Still Walking Dove crawled steadily forward, only pausing once to glance over his shoulder toward his truant companion in the adventure. A high admiration for the Cheyenne rose up in the breast of the thief, so that he knew that if they both survived this night he would have a greater regard for the Indian than ever he had had for a white companion.

He felt a trembling assurance, however, that when he had

44

attempted this scheme of his, he would strike even the courageous Cheyenne with wonder and with awe, and with a still deeper admiration.

He went forward a little to the spot where the robe had been discarded by the uneasy sleeper, and there he lay down again with his forehead touching the stock of an ancient musket, heavy as lead, and uncertain in its fire as a blunderbuss.

The sentinel, in the meantime, had reached the nearer end of his promenade and paused there with one hand resting on the haft of a war spear, turning his head slowly from side to side and scanning the broken edges of the badlands, and the horses in the meadow, and the black shadow of the river, out of which the two unknown dangers were crawling upon him—a thing to make all men doubt the value of their dearest vigilance, and suspect the eyes of watchers, and the strength of walls.

So thought Cashel, cowering agains the grass, and breathing the smell of the crushed turf and the ground itself. Then he saw the sentinel turn for his backward march, and knew that his time had come.

He told himself that he would not and that he dared not. But the next instant he was on his knees with his rifle slung by its strap over his shoulder, and the revolver stowed in his water-soaked belt, while he picked up the robe which the uneasy sleeper had discarded and draped it, as his pattern had done, over head and shoulders, and the whole body.

It was a new robe, a good robe, of the hide of a young cow, dressed with a softness that white tanners could never rival. Cunning hands had fleshed it and pounded marrowfat and brains into its texture until it had worked as soft and pliable as cloth, with a velvety surface to the touch.

It was a weight, added to that of his soaked clothing, but now that he was garbed as he wished, he gripped a knife under the folds and went forward with bowed head.

The sentinel had turned at the end of his beat and was coming back toward him. By the grace of bad fortune, the moon chose that moment to slide down through the veiling clouds, not entirely into the clear, but bucking through the sea of transparent mist like a laboring ship.

The white mares were close by also, one of them standing close to the fence of the corral with her head hanging, and one back foot pointed, as though she intended to sleep there on all fours, without lying down. She was white as milk. She shone in the moonlight with never a flaw. One would have said that she was made of some polished or translucent substance, so brilliant was she, with a sparkle in her long, well-combed mane and the sweep of her tail. The other, at a little distance, was almost as beautiful; and Cashel with the eye of a horse-lover judged them in spite of his fear. They had not the leg and the bone and the fire of Clonmel, but he judged them the highest type of the true prairie horse, tough as iron and easy as a rocking cradle. They were not kings like Clonmel, but princesses of the great plains.

He told himself these things with a curious detachment. His important occupation was in moving slowly forward through the last of the sleepers, stepping carefully in a litter of accouterment and weapons which would be caught up by brawny and skillful hands at the first alarm.

But the imp of the perverse drove him onward upon this danger as it had driven him that other night, far away in the New York theater. He moved with precision, and timed his arrival to chime with that of the sentinel, at the nearer end of his beat.

And there toward the right lay the brave Cheyenne. What wonder was in his brain as he saw his companion arise thus and go forward? What madness did he think possessed the white man?

Cashel was trembling with terror, and yet he could smile with a cold satisfaction at this thought.

He came straight before the guard, and the latter halted. He had a good rifle in his hands, held ready as he faced the robe-shrouded form. He was a big young man with good, wide shoulders, though his hands looked too large for the thickness of his arms. He was not more, say, than eighteen or nineteen, though his face was as fierce as his breed and that single feather trembling in his cropped hair certainly mean some great battle deed.

But what Cashel noted above all was the hollow of his throat, deepened by shadow, with the bone standing out, and the skin glistening over it, polished by the flow of the moonshine as by water.

He was hardly a step away when the sentinel took the gun barrel by one hand, and pointing with the other toward the sleepers, said a word or two in a harsh guttural which sounded almost familiar to Cashel, so like was it to the Cheyenne speech.

Then for the first time something more than a perverse rendering of himself to danger drove Cashel. He felt the leap of hope in his breast, and letting the robe part in front of his hands, he drove the knife at the hollow of the Pawnee's throat. He saw the gleam of his own weapon in the moon, and the horror that glinted in the eyes and parted the twisting lips of the warrior. Then the blade went home with wonderful ease, glided and stopped with a shock against bone, and his fist went on, dislodged from the hilt and striking heavily into the throat of the brave.

The rifle fell without a clatter. The Pawnee fell with it, striking wildly with both hands, but throttled by his own blood and the knife-blade. The boy caught the body in his arms; the struggling weight fell through them, and he saw the young brave lying on his back with a dreadful, writhing face turned up toward the moon.

Something gleamed behind his shoulder. It was the wet, naked body of an Indian, brilliant as hand-polished bronze; but as the heart of Cashel died in him, he looked up and saw the face of Walking Dove, exultant and fierce, with distended nostrils.

All was so far well, by miracle.

So the thief leaned and tugged the knife from the deep wound, and saw the Pawnee die as the steel left his flesh. Then he turned to the fence of spears and lariats, and slashed through the rawhide strips—not easily, they were tough as steel cable, and the bloody knife slipped in his grasp.

CHAPTER XI

FORTUNE which had seemed to leave them as the moon looked down through the clouds now struck for them again. A heavy drift of cloud spume washed across that silver ship in the sky and made it at once no distinct shape, but a far-away ghost, as the white man picked up from the spear shaft on which they were hung the pair of bridles. They were heavy with beadwork, and bright with porcupine quills. They were works of art, fitted to the sacred nature of the mares. And the two white beauties stood patiently, lifting their heads a little toward the stranger, but fearless of man, as having received no harm from them, ever.

Still Walking Dove was not at the side of Cashel, and the latter looked back with an impatient glance, in time to see his companion straightening above the body of the fallen warrior.

In one hand was a knife with a tarnished blade, and in the other, what looked a shapeless rag, though Cashel could guess well enough what it was. He was not horrified—merely amazed and irritated that the Cheyenne should stop for such trifles at such a time. Then Walking Dove came to him with long, swift, silent strides.

He was laughing noiselessly. It was more horrible to look at his face, Cashel thought, than to see the Pawnee choke and die.

47

They went on together. The two mares did not run. They even came forward to let the bridles slip over their heads, and Cashel was big with hope when the smell of the blood on his hands or the scent of his clothes made the one he was bridling jerk up her head with a loud snort and a stamp of a forefoot.

He turned his head, breathless, toward the sleepers.

One of them, rising on a stiff arm, rubbed a hand across his eyes, and Cashel dared not look again to see what would happen next, for he saw Walking Dove vault onto the back of the other white beauty, and he followed. But fear made his legs heavy and his arms numb. He only succeeded in throwing himself weakly across the withers of the mare and dangled there, holding barely by the pits of his arms.

And then came the war cry.

It entered his ears like a poisoned knife; it curdled his blood. And as he saw Walking Dove shoot through the gap in the fence around the corral, swung low on the back of the mare, he himself strove to swing his right leg over the hips of his own mount.

He failed, and she, startled at last, fled away after her sister, with Cashel flopping on one side of her, like a single saddlebag poorly secured. With all his might he clung, but felt himself constantly slipping.

He knew that he was through the gap in the fence, but he did not see what was happening in the encampment, for it was at his back. He could hear it, however.

If thirty-one devils had burst out of hell they could not have shrieked with more fury, in more differing notes of rage and astonishment. Guns sounded. There was one so close that he could have sworn he smelled the burned powder, and that the bullet must have struck his body or that of the sacred mare which carried him.

The mare swerved to the right. His arms half dragged from their sockets as she broke into greater speed, and looking ahead, half blinded with agony, he saw Walking Dove drive his mount in among the horses that were scattered about the meadow. He sat erect, waving his arms, yelling, apparently able to control the white mare with the mere grip of his knees and the swaying of his body; and as he yelled, the Indian ponies started. Those on the ground pitched to their feet and into full gallop at a bound. The others still grazing whirled away like dead leaves in a wind, this way and that.

And the moon came out to see that rout—or was it to point the guns of the Pawnees toward the thieves?

Cashel, looking up, was vaguely aware of how the clouds were torn apart, and with the fierce brightness of the moon

48

among them swept across the heavens with the speed of the galloping mare.

Guns still sounded behind him. Once and again bullets whirred past his head, but overmastering the noise of the shooting, and the echoes that flung back from the abrupt faces of the hills about him, he heard a great wail from the war party.

He heard it dimly, for the strength of his arms had failed him now. He hung on for another instant, slipping, slipping, and then attempted to cast himself free so that he might land running.

As well try to leap so from a train at full speed.

Down went Cashel on one shoulder and spun twice over. The moon went out.

The sky turned black. Only, on the margin of his brain, he heard the shouting and wailing of devils, and the sound of guns popping at a great distance.

Then great hands caught him beneath the shoulders and jerked him erect with a force that snapped his head hard back, and he raised one hand freebly, blindly, to ward off the death stroke.

"Quick! Quick!" panted the hoarse voice of Walking Dove. "There is still time, brother!"

Still time?

He wakened fully. The light of the moon seemed blinding bright as it plunged through the clouds, scattering them to either side like bow waves from the prow of a great liner. He saw the Indian ponies scattering before him, and to the right, low-running frantic forms of the Pawnees in pursuit.

Beside them stood Walking Dove's white mare, but the second one was at hand, also. She must have slowed to a halt the instant she felt the weight of her rider fall free, and now Cashel was flung unceremoniously on her back.

His head reeled with this second shock. He was vaguely aware that half his limbs were numb from his fall and that his head felt swollen, but his task was to cling with the full grip of his legs, and with one hand clutched in the mane as it flew back with the wind of the gallop. For she was off like a swallow in the rear of her sister, which the big Cheyenne hurled forward across the meadow.

It came to Cashel, strangely at that moment, that the mares were larger than he had thought at first, for the Cheyenne did not seem as bulky as when he sat on the back of his own war pony.

They were across the meadow. They plunged into the sweet darkness of a gully, and looking up from it, Cashel saw a flight of horses streaming across the hill crest on his right. They ran under the spur of their fear, stampeding wildly—

little, ragged-maned, stumpy-tailed ponies with thick legs, such as he had seen the Indian hunters of the caravan riding, but one among them was of a different mold.

Up from the rear it came and passed the rest so swiftly that they seemed to be bobbing up and down in one place. Gloriously it went, with high-flinging mane, and the lofty head and the proud neck of a stallion. What a stride was that, like a beat of wings, and then sailing forward against the lighted sky, and suddenly cleaving across the round body of the moon itself.

Cashel forgot to grip the mane of the white mare.

He flung out his hands to the flying stallion and shouted in a wild voice, "Clonmel! Clonmel!"

He made no more than a whisper with that shout. He tried again, and the sound screamed and screamed at his own ears like the cry of an eagle.

However, it was not the sound of his name that Clonmel had responded to, but the curious little whistle which the thief had taught him to know. He strove to render that whistle now, but his lips had blown dry. He wetted them, but the sound was all breath with no shrill in it.

And Clonmel was gone, sweeping over the top of the hill and flinging boldly down the farther slope. One flirt of his tail, bright in the moonshine, and that was the end of him. The earth had swallowed him from the thief's eyes.

With all his might, Cashel strove to turn the mare. She was a rare thing, with a sweet movement, and the temper of a dove; but how was she to be compared for an instant to the great soul of the stallion, and the pulse of his gallop? He must have Clonmel, if only the good white mare could bring him in sight of the big fellow!

But though he tugged and pulled and cursed and raged, and nearly toppled from her back again and again, as she dodged among the rocks and through the bad going, he could not swerve her an inch away from the trail of her sister.

Cashel groaned so bitterly that his eyes closed, and he almost went off as the mare made a right-angled turn. Tears of impotence sprang into his eyes.

And then he strove to give himself cold comfort by vowing that it could not have been Clonmel after all. Fate would not, like a devil, have brought him so close to the great horse, only to lose him again. Besides, there were other great horses in the world, and on these prairies stolen thoroughbreds of the Kentucky and Tennessee strain might have made such a silhouette against the sky. What chance, moreover, was there that this very band of the Pawnees should have captured him? Or, granting that they were wonderful horse thieves or horse catchers, was it possible that such a mount would be allowed to go free with the common ponies of the herd, without the hobbles of some great chief to control him? Ay, and with the chief's son to guard him like the apple of his eye!

So argued the boy, but as he ended, he knew that he was wrong, and his eye and his heart had been right. They had recognized the galloping form of Clonmel, and they could not fail. He could tell Clonmel by his gallop as the musician tells the song by its first phrase. And like music the love of the great horse went through him, and the yearning for him was greater than the yearning of a man for a woman, great as the desire of a child for the great tomorrow and the kingdom of the fairies.

But he was swept on at full gallop, brokenhearted, weak with disappointment and grief.

Straight back to the spot where they had left the rest of their equipment and the cached horse they went, and as Cashel came up, he saw the chief already stripping the saddle from his pony, and flinging it upon the back of the white.

Cashel threw himself to the ground and cried: "Do you hear? I've seen the stallion I told you of! Come back with me, Walking Dove! Listen to me! One minute of him is worth a thousand years of these little mares!"

"Go back?" said the Cheyenne, stopping in his work for an instant, and turning, agape. "Brother, brother, they already have caught some of their tamest horses. They are on the backs of their ponies, and are riding after us. And we have taken the sacred mares, we have ripped away the scalp of a Pawnee chief, we have stolen through them by night, we have made the moon blind them, the sky people laugh with pleasure because of what we have done. . . ."

Cashel said no more, for he saw that his companion was drunk with something stronger than liquor.

CHAPTER XII

As THEY rode through the broken country, sometimes in black shadow, and sometimes in the white of the moon, the Cheyenne made no effort to put a great distance behind them, in spite of what he had said of the pursuit the Pawnees would organize. He had given the saddle to the use of the white man, and he himself rode bareback, with a loose rein, given over to a debauch of pride, so that as they went along, he could not keep from breaking into a chant of which his companion understood very little. However, the thief did not insist on returning to make a final attempt to get Clonmel, for he realized that what Walking Dove had said was very true; there would be Pawnees in plenty in the saddle by this time, as angry as hornets around a broken nest. But for his own part, there was no feeling of exultation in the breast of the thief, for he felt that he had picked up a paste imitation and allowed a diamond of priceless value to escape from him.

They went on until they came to water, before the dawn, and having let the three horses drink and having filled their canteens, they made another good ten miles or so, and reached a secure camping place in a little oasis of stunted shrubbery. There they halted, and as quickly as he could wrap himself in the blanket, Cashel fell asleep, exhausted. He had done more in this day than ever before in his life.

In the morning, they had jerked beef and parched corn, which made a hearty meal, but one that took chewing until their jaws ached. They made their future plans in the meantime. But first of all Cashel wanted to know how his companion had been able to strike under the line of the Pawnee march with such exactness. Walking Dove had recovered from his excitement of the evening before. It was true that his eyes were a little brighter than before, and that a smile seemed continually to hover about his lips, but he replied in his usual frank way that it had been no exhibition of prescience. He simply had guessed that the Pawnees would be striking toward the Cheyenne country at about this time, and he had moved off to hit their probable line of march. Cashel admired the quiet way in which the chief refused to make a mystery of himself and of his actions.

"You were wrong about one thing, Walking Dove," said he. "You said that the white mares could not turn the bullets away, but they surely turned them from us last night."

"Certainly," said the chief, with a grin. "And they shall be sung about when I do my scalp dance in the village of the Cheyennes. But you know, brother, and so do I, that what spoiled all those shots was the moonlight, and the shaking hands of the Pawnees, for *they* believed that the mares were miraculous in their powers, and of course that made them miss. A gun is like a good horse; it can't win unless the owner believes in it. But you are sad, brother, and I would think that you had done nothing that interested you, and that last night was no more than a dream to you!"

"We've lost Clonmel," said the boy. "I saw him running over the hill. We've lost Clonmel, and I tell you, friend, that Clonmel is worth ten mares such as these."

"Does he turn bullets?" asked the chief, smiling.

Cashel did not answer, he was too busy in calling up again the picture of the great stallion striding against the moon.

And the Cheyenne went on: "An open wound is afraid of the wind. These Pawnees will be hard to touch during the rest of their march, because they will have more eyes than a fly, and more stings than bees. But you can be sure of one thing—we shall see them again."

"I thought you were only a wise man," said the boy dryly, "but I see that you're a prophet, Walking Dove."

"They will ride straight on into the Cheyenne country," said the Cheyenne, "because they will not dare to return to their city with the medicine mares gone, and the Owl dead."

"Was that the name of the dead man?"

"Yes. You know that the Pawnees are always fighting the Sioux even more than they fight the Cheyennes, and in one of their battles, that young brave rode straight through the Sioux line of horsemen and counted a coup as he passed them. He was called the Owl, for that, because the owl comes silently, and has flown past you before you know that he is there."

He leaned a little and looked at the scalp, which was not drying, tied to a bridle rein.

"He was a famous young warrior," said Walking Dove with complacence, "and the Pawnees will try hard to take something from us that will be equal to the value of his scalp, to say nothing of their magic horses. Now then, when you and I return to the Cheyennes, it will be easy for me to get young men to follow me. They will forget that I twice failed on the warpath and they will only think of the two magic horses I have brought home, and the scalp. I shall make medicine at once, and you will ride out with me at the head of a good party. They will be glad to follow me and they will be glad to follow you, brother, when they hear how you go down the river, and like a water rat slip up on the shore and kill the Pawnee frogs!"

He laughed a little as he said this.

"If they follow the Walking Dove, they will follow the Water Rat!"

Then he went on: "Be sure that we will find them, and when we have found them, every young man shall be told that ten horses go to him who brings you the stallion."

"How shall I pay for ten horses," asked the thief, "when I've only this white one?"

The chief looked at him in surprise.

"But *I* have horses still in my herd," said he, "even after I have paid off my debts to the moon and to the Sky People, and to the river spirits. Or, for that matter, don't you suppose that you could exchange for the stallion a mare who turns bullets and will make the scalp of her rider safe on his head?"

He waved his hand.

"The young men and the wise chiefs would all be trying to get her. Be sure of that!"

And that was how Cashel came to ride north again with his Cheyenne friend.

They went cautiously, for as Walking Dove said, the Pawnees were sure to be abroad on the prairies, looking for vengeance and a chance to cut the two thieves away from their return. But using the three horses alternately, and working them until the shadows of their ribs worked up through the sleek sides of the mares, they came at last, a good week later, within sight of a white cloud of tepees ranged in a great circle not far from the bank of a river, and looking pure as new-fallen snow against the green of the prairie.

"My people!" said the Cheyenne, pointing.

He insisted on stopping here, though the white man was for getting on, now that safety was in sight for them. But a casual entrance was not in the mind of the chief.

He urged Cashel to furbish his accouterment, and set him a very good example by cleaning the dust from his clothes, rubbing up the blade of his knife, and especially the fine new revolver which Cashel, having given for the battle, would not take back. The Cheyenne looked on it as a jewel, for it was at a time when the Colt's weapons were still something of a novelty on the plains. He polished that gun until it glistened like water. Then he took out of his saddlebag a gaudy pair of beaded moccasins which he fitted on his feet. He tied the scalp to the point of his war spear, and he gave to his face such a painting and streaking that even Cashel was half frightened. But last and most important, the long black hair of the chief was well combed out over his shoulders, where it flowed in greater abundance than the hair of a woman, and in the crown he fixed the two red-stained eagle feathers.

Cashel could not disdain some trouble with his appearance. In the "gang" he had been considered rather a dandy, and now at least he brushed off the dust.

Toward the end of this preparation, the chief began to stare anxiously toward the village.

"Will no one see us?" he asked of Cashel, in a growling murmur. "The young men among the Cheyennes are blind, and so are the boys and the girls who are swimming now in the river. Can't they see the white horses from the edge of the bank? Do they think that these are two bright clouds that have fallen out of the sky? They have lost their eyes, and one of these days, they'll lose their scalps! We shall have to go in and rap at the knocking boards before the tepees and ask the braves to kindly come out and see what we bring with us, for the good of the tribe. We shall have to invite the little girls and boys to come and watch our scalp dance!"

His anger and disdain increased to a great heat before the end of this speech, when out from the river bank a cloud of a dozen half-naked youngsters came spinning, whipping their ponies to a furious speed. Walking Dove was so pleased by the horsemanship they displayed in this race that he almost forgot his own anxiety and importance. The race itself took the eye of that born gambler.

"Which horse? Which horse?" he asked rapidly of the white man.

"How far do they run?" asked the thief.

"To that mound! Which horse, brother?"

"The pinto," said Cashel.

"No, that muddy-brown rascal that looks more like a bear than a horse. Watch, watch!"

The shaggy horse in the rear, in fact, now came swinging up on the others with a great rush, and fairly passed them all before the mound was reached.

"You have a good eye for a horse," said Cashel in admiration. "No," said the Cheyenne with his customary frankness, "but I guessed that lump of a horse was one of those that Spotted Calf stole from the Blackfeet last year. They look like grizzlies and they run like antelope. Here they come!"

He started on toward the village as he spoke, drawing himself erect in the saddle, and putting on a look half blank and half stern as though he saw not a thing between himself and the limitless horizon. The boys, in the meantime, having finished their race were now so close to the two riders that they could not help marking them, and they came with a rapid drumming of hoofs to see if these were not two returned from the warpath.

In a loose cloud they swept up around Cashel and his companion. At the white man they stared agape; but when they saw the two mares, and the obviously new scalp that hung from the war spear of the chief, they set up a screeching that ran needles into the brain of the thief. Their voices were so quick and shrill that though Cashel, by dint of constant conversation with his companion, now had a large vocabulary in the Cheyenne, he could not make out more than a word here and there. He could only be sure that they were asking the chief if these were actually the white medicine mares of the Pawnees, and if that were a Pawnee scalp of his own taking.

But they might as well have talked to a face of stone. The chief went on as though he disdained utterly the very thing which he had been demanding a moment before. His silence seemed to answer for him. Presently they turned of one mind, like a rising flock of birds, and winged away for the village, yelling and screeching as they went.

CHAPTER XIII

A FINER lot of boys Cashel thought he never had seen, muscular, straight backed, deep chested; and certainly he never had seen better riding than this barebacked performance. Even the placid white mares were a little excited and began to prance, as though they wished to follow the flight of the youngsters. But the chief insisted on a slow, walking pace.

He turned to Cashel and permitted himself the luxury of a smile, now that they were alone.

"Let the boys have a little time," said he. "In ten breaths they will turn our two mares into ten, the white man into five, and the scalp into a dead Pawnee army. Well, the village has been sleeping long enough, and it is time for it to wake up!"

It wakened with a vengeance.

But by the time they had waded the horses through the shallow stream, and climbed the farther bank, the whole population was pouring out to greet them. Men came on the war ponies which were often kept tethered close to the tepee, too valuable to be risked afield under ordinary conditions. Women came hurrying out, and little naked children flashed brightly in and out through the crowd, making a shrill din that seemed to be sweet to the ears of the returning chief.

However, he had draped himself carefully and gracefully in his buffalo robe, and the former immobility of his face was laughter and tears compared to the stony senselessness which he now put on.

The crowd rolled rapidly closer, a thin dust cloud tossing up behind them as they went over the worn ground near the village; and now Cashel could distinguish faces of the men and women, and the girls. He thought that he never had seen finer men, or bigger, or more brawny. They seemed six-footers, every one of them; and though the women looked a little dusty and dark skinned with time, the girls were radiant, with clear eyes, and translucent skins, and here and there features of actual beauty which he had not expected to find.

This crowd pooled about them in the most hazardous fashion. The warriors rode up close, but left a little interval which was filled by a swarming, scrambling, shieking, laughing, dancing, maddening mob of the naked children, so that every step his mare made, he expected to feel the hoof sink into soft, human flesh. He looked about him with a curiosity as frank as that with which they stared at him, and touched his leg or stirrup leather as they asked questions. However, he did not answer, even though he possessed enough of the language to do so.

That was for Walking Dove to do, since he obviously wanted the privilege of a little first-rate boasting and description. What amazed Cashel was the exultation that flamed in every eye. These people seemed on fire, every one of them, because they were seeing two stolen horses successfully brought home, together with a token of an enemy who had been murdered at night! However, he could guess that there was something more than the mere fact that was of importance —the superstitious significance that they attached to the mares, for one thing, and above all the fact that Walking Dove had gone out singlehanded and accomplished the thing for which he strove. Besides that, no doubt it was the national policy to encourage brave deeds by giving extravagant praise and fame to all who performed them.

With that, Cashel forgot some of the contempt with which he looked on savages; for he could not help wondering if, raised among such a people as these, he might not have been something more than a skulker on the edge of society. He had had honor from the "gang," but what was that, compared with the honor that a whole tribe was paying to Walking Dove?

Ay, and to himself, in a curious measure, smiling at him with wonderfully bright eyes, though they had not yet heard a word about him—though he might, for all they knew, be a mere prisoner in the hands of the returning chief. What, after all, would Walking Dove say about his part in the affray?

The sun had been well down in the west before the mob moved out toward them, and it was sunset before they struggled through the mob to the verge of the circling tepees. Then a brave, past middle age, came riding out on a tall horse, and before him the others parted so that he came easily up to Walking Dove.

"Two Antelope!" muttered the crowd, and Cashel could guess that was the name of the newcomer. He must be a war chief or a great medicine man, from the awe with which he was received.

When this fellow raised his hand and groaned a word of greeting, Walking Dove spoke for the first time. Two Antelope promptly turned his back and rode off. In disgust, or in jealousy, Cashel wondered? It appeared that both surmises were wrong.

The space behind the war chief and Walking Dove did not fill in again with the curious mob, and through the red of the sunset they could go on their way with a decent amount of ease, though there were still people hurrying before them and behind.

Down the road this opened. Cashel saw a cluster forming thickly in front of a tepee whose entrance was open, though no one stood at it. Up to this lodge rode Walking Dove, and dismounting struck the board that hung beside the open flap with the butt of his spear. He then stabbed it into the ground and left it sticking there erect and trembling, with the pendant scalp swaying back and forth.

Then into the black triangle of the tepee entrance stepped a handsome, copper-skinned young woman with a little bare boy of two or three years perched wriggling on her shoulder. It shrieked with pleasure at the sight of the tall form of Walking Dove. It yelled again with greater delight when the chief seized it from the woman and threw it up into the air —yelled, and quite unthinking of a fall, lifted its small hands to clutch at the dangling scalp.

It seemed a reasonably horrible thing to Cashel, but the Indian crowd shouted their satisfaction.

"A brave father makes a brave son!" said an old warrior close to Cashel.

But Cashel was watching the joyous excitement that trembled in the face and body of the wife as she greeted her husband. She was no beauty. She had cheekbones and a jaw that a prize fighter might have envied, but Cashel guessed at as much virtue and truth in her as he ever had seen in a woman of his own race.

Walking Dove went on, and the woman carried her boy on her shoulder into the crowd, which everywhere gave way with the greatest respect for her, and even turned a part of their attention and smiles upon her. Certainly a share of reflected glory fell brightly on the entire family of a Cheyenne hero!

The "gang" seemed farther away to Cashel than ever before, and Manhattan's streets and dark alleys were as unreal as an image wavering in the depths of water.

They had got by this time to a large, open circular space in the center of the village; and it was sufficiently dusk for the light of the day to be less than that of the fire that had been built in the center of the open space. It was a big pile of wood that had been kindled, and Two Antelope was on his horse in the background, still giving directions and orders, while more men carried in excess fuel and piled it within easy reach of the flames.

The whole population of that village now spilled around the outer edges of the circle, packed in thickly, and in a certain order. That is to say, the children were in front, their bodies gleaming, their eyes and teeth flashing as the day died and the fire seemed to light them more strongly. The warriors stood behind, and the squaws swayed from side to side, getting what glimpses they could of the show between the shoulders of the warriors.

And a show it was. With the fire lighted and the stage set, Walking Dove, like a leading actor delaying the performance in order to build up expectations, still lingered on the outskirts, pretending to see to the accouterments of the white mares. This delayed worked strongly on the nerves of the audience. Where were the stern, repressed, laconic Indians of whom the boy had heard so much? These fellows were like children grown big in body but not in mind. Presently the restraint and waiting grew too much for one of the braves in the circle of spectators. He could not wait to hear the story of the deeds of Walking Dove, and with a loud yell, he broke from his place and began to dance and chant.

He bounded like a big copper-skinned wildcat. He yelled. He whooped. With a good broad-bladed hatchet he cut down imaginary enemies with terific sweeping blows. This example was followed by half a dozen other braves who came out and began their individual dances. Their yelling made the thief think of an orchestra playing an overture; the play was about to begin! But as the excitement of the dancers increased, they left off their bounding and whooping and began to turn in smaller and smaller circles with a peculiar broken, syncopated, jerking step. All the time they chanted in rather subdued voices, for all the world like so many roosters gyrating and showing off before an admiring circle of hens.

No one seemed to be bothered by these exhibitions, and no one seemed greatly interested in them. The half-dozen young men simply were letting off steam, and the instant that Walking Dove strode into the circle of the firelight, they immediately withdrew behind the children to watch and to listen. Cashel himself was drawn into this entrance, for the chief begged him to lead the horses on. He himself would do the dancing and sing the narration, but he wanted his white friend to have some part in the picture. Cashel resisted. It was not his habit to take a share in any public appearance. He was more accustomed to lurking in corners among the shadows, from which he could look out at the follies of franker and more jovial men; and he was only persuaded by a most unexpected voice which said in good English at his shoulder: "Go on in, son. They won't eat you. They're going to make a hero of you, and Walking Dove will tell how strong your medicine is!"

Cashel turned and saw a long, lean-faced man who looked almost as dark skinned as an Indian, and fully as ugly as the homeliest of the braves. He was dressed, like them, in deerskin, heavily beaded and glistening with quill work. His hair flowed down over his shoulders in the Cheyenne style. There were feathers in his hair to indicate his Indian rank in the tribe. But still a humorous squinting at the corners of his eyes, and something about his mouth was inimitably Caucasian—Yankee Caucasian, at that.

He clapped a huge, bony hand on the shoulder of Cashel. "Go on in," he repeated, laughing a little in a nasal, drawling tone. "Stand up and let 'em see you. And by the time that Walking Dove gets through lying about the pair of you, every pretty young chief's daughter in this layout is going to want to do your cooking and sewing!"

Cashel, bewildered at hearing this voice, allowed himself to be urged forward, and actually let the mares out into the circle of the light. There he paused and took no further share in the celebration. He was not needed, however. Walking Dove was quite adequate to the work that lay before him.

CHAPTER XIV

THE CHIEF began with the greatest dignity.

The minute he stepped out, with his war pony behind him, several drums began to throb with deep, hollow, mournful notes, and a flute and several other horns blared. There was no attempt at a tune. At first it was merely a confused crashing on the ears of Cashel; but presently this confusion ordered itself a little and sounded to him as though some controlling rhythm were in it, like the roaring of breakers on a long shore, and the screaming of sea birds in the wind.

After the first blare of this "music," it sank away somewhat, and the drums merely kept up a subdued pulsing which was wonderfully exciting. Cashel himself felt his nerves drawing taut, and breathed with difficulty, while all around the circle, he was aware of terribly bright, hungry eyes fixed upon Walking Dove. The horns had died out completely, only now and again, at high points in the story, screaming all together like eagles in a storm.

But as the first riot died down, Walking Dove stepped a few paces to the right and planted the slender butt of his lance strongly in the ground. After this he turned and walked a few solemn strides to the left, holding out his arms as he paused.

He kept this position for a whole tense minute, and then spoke: "Oh moon, you have helped me. Be my witness now.

60

If Walking Dove tells lies, cover your face and refuse to hear him!"

It was an excellent effect, and well did Walking Dove know it. Cashel could understand why the warrior had delayed until this moment, for now the moon like a big yellow wheel was rolling up the side of a large tepee on the western half of the circle—exactly as though she were climbing into the sky in answer to the call of the chief! But if the effect upon Cashel was strong, it was immense with the Indians. Cashel saw them swaying from side to side, and heard a gasp, followed by a deep, long murmur of fear and satisfaction. The drums beat loudly one stroke and then fell back into their throbbing accompaniment, like the beating of frightened hearts.

Having started off in this excellent style, Walking Dove warmed up to his work gradually, beginning to walk in circles around the fire, his pace gradually increasing until it became a dancing step, jerking and syncopated like those of the others who had danced there before him. A good part of what he said was lost to Cashel because the tongue still was not perfectly familiar in his ear, but he got every word of the opening, which went as follows, in a good, grave prose style:

"Brothers, listen to a man who is a truthteller. He tells you how he lived among you with a broken heart because twice when he led out the young men on the warpath they were broken and scattered by the Pawnees and by the two white mares whose riders are kept from harm. His heart was broken. He could not raise his head. The young men deserted him. The women scorned him, and the chiefs no longer were glad to sit in his tepee. When he gave a feast, everyone was busy, and when others gave feasts, their lodges were too small to hold him! At last he said that he must do a great thing or die. He must do it alone, because none of the young men would follow him. So he took his best horse and rode out with him into the prairie. There is the horse! He remembers how we went out together, and how we killed the deer on the second day, and jerked the meat off it. He knows that we were riding to find the great Pawnee war party of which he had heard—the war party which the best chiefs among the Pawnees were leading out against the Cheyennes, laughing at my people because they knew that the medicine horses would turn bullets and knife strokes away in the battle. Do you hear me, brothers?"

Every throat in that assemblage opened wide for a shriek of assent that split the dary sky over them and made a light flash before the dazzled eyes of Cashel.

"We knew that seventy good warriors, practiced braves,

61

wise serpents on the trail, sure hands in the battle, were coming under famous chiefs."

Cashel made mental note of this "truthteller" who already had a little more than doubled the facts.

"And among the warriors there was a famous young man. He had ridden through the Cheyenne line in battle. He had counted a coup on a living man. There stands Gray Willow, on whom he counted coup! His name was the Owl!"

He got no further. A terrific din of excitement drowned him out, but having given this obscure foretaste of what was to come, he returned to his journey across the prairie, always emphasizing the singleness of his hand, and the number of his enemies, which would be counterblanaced by the strength of his medicine.

Then Cashel himself was introduced to the narrative. The Cheyenne sees him far away, and catches the glint of his glass, and stalks him through the grass, and raises out of it behind him, and then the good rifle is shot out of his hands by a conjurer's shot.

It was a moment not to be skipped over lightly by such a narrator and brazen-fronted liar as Walking Dove. He developed it in these words.

"I stood with empty hands. Another bullet lay in the curl of his finger. He could have sent me to my forefathers to hunt the ghosts of buffalo across the sky. But now he stood up and smiled on me, and he said: 'Walking Dove, have no fear! Your medicine is very strong. The Sky People love you, and they have sent me here to do everything that you wish. You shall have the two magic horses. I myself shall get them and give them to you, and you shall bring them home with a scalp!'"

This little improvisation left Cashel somewhat out of breath. He looked down at the ground, bewildered and uneasy, and expecting a loud shout of laughter to greet this open-faced lie, and this boasting he was assumed to have made. On the contrary, there was an ocean of applause at once. He ventured a glance around him. Every face smiled at him. He saw warriors with axes and spears and guns lifted and shaken toward him, as though they were pledging him their brotherhood in arms. He saw the children scrambling to their feet and dancing with excitement as they pointed their skinny arms at him. He saw, between the wide shoulders of two warriors, the face of a girl smiling at him. Indian style, her hair in two long braids flowed down past her throat, but that hair was not black. It turned to running gold in the firelight, and her face was pale.

Cashel gripped the reins of the horses a little more firmly. There was no ridicule in that smile of hers, but an open, warm admiration. Far otherwise the keen-witted girls of Manhattan would have smiled in mockery at such a tale as this!

But they were far away. The broad, green sea of the prairies fenced them off, and the big rivers between. He stood in the center of a new world where there was space to spare for good, big, mouth-filling, childish fictions such as this one of the chief's.

That warrior went on with his story on the heels of the noisy applause that had been given his last statement. The wave of excitement carried him along with it. His imagination wakened. His dance quickened.

Now they saw the line of the Pawnees against the sky; and the two white mares gleamed like milk in the light of the dawn. Now they were crouched in the ravine, and heard the shots of the hunters. Now they lay on the ridge above the camp.

"My heart grew small," said Walking Dove. "My heart grew as small as the heart of a child. It shrank and turned cold in me. I was afraid. I felt fear run over me like water in winter. I did not know what to do, but my friend laid his hand on mine.

" 'Have no fear,' said he. 'If your heart is weak now, your medicine still is strong. I shall show you the way into their camp. We shall take the mares from the fence of spears and lariats. The Sky People love you. They scorn and hate the Pawnee wolves. They know that you are a good man, and they have made your medicine strong.' "

So had the Cheyenne chief exactly reversed the facts of the case that Cashel could have laughed. But he could not understand, at first, why Walking Dove chose to minimize his own iron-hearted courage while talking up the bravery of his white companion. Only gradually it dawned on the mind of the thief that among these people courage and skill with weapons were all very well, but the wizard and medicine man was greater than the chief, and that by taking his present line, the warrior was laying claims to what he considered the greatest power in the world. The mysterious "Sky People" he was reducing, as it were, into boon companions and body servants!

The grandest of the warrior's lies now commenced.

" 'We shall go down the river together,' said my friend the white man. 'The underwater people love me. By them I am called the Water Rat. That is my name among them. They will keep us safe and warm in the water. We shall walk down the river behind a log, and when we come to the bank, I shall push the log away and we will go ashore. There we shall meet a dog. If you hesitate and are afraid, the dog will tear your throat and drink your life. If you are strong, you will take that dog by the throat and kill him and give his blood to the Sky People. Then crawl up the bank close behind me. I shall pick up a robe and walk forward with it draped over my head. Crawl close behind me. I shall kill the guard and leave you to count the coup and take the scalp, then I shall cut the lariats of the fence and go to the mares!' "

This almost complete misstatement the warrior delivered in a continuous yell of excitement, but the audience returned not a whisper of applause. It could not speak. It was enchained with delighted expectation. Of course the white messenger from the Sky People would do all that was promised, but still, it was delightful to hear the prophecy turned into the fact.

And Walking Dove made the most of the fairy tale he had created. He made his audience go trembling with him through the ranks of the Pawnees. He named off-hand the warriors among whom they passed, touched a little on their deeds, and made that Pawnee band seen like a hundred sleeping dragons.

For the number had by this time insensibly mounted from seventy to a hundred!

The white man stood up; struck down the Pawnee with a knife stroke—or was it a bit of raw, white lightning that flashed from his finger tips?—and then the scalp was seized by Walking Dove.

Here the chief seized his prize from the shaft of the war spear and began a wild dance, a true scalp dance. This was too much for the other warriors. They poured out into the circle. A mad clamor began as they pranced and leaped around the fire, their wild bodies flinging up against the red light, their faces contorted with battle hysteria. Cashel watched them with amazement. Over the hubbub, he heard still further screeched fragments of Walking Dove's chant, a chant of glorious victory, and the speed of the matchless white mares bearing the victors away. The whole audience broke into a frenzy. The very children were dancing and yelling and taking imaginary scalps, and the women tossing their arms. Only, looking across the dimmer sea of light, Cashel saw one composed face, now fainter and farther away; it was the girl of the golden, braided hair, thick and heavy as metal; she was untouched by the uproar; she still smiled; and her eyes dwelt on him steadily as on a daydream.

CHAPTER XV

THE RIOT that started with the scalping story, and the vivid description of the end of the Owl very soon drew into it every man and most of the boys of war-trail age in the entire group. Cashel was looking on at this strange exhibition of madness and mental drunkenness, when his arm was touched from behind, and he looked around to see that the tall white man was again with him.

"This here will keep on a mighty big part of the night," said the stranger in his drawling voice, "and I reckon that you'd better come home with me and go to sleep. I've got a tolerable bed for you, and a squaw that can cook some, and a backrest that'll do your innards a lot of good. Give the hosses to this boy to hold. He'll thank his stars for the chance."

He beckoned to a stripling who reecived the reins as if they were made of gold, and looked at Cashel as though at a demigod; then the latter willingly followed his new-found friend, partly because he was very tired, and partly because the taste of English, spoken even in this fashion, was sweet in his ears.

They went back down a lane through the crowding tepees, attended by ten or a dozen dogs which had detached themselves from a mob of their fellows that had been howling in sympathy with the humans at the scalp dance. These dogs were on the whole big fellows with the look of wolves, so that there was no doubt about their ancestry. Some of them looked strong enough to pull down a buffalo, and a decided chill went up Cashel's back when the shaggy monsters came sniffing at his legs.

His companion was one of those slow but steady talkers who allow few interruptions because they either are completing a sentence or have their lips parted to begin a new one. His thoughts did not come fast, but they came faster than he was able to utter them.

He said: "That fellow Walkin' Dove they oughta hire regular and pay him a hoss a week to put on shows for them, because he's as good as a theater, any time. That fellow could kill a chipmunk and get the whole doggone tribe whoopin' and dancin' over it, and claimin' the help of the Sky People, which I reckon that you didn't see a terrible lot of the same, anyway, did you?"

Cashel laughed softly.

"We needed them, though," he admitted.

"And that crawlin' through the camp," said the other. "That was a good dodge, too; it takes a Walkin' Dove to thing up things like that. Storybook things, that'll make good tellin' the rest of his days, and they'll always be glad to hear him count that coup when they set around and swap lies in the winter nights. You must of give him a hand, though, or he wouldn't give you so many wings. Did you run onto that poor sucker, the Owl, all by himself and do for him, and grab the white mares?"

"We did for somebody that wore Pawnee hair and a feather," said Cashel quietly. "That's all I know."

"But that about the fence of war spears and the Injuns lyin' around thicker than corn shocks in a cornfield—you wouldn't want me to believe that, partner?"

"I don't ask you to believe anything," said Cashel. "There were plenty of Pawnees lying around, though."

"A hundred, eh?" asked the other.

There was no sneer, merely laughter in his voice.

"There were thirty-two," said Cashel truthfully.

"And you done just as he said—got up on your hind legs and walked right through 'em?" asked the other.

"Yes," said Cashel, yawning a little as he saw the impossibility of having this true story believed by any incredulous white man, no matter how Indians could trust in a narrator. "Minus the Sky People, and such rot, Walking Dove told the truth, as closely as I could follow him."

"And you stabbed that there Pawnee with a lightning flash, too?"

"I stabbed him with my knife," answered Cashel, "and there's still a nick in the point of it where it chopped against his backbone."

The other paused suddenly and faced his companion in the dark, faintly lit with the quaverings and leapings of the firelight from the center of the camp.

"D'you mean it, stranger?" said he.

"If it weren't true," replied Cashel, "I tell you that I wouldn't be able to make up a thing like that. I'd made a lie closer to probability. The main thing that Walking Dove left out was simply that I was scared sick, and he did the leading. Somehow, I had to keep in his shadow, until I got the idea of wrapping myself in that buffalo robe. I've still got the smell of it in my nose and I wish that the scalp we took had been that of the fellow who owned the robe."

The other broke out into loud daughter.

"I believe you, now," said he. "Scared I reckon you were. Walkin' Dove was so mighty bent on getting back some reputation that I suppose he would have walked up and batted a grizzly on the nose. My name's Jim Diver to white folks, and Long Bull to these new people of mine, which ain't a bad name for me, considerin' that I shade six foot four. They're kind of stretched out themselves, but nothin' quite so extravagant as that. Who are you, stranger?"

"Bandon Suir Cashel," said the thief, looking steadily toward the night-darkened face of the other.

But apparently this name meant nothing to the other.

"I'm a squaw man," he went on steadily, "and as long as you wanta hang out with this tribe, my woman'll make you comfortable. There ain't a better squaw in the tribe than Lucky, which is short for Lucky Buffalo Bird. You translate that into Cheyenne and you get a five-minute talk before you begin to say what you mean. A name as long as that is in Cheyenne you couldn't afford the time to say moren than once on your marriage day. A name like that would plumb stop conversation, and so I call her Lucky for short, and lucky she is, and always has been for me. I come among the Cheyennes with the skin that God give me, and a ragged piece of old antelope hide to cover my shoulders, and a couple of bird snares and a broken hunting knife. And now, you wait till you see how I'm fixed, Muskrat!"

"Muskrat?" queried Cashel, a little angered by this familiarity.

"Well, ain't that the name that Walkin' Dove give to you?" asked Diver. "Water Rat, he called you. And Muskrat is likely what Injun politeness will make of that."

"I'll see Walking Dove about that," said Cashel, whose pride in his name was as fierce as a fire.

"Don't you go getting upset," answered Jim Diver. "The fact is that names don't mean nothin' to an Injun. It's how you get your name that counts, and every time that the Cheyennes hear that name of yours, or speak it, they'll have a picture of you sneakin' down the river, and then slidin' in amongst a couple of thousand man-eatin' Pawnees and snatchin' off scalps and stealin' magic hosses as you go! That name ain't no insult to you, and as long as you stay with the Cheyennes that name'll do you a lot of good."

This version of the name and its possible meaning amazed Cashel and effectually silenced him. At any rate, before he could speak again they had come to a good-sized tepee made of new, cured hides as white as milk, and glimmering in the darkness as brightly as one of the enchanted mares. At the board hanging near the closed entrance flap, the squaw man rapped, and then drew back the fold of skin and waved Cashel in before him. So he stepped into the first lodge interior he ever had seen.

It was surprisingly roomy. Straight, slender ashen poles extended around a circle and over them the skins fitted neatly and taut, rising to the opening at the top, with the flap of skin above it to make the draught. The top of the tepee was a little obscured with smoke, but the lower part was clearly visible in the light of the small fire which burned in the center of the floor and kept steaming a good-sized iron pot out of which issued a fragrance of cooking meat. Two beds, deep with robes, were made up against the wall of the tent, with a partition of deerskin in between them, and a small pole at the foot of each from which hung pipes, clothes, a feather headdress, and a crowd of other things. More racks appeared against the sides of the tent, littered with bridles, saddles, hatchets hanging by wrist loops, and such a quantity of other camp furniture that Cashel could imagine a man being comfortable here the rest of his days; and after sleeping out so long on the hard ground with only one thickness of blanket between his hipbones and the sod, his very soul ached to stretch himself in such comfort! There was only one feature of the tepee that jarred on him, and this was a series of paintings that covered the interior of the lodge in a style that a five-year-old white child might have duplicated, except that here and there appeared a bison or a horse drawn with some sense of anatomy, but with pipe-stem legs, and stretching, pulled-out necks.

A big, broad-faced squaw rose to welcome them, still holding in her hand a moccasin she had been beading. She gave her husband and Cashel a scowl and a "How!" and then she turned on Jim Diver and let loose a stream of Cheyenne that staggered the other white man with its eloquence. It was so rapidly spoken that he could not follow all of it, but merely gathered, uncomfortably, that she was saying that other warriors brought home new supplies of venison and buffalo meat when they came home, but that her brave merely supplied extra mouths to devour the provisions.

In return, her white husband replied in a murmur which Cashel quite missed, pointing toward his guest. The squaw called "Lucky" gave her spouse a furious glare and hurried from the lodge at once.

"Your wife doesn't want me here," said Cashel. "Besides, I suppose that I ought to go to sleep with Walking Dove in his home."

"Don't be a fool," replied the squaw man. "Walkin' Dove lives in a lodge with two other families, and so full of poles and dogs, and squallin' babies that you wouldn't get two winks of sleep in a week. There's so much cookery goin' on inside that lodge that the sides of the tent are always wet with drops of water, and the sour smell of cookin' buffalo meat. Set down over there and rest your feet, will you? Make yourself easy, partner, and don't bother none about my wife's tongue. I used to have her sister, besides, for a second squaw. That other girl, she acted like a lightnin' rod, and absorbed most of the shocks for me, but she died last year, and since then Lucky ain't had a chance to work herself out except on me. She don't mean nothin', but she's gotta make her share of the noise. Besides, you seen how I shut her up?"

"What did you say?" asked Cashel, amused.

"I told her that she'd better go out and find out for herself what sort of a man I'd brought home; because she's so dog-gone sour that she won't go out and waste her housekeeping time on scalp dances and frolics like that. And then I wound up by tellin' her that you understood Cheyenne!"

He laughed, and added: "She's gonna hoof it down to the dance, and in five minutes, she'll be settin' in the dark pullin' out her hair in hunks and pourin' dirt and ashes on her head for havin' made a fool of herself."

CHAPTER XVI

IN THE meantime, the squaw man was pulling out an extra willow bed, unrolling it, and heaping it with blankets from a stack of robes that was piled in a corner of the lodge, and all the while he worked he was piling encomiums on the head of his wife. She was, he declared, the best woman in the world, the most industrious, the quickest and neatest in the beading of moccasins or the adornment of clothes with quillwork, the swiftest in fleshing hides, the most dexterous in curing them, the tidiest cook, and the most faithful laborer. Her pemmican, he swore, was the finest in the Cheyenne nation, and her vocabulary, he wound up, equal to that of a poet.

"If she was back to New York or Boston, she'd be a she-writer in no time," declared Jim Diver, "like Harriet Beecher Stowe, and the rest of 'em. She's a girl of parts, that old woman of mine, and she'd be the happiest woman in the world if it wasn't for one thing."

"What's that?" asked Cashel.

"Why," grinned the other, "she suffers a good deal from havin' only one tongue to dress me down and give me advice. But you get used to a talky woman and there ain't nothin' so dull as a quiet one. It's like a Sunday band; there's always somethin' in the air, and it don't mean nothin' but noise. Watch her come back in a minute."

He laughed, and added: "She's gonna hoof it down to the that was stewing in the pot, and offered it to young Cashel. It lacked all salt or other seasoning, but he had been eating unseasoned fresh meat so long that this was almost a relief. Besides, he possessed that best of sauces.

Jim Diver sat down, stretched his long legs, leaned himself against a backrest, and filled and lighted a pipe. Through the smoke that rose from this he observed the newcomer with little, twinkling eyes, and answered at great length the questions Cashel put to him.

He had been on a freighter, a Mississippi steamboat hand, a guide, a trapper, a small farmer in Illinois, a horse hunter in the land of the Comanches, where he nearly had lost his scalp, and finally he had become a trader, and while in that capacity had run from a raiding party of Pawnees who scooped up his entire profits of two seasons.

"After that," said Jim Diver, "somehow I got a hankerin' after Pawnee scalps. There never was no tanner that wanted to tan hides no moren than I wanted to smoke Pawnee scalps over my fire. So I come to the Cheyennes and settled right down among them, because when it comes to catchin' Pawnees, they're the outcatchin'est pile of folks that you ever seen."

"And you took scalps?" asked Cashel, his mind flashing back to the picture of Walking Dove as the latter had straightened above the dead body of the Owl, with the blade of his knife tarnished, and a shapeless rag of something in his other hand. "You took scalps, Diver?"

"I never was nothin' like Two Antelope," said the squaw man, "and I never could hold a candle, of course, to that outstandin' hellion of a fightin' man, Broken Arrow, but in my own little quiet way, I done tolerable!"

He lifted his eyes as he spoke, and high aloft, obscured and almost lost to view in the smoke of the fire, Cashel saw hanging five small objects, suspended from the upper parts of the tepee poles.

Said Jim Diver:

"They ain't much to see. They don't match up, say, with the scalps that you get from a Cheyenne, or a Kiowa, to say nothin' of them Crows, with the hair a-hangin' down to their ankles, pretty nigh, but the beauty of a Pawnee scalp, it ain't in the looks. It's in the takin'!" The way that a Pawnee scalp is fitted on, it's one of the toughest things in the world to get at, and you lay awake at night and gotta figger out ways of snatchin' it off the head that wears it, and mostly you only break your fingernails and don't get no where in the game!"

He said this in such a matter-of-fact manner that half the horror was taken from his words; but still Cashel was conscious of a qualm in his stomach and a chill that went serpentwise up his spine.

70

Immediately after this, there was a tremendous additional outburst of noise from the direction of the dance, and on the heels of this great wave of sound, in came the good squaw of Jim Diver, and paused for a moment, with her hand still extended to the flap of the tepee, and her eyes fixed upon Cashel's face. He eyed her back with one swift glance, for that was his fashion. One who does not wish to have his face remembered, one who preys on society and prays that society may not note him, is not apt to stare fixedly at other faces. Instead, he learns as Cashel had learned to see everything with a glance as swift as the flick of a whiplash, or a mere touch from the corner of the eyes.

But the squaw stared heavily at him, until even her easy-going husband was roused enough to raise an angry finger at her.

Still she said not a word, but went over to the seat she had occupied before and sat there in a gloomy silence.

"There is a guest in our tepee!" said Diver at last, thoroughly angered. "Have you made him welcome?"

She merely set herself to the threading of her needle in order to continue her beadwork, and at last, lifting her head from this occupation, she glared again at Cashel, and the impact of her eyes made him wince and shift a little. He could not tell what her expression meant; only, that whatever her emotion was, it was strong.

"Don't mind her," said her husband. "She has on one of her fool streaks, and when she gets that way, the best thing is to leave her alone. I learned that early in our happy life together."

He puffed some smoke toward the top of the tepee and grinned as he watched it rise.

"I tried to use a little discipline one day and she picked up a handy meat cleaver and tried to use the edge of it on my head. I dodged, and she went for the door. I let her go."

"How did you get her back?" asked Cashel, thinking that this was a helpmate that a man could have done very well without.

"Why," said the squaw man, "I got word from her old father that the idiot was sitting in his tepee with a robe over her head, not eating or drinking. He thought I'd beaten her. She wouldn't talk. Well, that made me think that she wasn't all teeth but maybe was fond of me. I went over to the chief's tepee and spoke to her, and she got up without saying a word and followed me back here. She never spoke about it afterward, and neither did I, but I learned to respect her little whims that crop up now and then. If you don't push her too far, she leaves off at words, which don't break anybody's skin; but if you get her really angry, I think she'd as

71

soon slide a knife under your left rib as take a drink of water. She's got the name of being the roughest lady in town, but she's also the best housekeeper, and that's what counts. If you marry one of these girls, don't hunt for the pretty faces. They cost you more hosses, and they don't hoe the corn or flesh the hides as well. And you can't eat sweet smiles if you're my kind of a man!"

"You like this life?" said the thief.

"It's the only one for me. It gets me a Pawnee once in every couple of seasons, and the rest of the time, it's no work, and plenty of chuck and nobody to give you orders. I eat the best, dress warm, ride smart hosses, get my fun chattin' with the old braves, or huntin', or gamblin' on winter evenin's, or listenin' to the yarnin' of some of the professional liars and medicine men of the tribe, or sneakin' along the war trail with a lot of the rest of these varmints lookin' for a good fresh crop of Pawnee hair."

He looked up again at his prizes with the same faint smile of appreciation and, apparently, amusement, as though he enjoyed his victories, but also was willing to laugh at them a little. He seemed to the boy a character with a good many phases, and certainly a white man wise in Indian ways.

The uproar of the dance had ended, at last, and broken up into many separate currents and islands of chatter as the people moved away toward their tepees in various parts of the camp. A moment later there was a knock at the entrance and then the deep voice of a brave speaking. This time even Lucky showed some animation, and going hastily to the flap, drew it aside and stood back. It was Two Antelope who entered. He greeted his host and the white man, and readily accepted a backrest against which he made himself comfortable. He was in no haste to talk, but first took out a red-clay pipe bowl, fitted a stem into it, and accepted the tobacco which his host proffered. His first puff he blew with a ceremonial air toward the top of the tent, his second toward the ground, after which he was able to enjoy his pipe in peace.

All this while, the thief had been eying him covertly, and askance, and he thought that he never had seen a harder face, or a grimmer eye. Two Antelope struck suddenly into the heart of his purpose by saying to Jim Diver: "I am glad to see the Muskrat in this tepee, Long Bull. You can tell him that the Cheyennes are not a bad people, and that they love their friends. Their braves have strong hands and their women have faithful hearts. If the Muskrat will stay with us, we shall try to be good to him and fill his hands with everything he needs."

He turned suddenly and directly upon the white man.

"Friend, what is your thought?" said he.

Cashel stared at the fire, and then raising thoughtful eyes, he encountered the glance of the squaw, and found her eyes as big and bright as the eyes of an owl. But he could not tell, again, what her emotion might be—whether it was anger, scorn, contempt, pride, or hate. He let his mind fly forward. There was a sense of self-abandonment that was exciting to his gambler's nature, in the thought of remaining here among the savages and making them his people for a time. When he cared to, he could leave them again.

And he saw again, vividly, the golden-haired Indian who had smiled at him; and Clonmel sweeping over the crown of the hill. If he remained with the tribe for a time, they would help him to the horse, at least. As for the girl, he would not bring her out of the back of his mind, where she remained guiltily hidden.

He said bluntly to the chief, "There is a horse . . ."

Then he hesitated, realizing that one does not bargain about such a thing as a tribal adoption.

"Walking Dove has told me," said the chief. "If the stallion is stolen by any of our braves, he will bring it to you gladly."

"If that happens," said Cashel, "he can change his bridle onto the white mare that I rode in this evening."

Two Antelope parted his lips to speak but could not utter words—as though his jaws suddenly had frozen with rust. Then a cunning light gleamed in his eyes.

"Brother," said he, "within seven days I shall place the stallion in your hands!"

CHAPTER XVII

LIKE a man with a great purpose in hand, Two Antelope left the lodge at once, and Jim Diver remarked:

"He's a rich chief, Muskrat, and he'll give nine-tenths of everythin' he has to buy the stallion from the Pawnees. But you'll have an unlucky name around here among the Cheyennes if you give up one of the white mares. However, that's your business. And it's time to turn in."

Utter weariness closed the eyes of the thief as soon as he had stretched himself on the comfortable bed of willows. But he enjoyed no more than an hour of leaden sleep before he was wakened by an explosion of noise. It sounded like a shrieking of the wind and the braying of mules blended, and he was so alarmed that he started up from the blankets with his heart beating wildly.

The quiet, drawling voice of Long Bull spoke near by, through the fire-stained dimness in the lodge:

"That ain't a murder. It's only some of the young bucks serenading a gal near by. She's got a name that means One-that-never-trips-when-walking. Put that into Cheyenne and it's so doggone hard that it brings tears to your eyes and makes you sneeze to say it. She's got a face like an accident, but she sure appeals to the young bucks, and they're tunin' up for her sake."

Cashel, listening more carefully, could pick out the sound of the flutes, now, and afterward the roar of the singing braves.

He lay back on his bed, half laughing and half groaning, for he was dizzy with weariness. In spite of that noise, he was almost asleep before the end of it and would have been deep in slumber the next moment if it had not been for a dogfight that started so near at hand that the brutes seemed to be wrangling and snarling in the very lodge where he lay.

That tumult swept away, and yet it was only the beginning, for other fights began, as if in emulation of the first one, and a hubbub roared from one end of the camp to the other. In the midst of this inferno, he made out that Jim Diver, alias Long Bull, actually was snoring in the most peaceful slumber! So was the squaw, in a higher key.

The dogfights continued for some time, and when they ended, Cashel was almost asleep. But a newer sound broke out close at hand—the single voice of a squalling baby, somewhere between colic pains and furious anger. Needle-like it shrilled into his brain.

He turned on his face and clapped his hands over his ears, but not until the baby had ended, an hour later, could he actually sleep. And all through the rest of that night, which seemed as long as ten days, he started up wide awake, from time to time, roused by a turbulent outbreak of one sort or another.

He had a thorough idea of the pleasures of the wild life when he was finally roused in the morning by Long Bull, nodding and grinning down at him, as fresh as could be.

"You got your ears sprained last night," said Diver, "but you get used to it, after a while. Come along with me, and we'll have a plunge."

They walked down to the riverbank, where Diver pointed out the water plan of the camp. First was the place where water was drawn and carried to the camp. Below that began a point where swimming was allowed, below this laundry was done, and last of all came the section where the animals could be brought to water.

They swam in the appointed pool, where half a dozen

young braves already were disporting themselves in the water, active as brown seals, and such pictures of muscular manhood that the thief was ashamed to strip before them. However, he felt better after he had splashed clumsily about in the water for a time, and when he had shaved and rubbed down and dressed, an appetite came to him and the world once more seemed a comfortable place—even the Indian world which was absorbing him for the moment.

He confided his embarrassment to Diver.

"I felt like a peeled carrot in front of those Cheyennes in the pool," he said. "Did you see how they laughed?"

"I saw how they laughed," said Diver. "You mean that you felt scrawny beside them? Well, Cashel, I'll tell you how it is. A man ain't known among the Cheyennes by the size of his biceps. He's known by his medicine, and by his courage. Those youngsters were all good fighters—warpath braves. But they were laughin' to cover *their* embarrassment. You should have waved your hand to them and saluted them in some way, as if they were just important enough for you to notice them. You didn't pay any attention to them, and they're feelin' pretty sick about it. You see, Cashel, you're now a great brave, and your medicine is a hundred per cent. By the time that Walkin' Dove got through talkin' and lyin' last night, he had painted a picture of you that every brave in the nation would give his eyeteeth to call a portrait of himself. You're such a great man in this nation, right now, that there ain't a chief who wouldn't *pay* you to marry his daughter! When we get back to the tepee, you'll have some surprises ready for you, or I miss my guess. No, sir, there ain't a brave among the Cheyennes that wouldn't change his list of coups for the sake of the thing you did to the Pawnees. I leave Broken Arrow out of the count."

"That's the second time you've spoken of Broken Arrow," said Cashel. "Who's he?"

"Him? Ain't you heard of him?"

"Never a word, I think."

"You've had wool inside your ears, then. Broken Arrow is the sure poison, the center-fire hell raiser of this outfit. They say that he's taken thirty scalps, and I've set in the circle and heard that red devil count twenty-eight coups. All first coups, and no seconds and thirds, because they're beneath his dignity to notice."

"What does coup mean, anyway?"

"Why, it's when you touch an enemy. If he's alive and on foot and you're on a hoss, that's the finest coup you can count. You touch him with your hand, or a coup stick, and holler out that you count coup, and it's a lot more important than his scalp, even. If you kill a man, that don't count as a coup. You might shoot him from a distance. But if you can come up close and touch him with your hand, then that counts coup, and it's the thing that you talk about when the coup-countin' starts in the winter evenin's. Three coups can be counted on every man, alive or dead, in the enemy's outfit. When a Pawnee drops, you'll see a flock of Cheyennes charge for him, for the sake of touchin' him first. That's why this Broken Arrow is such big medicine. He's a queer fellow, and he never leads parties out on the trail. He's the best lookin' upstandin'est Cheyenne in the tribe. He's the handiest with a bow and arrows, and the slickest with a rifle, and uses a pistol like a white man. He can run faster, last longer, ride harder than any other brave on the plains, I reckon. He's stole enough hosses from the Comanches, and Sioux, and Crows, and Pawnees to haul New York into the East River; but he gives away his stuff as quick as he gets it. He keeps himself poor. He lives with the young unmarried men in the big lodge. He's never looked at a girl for a wife. And usually he don't never own more than three hosses—all first-rate—a rifle, a brace of pistols, a couple of knives, and the clothes that he stands up in. No, Broken Arrow wouldn't trade his glory for the job that you done on the Pawnees the other night, but I reckon that any other brave in the tribe would."

They came back to the lodge, as this was said, and here they found a crowd of fully fifty warriors waiting. Each had something in his hand, one a saddle, another a bow, another a pipe, and some the lariat that led a horse, and some had ordinary or painted robes. Each of these came up to the new white man with a dignified greeting; each was duly presented by name by Jim Diver, and each gave his gift by putting down the article at the feet of the new addition to the tribe. Very soon the heap grew huge. And Diver himself was holding four horses to leave free the hands of his guest. Walking Dove himself was there, coming up among the last with a very broad smile and pointing with some excitement to his gift. It was a princely one. Two good horses pulled strong travois, and upon these were heaped enough fine new skins of buffalo cows to make an entire tepee. They were shaped and sewn and ready to be fitted over the poles.

But last of all came a tall young brave who walked with a high head and the step of an athlete, but who wore no ornamental feathers in his hair, and who was wrapped in a tattered and battered old robe, thin and torn with long usage, and on his feet was a pair of moccasins unadorned by as much as a single bead. Yet in spite of the common cheapness of his outfit he held the eye with a face as finely cut and with an eye as open, and a brow as deep as that of any white

76

man. There was no brutality, no flaring nostrils, no heavy modeling of the lips, no outthrust of the cheekbones.

Cashel watched him with wonder and, when the warrior came closer, with a touch of awe, even, though awe was something that rarely came to that keen, hard-tempered brain of his.

From beneath his cloak, the brave took a single eagle feather, long, straight shafted, stiff with newness, just as it had come from the bald-headed eagle that had been killed for the sake of its plumage.

"It's Broken Arrow," said Jim Diver, excited as he spoke. "This is an honor for you, Cashel!"

Broken Arrow held out the feather and said, in an astonishingly quiet voice:

"This is the gift of a poor man, my brother. I have prayed to the Sky People that they may send us out on the warpath together, and that you may come home wearing many feathers like this."

He went off at once. The others scattered at the same time, for they seemed to have waited only to see Broken Arrow make his presentation, as the climax to this little show. Now Lucky Buffalo Bird began to carry the gifts into the tepee, and Cashel, staring at this heap of wealth, said to Diver, "What makes Broken Arrow go around like a beggar and wear no feathers, since they seem to be the highest decoration these fellows can carry?"

"He and a friend went on a skirmish and were mobbed by a whole crowd of Sioux. The friend was shot off his horse while they were running for it, and poor Broken Arrow left him for dead. But when he looked back, he saw the man jump up from the ground and fight the Sioux as they came charging around him. Of course the other Cheyenne was killed and scalped, but it left Broken Arrow with an idea that his partner had died defendin' him and that he had deserted a companion on the warpath: so he's sworn off pleasures of all kinds and never tackles any jobs except the hardest ones, never sings a scalp song, and only blows himself to one recreation, which is countin' coups when the coup stick is passed around at a feast. And I don't think that he does even that, except about once a year. After that day when his friend was killed, he broke all his arrows and swore he would never wear weapons again until he had killed an enemy with his bare hands. He did that a month later. Went out on foot, togged up in moccasins and a loinstrap, and came back ridin' a Crow hoss, with a long Crow scalp growin' out of the bridle reins. Come inside and look over this loot."

CHAPTER XVIII

LUCKY BUFFALO BIRD laid out the loot in rows, and then Diver had driven the four horses out into the herd, he came back and reviewed the gifts with Cashel. It was all, he assured the latter, of the highest quality.

"There is one thing left out," said Lucky, with a grunt.

"What is that?" asked Cashel.

"A wife," said she, "to take care of all this. I can't do it for you. Every rich husband needs two wives, but my warrior, he saves expense and keeps only one. You, Muskrat, ought to have a good, strong girl to come to work for you, and keep the knives and guns clean, and the robes in order, and set up your tepee, and cook for you. Already I have more work than I can do. And my husband won't take a young wife to help me!"

"She'd cut my throat if I did," said Jim Diver, "but this gives her something to growl about. She's right, though. Look over these Cheyenne girls and pick out one of 'em."

The thief sat at ease, lounging against a backrest. He could forgive broken nights, if the days held such things as these. It seemed a dream that there had been another Bandon Cashel who slunk down alleys, afraid to show his face. For now he was among the lords and could look down on life from a height.

"You had better pick out his wife for him," said the squaw in her usual bitter tone. "Otherwise the fool will want Chapa. They all do—the young men. Pick out a wife for him, Long Bull."

"Suppose that a man marries," said Cashel, "and then wants to leave the tribe, some day?"

"Been done a thousand times," said Jim Diver. "And the white man always leaves so much behind him that the girl's glad to have him gone. Then she can pick out some hard-handed buck who's taken a crowd of scalps, some brute that'll beat her twice a day. She'll be might happy with him, and forget you before you've trailed your shadow over the sky line. I know these Injun girls!"

"Suppose that you have children?" asked Cashel.

"You can take 'em with you, if they mean that much to you. Or else, you can leave 'em be, and the tribe'll take care of 'em. They ain't any fear of that. But I'll tell you this—I see that you like comfort, and comfort you ain't gunna have without that you got a tepee of your own, and a squaw to keep it for you! I'll pick you out a girl that'll work like a hoss, keep you like a king, and be doggone glad of the chance to slave all day and sew half the night. And the only thing that she's likely to ask of you is to let your hair grow long and wear feathers in it, which don't break no man's back to do!"

Cashel laughed.

And, looking forward into the future, he felt that life among the Cheyennes could be a pleasant thing, indeed.

"I'll tell you," said he, "that I've already got a girl half-way in mind. Unless she's married already. The other night, at the scalp dance, I saw one with a white-looking skin, and yellow hair. . . ."

"Chapa!" broke in Jim Diver.

And he shook his head, with a frown.

"Who is Chapa?" asked the thief, his interest suddenly taut.

"That's Sioux for Beaver. She was captured from the Sioux by a raid, and the brave that got her—she was a baby then—raised her like his daughter, and adopted her. She belongs to old Rain-By-Night, the sourest old devil in the camp."

"And he won't let her marry?"

"He'll let her marry. But his price is high. Ten good hosses was what Sandy River offered for her, and a saddle on the back of every one, and a bridle onto its head. A whole flock of horses he offered, and some robes besides."

"That wasn't enough for Rain-by-Night?"

"That was enough for him, and he drove the hosses out into his herd, which is the sign that he would accept Sandy River for a son-in-law. But Chapa herself had some say. For ten days, Sandy waited for her in the evenin' when she went down to carry up water, which is the regular courtin' time for the Injuns. Well, for ten days, he popped his blanket around her and stood there and told her how much he loved her and asked her to marry him, and for ten days she looked him fair in the eyes and said no. He got his hosses back, and Rain-by-Night flogged Chapa, they say, so's she couldn't walk. But I don't believe that. Anyway, Sandy River didn't get her. Neither did Waiting Bull, that offered a whole tepee full of stuff. She wouldn't have him."

"Maybe she wanted something better."

"Wait a minute. A couple of years back, Broken Arrow seen the girl gettin' taller and prettier every day, and he forgot about his resolution to stay poor and have no wife. He went and talked to her, and he offered to collect a whole tribe of Sioux and Pawnee and Comanche ponies to pay her father, if she'd consider takin' him for a husband. But she looks *him* in the eye, and says no. Now, son, if you think that can you can win out where Broken Arrow lost, go right ahead and bump your head against a wall."

The thief closed his eyes in heavy thought.

He was not tall, like Broken Arrow. His fame was not like that of the great warrior. He was not swift and powerful. He was not handsome to the eye. But behind his wide brow there was a brain, and by the cunning of that brain, all his life he'd been able to steal what he could not honestly win or buy.

How, then, could he steal the girl?

He felt the hugeness of the obstacle, but he was not willing to let that difficulty make him surrender with the prize unattempted. The higher the wall, the more excitement in the scaling of it. But how could a woman be stolen? So, with his eyes closed, he pondered.

He heard the squaw growling: "The young man will not pitch his tepee in a hollow which is safe from the wind. He must go to the top of the ridge where he is seen by his enemies against the sky line, and the wind comes up in the night and takes his lodge to pieces above his head!"

It was easy to translate her words into the meaning that Chapa was a high place where dangerous winds blew. But what was that to Cashel? The Bentwell diamonds had been guarded day and night, but he had taken them.

At that thought, he touched his shoulder, instinctively, where a pistol bullet had driven through and put him to bed for two months of misery. But, nevertheless, the diamonds had been his.

He had seen the daughter of the family at a concert, her throat and arms loaded with the brilliants, and they had burned in his mind until he had them in his hands. And now the eyes of Chapa rested on him day and night, with a persistent smile. Besides, the ways of women are strange, and surely since she had smiled so kindly, she might give him a better audience, even if he were no Broken Arrow in fame and in beauty.

He opened his eyes at last and encountered the bright, critical stare of the squaw.

"He has seen fire burn wood," said she, "but he won't believe that it will burn flesh. Well, take it into your hands, then, Muskrat!"

"We'll see," answered the thief calmly. "Diver, tell me some more about these evening courtings."

He listened to the tale, at length, and all the ways of the wooers. And that day he spent quietly in the tepee, lounging and smoking, and turning the problem back and forth before his mind's eye. There is a solution to be found of every difficulty. This fact he kept before him, and refused to be disconcerted.

The day wore on.

Two feasts were to be given. The announcers went through the camp, loudly bawling the names of the invited.

And the Muskrat was invited to both the lodge of Walking Dove and to that of Two Antelope.

"Tell them I'm sleeping," said Cashel to Jim Diver. "Tell them I'm tired out and asleep."

"A good brave," said Diver, with a grin, "is never tired, and never needs to sleep."

"Then I'm not a good brave. I want to stay here and think."

So Diver went off to the feasts, and Cashel lay on his back and cupped his hands behind his head, and thought long thoughts that twisted and turned in his mind like the path of a snake.

If only the soul of a woman were like a treasure locked in a great steel safe!

He waited until the fall of the afternoon, when the sun was low in the west and the heat of its rays no longer soaked through the strong sides of the lodge. There was a stir of evening breeze, also, that crept along the ground and made him restless. The time had therefore come, and he stood up from the bed where he had lounged.

He buckled on a belt and revolver. He fastened a sheathed knife at one side of it. And then he swathed himself in a light robe, made from the hide of a young cow, and scraped thin for summer wear.

It was a gaudy affair, painted on both sides with terrific designs in yellow and ocher and crimson and green. Vast suns burned on it, and huge blue heavens extended, and fires leaped, and buffaloes died in the crude picturing of the Cheyenne artist who had decorated that robe. But the thief felt secure that an Indian eye would be pleased as much as his own was staggered by this display.

He walked out, and instantly found himself the center of a mob of twenty boys. They chattered like so many magpies. They followed around him like a swarm of bees, buzzing, murmuring, talking so rapidly that he could hardly understand a word they said.

So he left the edge of the camp, and still they followed him, until they saw the direction he was taking, toward the upper section of the river where the water was drawn.

Already he could see half a dozen forms of young braves shrouded in robes, and at that very moment a girl, walking down toward the river's edge, was stopped by a hooded form and gathered suddenly into the folds of the robe.

There was a loud yell of derision and scorn and mirth from the youngsters when they saw the purpose of the new warrior. They scattered away from him on either side, laughhing, jibing, pointing, but Cashel went on, undisturbed, and even chuckling a little. After all, Indian children were not very different from their white brothers. Perhaps Chapa would understand a white man's wooing, also.

On the edge of the slope he took his stand and waited, while the sun dropped, and the river ran golden and green between its banks; and then he saw Chapa coming from the verge of the village.

CHAPTER XIX

No less romantic young man ever looked at a girl, but now the Muskrat was stirred to the cold depths of his heart. Some hot sirocco of passion blew through him, and such a giddiness came that he shook his head violently to clear it.

He looked back toward the other three or four couples who stood on the green slope, wrapped in the robes of the lover. And now it happened that one of these separated, and the girl went on toward the river with a high head and a quick, impatient step, while the brave turned drearily away— a rejected man, beyond a doubt. But there was another couple separated, she moving off as rapidly as the first girl, yet with a bright, telltale glance over her shoulder that kept her chosen warrior a-tiptoe staring after her. So that Cashel could not help wondering which of these fates was reserved for him.

Certainly, in the very beginning, he could curse Walking Dove for saddling him with such a name as the Muskrat! Yet Cashel recognized an ironic propriety in the name, and could see that he had been among other men of his kind like a sort of keen-eyed rat, burrowing through walls into the savings of honest laborers.

He looked back at the girl, and she was breathlessly near. She came with a swift and easy step and such a grace as women have whose stride never has been chopped and staggered by high heels. Her head was high. She was sure of her way without ever a glance at the ground, and as she looked around her a smile went with her glance. He was not fool enough to take it for himself, since he knew well enough that it came from mere physical wellbeing; and perhaps that was the smile with which she had looked at him across the hurly-burly of the scalp dance?

Yet no matter how impersonally she looked at him, the heart and the spirit of the thief were raised, and the world about him was transformed. The mere runnel of water through which he and Walking Dove had trotted their horses the evening before now seemed to sweep on as a mighty river with glorious color on its face. The blue heavens were wider, and pure clouds of crystal rushed through a greater and bluer sky.

She was now very close, and turning a little toward her, Cashel stepped into her path. She made not the slightest effort to avoid him, but that faint smile of high spirits faded from her face and left he cold. She stopped short, and only by a great effort of the will did Cashel step forward and throw his robe clumsily about her, which brought their faces short inches apart, and left him startled and dumb with her nearness. His hands, holding the robe about her, trembled. He cursed the Indian custom which prescribed this fashion for a courtship.

But her own coolness upset him more than all else. Her color was not a whit heightened, and her eye was as steady as the glance of a man. She had been half embraced like this a hundred times, he told himself, and every time by a greater warrior than the Water Rat!

Another curse, and a heavy one, for the head of Walking Dove.

Then the Cheyenne words came to him. He had been saying them over and over while he waited, so that at least he would have some fluency in the beginning of his appeal.

"Chapa," said he, "now that I have become a Cheyenne, the chiefs tell me that I should marry into the tribe; and if that is true, certainly there's only one woman among them for me. I've come here to talk to you, Chapa, and ask you to consider me."

He heard her voice for the first time, and found it low pitched and a little husky, but it turned the harsh gutturals into music.

"If you wish to become a Cheyenne, marry a Cheyenne woman, because I am only a Sioux."

"There was never a Sioux," said he, "with a skin as white and pure as yours, Chapa. There was never a Sioux whose face shone as yours shines! Tell me the truth. You are no more Sioux than I am!"

"You mean that I have a pale face," she answered, no more perturbed by his nearness and his courtship than at first, "but I don't think that the color of the skin matters a great deal. I was happy among the Sioux. That is why I tell you to find another woman if you wish to become a good Cheyenne."

"And you are not happy here, Chapa?"

"I have an adopted father here who takes good care of me and gives me clothes and food and a bed. Why should I not be happy?" said she.

The thief smiled. There was so much feminine contradiction in this talk that he felt more at ease, and lost some of his awe of her. However, at this moment the fold of the robe that had been projecting like the rim of a poke bonnet above his face now fell down and blinded him. He had to shrug his shoulders violently to shake it back, when it dropped like a monk's cowl between his shoulders, and left both their heads exposed. A passing young buck looked curiously at them, and grinned with mischievous pleasure.

"Chapa," said he, "I am not such a fool that I think I can please you at once. I've come to talk to you today merely to find out what sort of hope I may have of pleasing you in the future."

She looked a little away from him, thoughtfully. He wished tremendously that she would show the least embarrassment, but even now that their heads were exposed to the eyes of all the curious, and he knew not how to recover them without releasing her—which would be the signal for her to leave—even now she was perfectly at ease. He looked down at the massive yellow braids that dipped over her shoulders and slid downward toward her hands, the fingers of which were pleached together. There could not be imagined a more perfect ease and composure than her whole attitude suggested.

"I don't think I could tell you that," said she, at last.

"You can tell me if there is some other man in the tribe—or outside it—that you're interested in."

"Why should I tell you that?" she asked him.

"For a good enough reason. It would stop me from bothering you, and if there's really another young fellow you'd like to marry, I'll help him to make up a present that will please your adopted father and make him want to let you go."

Her brows lifted a little at this, and her glance turned straight into his. It was always a strain to the thief to meet an eye honestly, and this was a greater shock than the look of any man. He could endure it only an instant and then his guilty eyes drifted away, like the eyes of a wild wolf.

"Do you give gifts to people you never have seen?" she asked.

"That sounds strange," admitted he. "But the fact is that once you're married I'll probably be able to get you out of my mind, whereas as long as you're not tied to another man, you'll haunt me, Chapa. Even last night," he added, "I couldn't sleep on account of you."

"Or was it the noise of the dogs?" she asked him, with the frankest of smiles.

He could not help smiling back, but he could tell himself now that she was clever enough and wide-awake enough mentally to make a mate for him, and the knowledge struck home in him like a plangent wave.

"You haven't answered about the other man?" he insisted.

"There is no other man," she admitted. "There never was, except once."

That turned him cold.

"There was once," said he.

"Once I saw a trader who came to the Cheyennes with a great train of horses loaded with goods. He was young and wise and a great warrior. There was no wiser man among all the chiefs of the Cheyennes, Rain-By-Night told me. I used to like to stand where he could not see me and watch him while he traded. I watched him so long that I could tell when he had traded a thing for ten times what it was worth, or only for three times. But he never lost, and that is a great thing in a husband."

He guessed at irony behind this speech, but he could not be sure.

"Well," said she, "I was falling very much in love with that trader when I asked some of the women about white husbands, and they all told me that a white man never stays more than three years, and then he goes off to his people and leaves wives and children behind."

"Even among the Indians there must be some bad people," said he.

"White men," she said, "want several wives. They want a wife to flesh the buffalo hides, and a wife who is a good seamstress, and then they want another one with a pretty face." She studied him with peculiar impersonality, like the page of a book, her eyes drifting from feature to feature. "When the pretty ones grow wrinkled, then they are thrown away and a new one is bought."

"I'm not such a man, Chapa," said he. "I would have only you."

She raised her brows again, but did not need to speak her incredulity.

"There's Long Bull," said he. "He disproves all your ideas. He lives with one wife, and he's been here many years."

"Long Bull," said she, "is a Pawnee hunter. That is why he stays. He doesn't keep a wife, but a cook."

This diagnosis was so swift and neat that it took his breath.

"You are dodging me, Chapa," said he, "as fast a dog dodges a wolf, but I haven't come here simply to worry you. Suppose that you tell me how I could prove that I would be good to you and true to you and you only? Don't you see, for one thing, that your skin is as white as mine, and that even if I ever left the Cheyennes, I would take you with me to live with my people?"

"You could call me a half-breed squaw," said she, calmly. "That would be better than a full Indian, I suppose."

"Give me some test, Chapa," he insisted. "Or else tell me that you're not interested in what I have to say. I'm not going to whine and beg. I have to know where I stand."

He saw a flash of emotion that might have been anger in her face. Then she said, "There are things that a man can do. If you counted coup on a Crow chief, and a Pawnee chief, and a famous Sioux, then I would have to say that you are a good Cheyenne, of course."

He shrank a little, but there was a bargain suggested by this.

"Suppose that I counted those coups?"

A revulsion of feeling, a positive distaste, flashed into her face too clearly to be doubted.

"If you counted them, then Chapa would marry the Muskrat. If they were counted, and other good warriors saw them counted in the fight, I'll be your wife."

The robe dragged down his nervous hands. She stepped past him as lightly as she had come, and the heart of the thief turned cold in him as if with fear. For he knew that she had looked through him and seen what he was worth!

CHAPTER XX

HE WATCHED her for a moment as she went on by him, carrying the paunch of a deer which she would fill with water, and then the Muskrat—feeling very much like his new name, indeed!—turned back toward the village, certain that she had not told him the full truth. She was not really interested, he could swear, in the pinchbeck honor of a coup counted, no matter on what chief's body, of the Sioux or the Pawnees, or the long-haired Crows. It was merely that this, perhaps, would show that he had committed himself to the life and the ways of the Indians. But what inspired her obvious scorn was simply that she did not believe in his courage. The narration of Walking Dove must have seemed purely fiction to her.

It was some comfort to know that she had underrated him. It might be that his eye was not firm enough to meet the eye of another steadily. But he knew that man to man his spirit was not less than that of other fighters. For even the chosen bullies and gunmen of the "gang" had avoided trouble with him after his ways had become known.

A loud yelling within the village lifted him out of his own troubled thoughts. The manifold shout was followed by a long and terrible keening cry of women that grew on his ear as he came closer, and almost the first tepee he passed showed him a nightmare sight.

A young squaw had slashed off her long hair and with the same knife gashed her arms, her legs, and her face, so that the wounds still were bleeding freely. She had ripped the lodge to ribbons and carried out the contents, and the audience, no matter how much it sympathized with her lament, now was carrying away the last of the property. Inside the wrecked and naked tepee the poor creature now sat on the ground tearing at her hair and actually bringing out handfuls of it, or pouring dirt and ashes on her head, or sometimes flinging herself face-downward, and always maintained the same piercing cry of sorrow until she became exhausted, and her voice was lost in croakings.

He had seen a Romany on a roadside near Manhattan lamenting after much the same fashion, and he could guess that there was a death in the lodge. From the mutterings of the bystanders in the twilight, he learned that it was her husband who had fallen, that he and half a dozen others had been surprised by a war party of Pawnees, and only one had escaped. That was the reason that other sorrowings were heard from different parts of the camp, rising in long, piercing wails.

"Why aren't the warriors gathering to ride out and strike in revenge?" asked the thief, for this was contrary to all his preconceptions of Indian character, seeing the fighting men standing mute and gloomy around the lament.

"Young Thunder, the great medicine man," said a young brave, "has made medicine, and says that no war party must ride out during this moon."

"Yes," said another, "but Walking Dove has made medicine for himself and is gathering a party."

"Walking Dove is a brave man," said the other, "but when was his medicine as strong as that of Young Thunder?"

This was news enough to send Cashel straight for the tepee of Jim Diver, whom he found inside the tepee, calmly smoking a pipe and apparently interested in none of the laments or the war party that was gathering to start out in revenge.

"You'll be ridin' out with Walking Dove because he's your friend," said the squaw man, "but I stay here."

"I thought you wanted Pawnee hair," asked Cashel.

"I'm kind of a collector of it in a small way," admitted the renegade, "but the fact is that I pick and choose the parties that I ride on, and this ain't the one for me. Young Thunder calls it bad business."

"Can he tell what's coming?" asked Cashel.

"Young Thunder's an old fool," answered Diver, "and he's got no more sense than a robber frog barkin' in a marsh. But what he's said is gonna have a weight with all the bucks that ride out on this trail. They may go along with Walking Dove, some of 'em, because he's worked himself up a reputation lately, but they'll all be quakin' in their boots; and if one Pawnee says 'boo' at 'em, these here Cheyennes will run. They's brave enough, but medicine counts more than guns, with 'em. Besides, they's a white hand mixed up in that Pawnee gang."

"White?" exclaimed Cashel.

"Ay. They's a white man ridin' of a big strappin' red chestnut hoss. Which it sounds like the same Clonmel that you're after, young feller. And where you got Indian hands and white brains to show 'em how, it's always hot water for the other gents. You better stay at home with me!"

But Cashel was already picking up his Colt's rifle. He had forgotten Jim Diver, and beautiful Chapa, and the whole Cheyenne tribe. What mattered to him was simply that Clonmel was somewhere near the camp, and a white man on his back.

He came out of the tepee and threw a saddle on the back of the white mare. He was barely ready for mounting when a noisy procession went by.

Walking Dove on the other captured mare led the way, and behind him were strung out forty or fifty braves in single line. Several of them carried torches to light the way, or perhaps rather to show their own faces to the people they passed. And here and there squaws ran alongside their husbands, catching at their feet, wringing their hands, imploring them to remember the warning voice of the great medicine man and leave this expedition to the others. But not a man would fall out of the ranks because of such persuasion. They rode on, keeping their faces sternly toward the front. Now and then one of them started a war whoop, but it was almost as though they did this to raise their own spirits, and the shouts were taken up only feebly and brokenly along the column.

But, at the very end appeared a rider on a tall, finely made horse, a man without feathers in his hair, and with a tattered buffalo robe blowing back across his muscular shoulders. However, the goodness of his horse and the gleam of the rifle that he carried balanced across the withers of his mount showed that he was someone out of the ordinary, and when he came closer, the white man recognized Broken Arrow!

He mounted, and would have fallen in behind that famous brave, but Broken Arrow reined back and waved him into the place before him. It seemed a token of the famous man's humility that he should insist on the least important place in all that train. But as he went by, all eyes were for him. Even the spectacular recent achievement of Cashel was nothing in the mind of the tribe compared with the greatness of Broken Arrow. A great shout went up when he was seen, hands stretched out toward him, braves brandished their weapons, and before the procession left the camp, half a dozen others had joined the ranks, daubing on war paint as they came.

It was Broken Arrow, beyond a doubt, who had inspired them to come, in spite of the black prophecy of the medicine man.

And Young Thunder himself appeared on the rim of the camp as the party rode out onto the plain.

He was by no means young, in spite of his name. He stood erect, but age had thinned his hair and starved his cheeks so that he looked like a gaunt bird. He held a robe loosely about him so that his skinny shoulders and fleshless arms appeared also, and he had a young boy on either side of him holding a torch so that his ominous face and the waving feathers of his headdress could be clearly seen by all of the riders.

There was little superstition in Cashel, but his heart sank at the sight of this. And he saw the Indians immediately before him turn their heads with a distinct shudder rather than face the gloomy apparition of their chief medicine man. He could have sworn that every man in the party felt his scalp fitting more loosely on his head as the group dwindled away into the dark of the plain.

After the flare of the torches within the village, the darkness of the outside seemed quite blind, and it was only gradually that the stars burned down brightly over their heads. Now, at a signal, the riders formed themselves into a ring fence of men and horses, and into the center rode Walking Dove.

He made a short and strong speech. He was convinced, he said, that the party that had struck the outlying band of Cheyennes was the same body that had been harried by himself and the Muskrat. If so, their spirits surely already were broken, and at the first sight of the white mares they would turn and run for their lives. Their only problem would be to get in touch with the Pawnees. By this time, he was sure, they would be scattering for home, and he proposed to maintain a brisk pace, heading straight for the Pawnee village. If they traveled at a good gait, about dawn they would come to the big bald-headed headland that rose about the curve of the river, and from this point of vantage, they would be able to search the plain for a considerable distance. Moreover, his good friend the Muskrat, of whose courage they all knew, possessed a magic glass, through which he could see things five times as far away as the average eye of an Indian could strike. And as the morning grew, they could be sure of spotting the fugitive Pawnees, with the five fresh scalps they were bearing back to their own country. It would be simple then to force them into battle, and with such a band of fifty famous braves behind him, with Broken Arrow and the Muskrat among them, he did not doubt that they would crush the Pawnees and bring at least one living prisoner back to camp in order that the Cheyenne women might sacrifice him and comfort the ghosts of their recently slaughtered husbands.

This speech of the young chief was well received. And, when he asked for advice from any of the better-known warriors, no one answered him except Broken Arrow, who modestly suggested that this was a beautiful plan if the Pawnees actually were in full retreat, but that if they were lying close at hand to the Cheyenne camp, they would simply follow on the rear of the war party and strike them when the opportunity seemed most favorable.

"True, Broken Arrow," said Walking Dove, "but when they come close enough to see the glimmering of the two white mares, you may be sure that they will turn and run as fast as their horses can gallop!"

Since Broken Arrow made no comment upon this answer, it was taken for granted that Walking Dove's plan should be executed, and accordingly the Cheyennes stretched away behind that leader.

They made excellent time, for in the rear of the warriors several boys were driving a herd of more than a hundred remounts, which every hour or so would be called upon by some of the braves. Their best ponies they reserved for the time when the enemy should be sighted. And so, constantly changing horses, and proceeding at a gait that racked the body of the thief painfully, they poured across the prairie until they came within view of the Bald Hill, rising dim and black against the first light of the horizon.

CHAPTER XXI

RIMMON was heaping thunderclouds in the west; the arch of the sky still was dark with night; but along the east they could see the shadow, as it were, of the rising sun, and against it Bald Hill was splitting the heavens.

It was a big, bold headland. It did not have the pyramidal outline of a mountain, but rather was like a great ship's prow, heaping the seas before it as it tore through the prairies, and with the gleam of the river like a thin bow wave around its stem. There was not a bush, not a tiny shrub on it, to say nothing of trees. Even the grass was too scarce for a sheep's grazing, and as the light grew, it appeared that Bald Hill grew nothing at all except a ragged scattering of boulders. If it was the prow of a ship, that was a vessel that had been swept clean by graybeards, and therefore the thief looked upward toward it with a little pinch of uncertainty and fear. He had been enough in the prairies to get the fear of the horizon in his blood, and that fear closed down on him again as the party began to ascend the slope, riding hastily through the rolling, bush-covered ground at its base.

And Cashel heard a voice near him murmuring, "Can fifty pairs of eyes see better than three?"

He looked hard through the dimness of the dawn light and made out the unmistakably erect and graceful outline of Broken Arrow, his bronzed body just beginning to glimmer like polished stone. But whatever his opinion of this maneuver might have been, he made no effort to retrocede, but passed on with the rest, close beside young Cashel.

They thronged up to the head of the upland, and from this point they had a magnificent view of the prairie that rolled around them, so that it was no wonder that their leader had chosen this point as a spy tower from which they might scan the horizon. There was a sufficient light now to enable them to see a scattering of antelope in a hollow not far away. Some alarm struck the little creatures, and they started away with such a burst of speed that they literally dissolved in the dull dawn light. A few moments more and they would not be able to see them at all as they dipped into every hollow of the surrounding country. Cashel already was able to make out the features of the braves nearest at hand when a rifle fired loudly at the base of the headland, followed immediately by a prolonged screech from one of the Cheyenne warriors, and Cashel saw a brave stiffen in

91

his saddle and then sway outward with hands that beat at the air as though he were a swimmer in deep water.

He fell, and his rifle dropped with him, with a brief clattering against the rocks.

Cashel heard a deep, subdued murmuring among the Cheyennes. The whole party swayed higher up the headland by a mutual impulse, and Cashel himself, borne along by the rest, whose horses were jamming about him, was carried far out on a spit of promontory. Looking down, he saw a sheer dropping of the face of the cliff. No horse could get down it. Even a dismounted man could hardly have managed that descent. And the circling river gleamed beneath like flat, cold steel.

He glanced back from the river toward the foot of the slope in time to see the entire line of the rolling ground at the base of Bald Hill blossom with little flowers of red fire, and the roar of many rifles.

He heard several of the Cheyennes yell like hurt dogs; two or more saddles emptied; they were helplessly cornered and milling back toward the edge of the cliff. Too close, already! For a great cry at the rear made him look downward, to see a Cheyenne on his horse hurtling down toward the river, the warrior with his war spear brandished over his head and a battle cry on his lips. He and his shout went out in an upward leap of graylighted spray; the water closed; and then, distinct as a clap of hands, he heard the sound of the impact.

But clearer than this horror, he could see the form of Young Thunder stand gaunt as a death's-head at the exit from the Cheyenne camp, propheysying the evil that would come upon this unlucky war party.

There was no headship. No one knew what to do. Some of the men began to dismount. Others swerved wildly here and there.

And then out in front of them dashed the well-known form of Broken Arrow, his rifle raised over his head by a stiff arm while he called back to them:

"Brothers, the only life is through the teeth of the Pawnees! Follow me!"

He knew that that was generalship, and generalship in the pinch. And no matter what folly Walking Dove might have shown, certainly he was the first to understand and follow the lead of the great warrior. Out he went, a white streak on the medicine mare, yelling like a spirit; and the whole rout of the Cheyennes followed the good example with wonderful suddenness.

It was a wild charge.

Straight downhill they had to plunge, scattering right

and left so that they would present a less solid target to the enemy, and with every stride of the horses they yelled frantically, with despair and with fury. And before them arose an equal inferno of whooping. No better riders, no braver warriors were on the plains than those Cheyennes, but they were terribly pocketed, cut off, and trapped.

Cashel himself was well among the last to start down the slope, and he was by no means anxious to go fast. But he had to devote all of his attention to clinging to the mare with hands and knees, and that left the swift animal free to go her own pace, which was like the swoop of a hawk. As they shot off the ragged upper face of the slope and straightened away on the lower rolling ground, he was able to master the reins again. He had never jerked his rifle from its case, but he had the good Colt's revolver in his practiced hand, and having drawn the reins taut with his left hand and regained some mastery over his mare, he was ready to fight like a cornered rat, to the death.

He could take stock of the situation around him in that last frightful moment before the impact.

The Cheyennes were thinned, but they were pushing the charge home with a frantic courage, lunging straight up to the smoking muzzles of the Pawnee guns. The latter, secure victors already in this battle, were exposing themselves recklessly. A very few were mounted. The majority had left their horses and crept up among the rocks and the shrubs; but with so many Cheyennes on the ground before them, with so many scalps and coups in sight, they were frantic with excitement and were standing erect, many of them, regardless of the charge. And he saw one crop-haired Pawnee actually dancing in a fury of exultation, and waving an emptied rifle above his head!

They were hysterical with joy and well they might be, because they had not yet lost a man, and the slope above was splotched and draggled with the Cheyenne blood.

Broken Arrow, who began that charge, would not be slack in pushing it home. First man down the slope, he still was first man as the Cheyennes closed on the enemy, and now Cashel saw him ride straight in at the enemy rifles, disdaining an easy gap among the rocks, but literally throwing his life away.

Far the first, riding erect, disdaining to take shelter over the side of his horse, the famous warrior plunged straight at the riflemen among the rocks, as though he chose by preference to take a hundred bullets in his own body, if that might let his comrades through.

It was the first time that Cashel had seen selfless nobility shown by any man at the risk of his heart's blood. It was a thing he thought really amounted to no more than fiction for books. But here it was in the fact and in the flesh. Here it was cased in the red skin of an Indian savage!

Something snapped in the very core of Cashel's being. A blinding wave of heat and light rushed through his brain, and dimmed his eyes; and when it passed he was seeing as he never before had seen. The yells that had been shaking all his nerves now seemed futile and small things. The crash of the long rifles he regarded no more than the popping of toy guns. There seemed only one thing to do, and that was to push home the charge of Broken Arrow.

Around him and behind him he sensed the Cheyennes sluicing away to rush off through the gap in the rocks and the brush; but all that lived and moved for Cashel was the form of Broken Arrow plunging straight ahead to meet his death.

Guns flamed before that undaunted warrior.

Cashel's throat grew tight and hard; his ears blurred; he only could guess that he was yelling at the top of his lungs, instinctively, for somehow he heard no sound from his own lips.

Then he saw the horse of Broken Arrow rear, strike, as it were, with his forehoofs against the rocky parapet of the Pawnees, and then topple backward.

They knew what had happened. Over the roar of the guns and the battle yells, he could hear the Pawnees shrieking: "Broken Arrow!"

Three men rushed out toward the fallen brave, and one of them never reached the goal, for Cashel brained him with a deadly sure snap shot. The other two, startled by this sudden death in their ranks, swerved away and bolted back for the shrubbery; while Cashel jerked the white mare far back on her haunches and brought her to a halt beside the fallen rider.

He lay with his horse dead above him, and both legs pinned beneath its weight; and yet even then Broken Arrow had the courage of a hero, and a hero's presence of mind, for he waved his arm violently to the white man and shouted in a ringing, cheerful voice, "Save yourself, brother. There is still tomorrow!"

And Cashel, with a groan, wrenched the head of the mare around and drove his spurs deep into her quivering, tender flanks.

He knew that he could not save Broken Arrow, but something made him wish to push home that charge the hero so gallantly had begun. So straight at the rocks before him he drove the mare. She winced under the galling stroke of the spurs, but she shot forward.

And then, above them—enormous, and like a giant—he saw the form of a great horse and rider looming, like black

94

demons against the glow of the distant horizon. But he knew the head of that horse. It was that of Clonmel. The wind in its mane revealed it, and the lordly lift of its head. He fired point blank. The hammer of the gun dropped with a leaden click upon a bad cartridge, and as the white mare rose with a grand sweep above the rocks, he saw a pale flicker of light in the hand of the rider on Clonmel, and knew that a sword was hanging in the air. Next instant he saw the face—it was that of Captain Fitzroy Melville!

Blindly he struck out, in a horror, as at a ghost. A livid flash of light dropped toward him, dazzled past his eyes, and then he was over the rocks, beyond Clonmel, beyond Captain Melville and flinging boldly down the slope.

CHAPTER XXII

ALL THAT lay of the land which had hampered them in their charge and favored the Pawnees was now fighting on the side of the Cheyennes. The very same rolling ground and brush and rocks which had screened the Pawnees as they stretched out at ease across the line of the retreat of Walking Dove's party now acted as an equal screen to the Cheyenne warriors who were sweeping through, with the downward slope to give speed to their striding horses.

But young Cashel still rode on, blindly.

He could not realize the thing that had happened, nor the fall of Broken Arrow, nor the strange apparition of Melville on the back of Clonmel like a gigantic ghost.

Every nerve in his body trembled, and then was still, for Broken Arrow was lost to the Pawnees!

He had not seen the man six times. He had hardly heard him speak a dozen words, but he knew that of all the men he had encountered on this earth, the Indian hero was without a peer.

They would have his scalp. Some brawny, crop-haired Pawnee would wear it at the scalp dance, while the other warriors envied his good fortune and shrieked their joy that such an enemy had fallen.

Worse still, they would take him alive!

Why had he not sent a ball through the head of the fallen brave? They could take him alive, unless their hatred made them brain him on the spot. They could lead him back to the Pawnee stockade, and give him over to the curious, devilish hands of the women, to be done slowly, artistically to death, while all the tribe enjoyed the exquisite artifices of the squaws, and relished the sublime patience of the prisoner.

But Broken Arrow, with his great heart, and his ragged robe, and his magnificently foolish vows, was gone from the Cheyennes!

It was more to Cashel, almost, than the loss of Clonmel this second time! Ay, it was more than the missing of the stallion.

So these thoughts darted through his brain, and looking to the left, he saw that no living thing moved between him and the river, and looking to the right, he made out that the rolling ground was streaked with the dark forms of riders, growing momentarily more visible in the increasing light of the dawn.

It had been a mere breath, he could realize then—a mere balancing upon the cliff, and then a rush downward through fire. And still he could see the contorted faces of the Pawnees as he burst through their line, and the stern face of the captain as he swayed the sword aloft!

While he thought of this, he ejected the spoiled cartridge, replaced it with a good one, and so tipped over the brim of a hollow and swept down into a swale literally packed and alive with the tossing heads of many horses.

He had blundered by the blindest chance into the chase of the Pawnee ponies!

He tried to check the rush of the white mare. But she was still irked by the griding of the spur wounds in her tender flanks, and the dip of the ground helped her forward against his jerk upon the reins.

Straight on she went against a veritable wall of horseflesh.

A silhouette leaped up dimly from the ground. A gun roared in the very face of Cashel. Had it been a grown warrior, that would have been the end of him, but it was only a herd boy; the men had gone to pick Cheyenne scalps like daisies on the bloody slope of Bald Hill.

Cashel clubbed the youngster down with the barrel of the heavy revolver and yelled at the top of his lungs.

Before him the ponies scattered. There was never a time when Indian ponies were more than two removes from wild antelope. This alarm, this rush of the rider was too much for them. Here and there Cashel saw lithe youngsters frantically striving to check the stampede, but they might as well have waved blankets in the face of a prairie fire, for the mustangs were still gathering headway, and now bursting out like a wave beyond its bounds.

One stripling, a young hero if ever one stepped, charged the enemy without a gun, but with no more than a lance. Twice Cashel covered the slender, naked young body with his revolver, then lowered his aim, and shot the horse. It toppled head over heels; the lad was flung far off and lay still—

neck broken, perhaps—and Cashel rushed on at the heels of the horses.

From the right, other warriors, aware of what had taken place, joined with Cashel and took over the herding of the horses into their more expert hands.

With a dull thunder they swept along over the soft green of the prairie grass, and Bald Hill dwindled behind them. The sun rose. The hill was lost beneath the horizon.

The sun grew hot. Even through the grass, a thin dust cloud was trampled up by the many hoofs. And Cashel looked right and left into downward, sullen faces, and drooping shoulders without strength.

They had lost.

This prize of horses was a scant sweetening of the taste of the disaster. They had before them a full hundred of the best war ponies of the Pawnees, but they themselves had left behind on the slope of Bald Hill and at its unlucky base fully seventeen warriors, whose scalps were now hanging from Pawnee bridles, or, their legs bound beneath the bellies of horses, the less lucky ones were being herded away toward the Pawnee town.

Walking Dove rode at the back of the entire party.

Since this was a retreat from a victorious enemy, his place was in the rear, as the commander of the last guard. Never had Cashel seen a more joyless face.

Cashel rode up beside him.

"Do you see what you are doing, Walking Dove?" said he. The chief raised his tragic face.

"You are riding away from your enemy," said Cashel, "and the Pawnees, on foot, are struggling off across the prairie to get to their town, while you could ride around them and cut them off. What are you thinking of? Turn back the party, Walking Dove. Send the boys on with the captured horses. Turn back with the rest and we'll make the Pawnee scoundrels sweat for this!"

With merely a dulled and helpless eye, Walking Dove regarded him, as one delirious hears important words and cannot comprehend them. Again Cashel repeated his idea, but the other shook his head, at last, and pointed to the despondent riders before him.

"You can speak with a high heart, Muskrat," said he. "You've done what even Broken Arrow failed to do. You've drawn the fire of the Pawnee rifles. You've broken through their line. You've counted coup on some living warrior, I suppose. And the braves say that they saw you shoot down one of the warriors who ran out to take the scalp of that man. You have stopped at his side, too, and offered him help. These things were seen. You have met with the white

97

man who rides the tall stallion, and passed safely away from him on level terms. This was seen, also, and then you have routed the Pawnee horses, and beaten down the braves left to guard them. . . ."

"Only a few boys, Walking Dove," said Cashel, amazed by this long recital of his deeds.

"However," said Walking Dove, "the only glory that has been gained by Cheyennes on this day has been gained by you. But I? I have led the flower of the nation into a slaughter hole, and not even a dog would follow me out to battle again! Three times I have gone out. But even the magic horses could not help me this time. The Sky People have turned their backs on me. They scorn me. They laugh at Walking Dove. I am going to face the scorn and the hate of the squaws, and then I am going off to live by myself like a lone wolf, and surrender my family, and let another man take my son! I am a miserable man, Muskrat."

"You are groaning," said Cashel, "at the very minute when you ought to be trying again. If you hit the Pawnees now, you take them by surprise, and sweep them off the face of the earth—and I have another chance to get Clonmel!"

The young chief shook his head.

"You think the Pawnees are on foot. You forget how many of *our* horses they have taken after the fight, and how many of theirs escaped through our fingers as you brushed them away. But even if they were all on foot, you could not make these men face them again."

"They have more courage than you think," suggested Cashel, doubtful as he stared again at the dejected band.

"They have courage," said the chief, "but they have seen that my medicine is no more than a puff of dust in the air compared with the medicine of the great Young Thunder.

"Who would listen to me now? Go speak to them, if you wish. They will not laugh at you, because now the whole tribe has seen you proved. But they will not follow even you, nor any other man, so long as this moon lasts. Young Thunder has put a blight on every war party for that length of time, and who would risk his scalp against such a prophecy now that he has been proved right?"

"Do you still believe," said Cashel, amazed, "that it was Young Thunder who caused your trouble?"

"He did not cause it, but he foresaw it, and he warned us all in town. He stood at the rim of the village and warned us back with his frown."

Suddenly he jerked the edge of his robe over his face so as to conceal the grief that, in spite of his self-control, now twisted and puckered his features, so that Cashel allowed the white mare to drift away, further and further to the rear.

Neither he nor Melville, he suddenly told himself, was worthy of sitting upon the back of Clonmel. But the red man was the chosen spirit—Broken Arrow, the hero, the selfless man!

He drew a great breath.

A great thing had come to the spirit of Bandon Suir Cashel. But he did not realize it. We cannot see our own faces even in a mirror, looking from day to day, so how can we tell when the heart inside of us has been altered for evil, or for good?

But one thing he knew; that he forgot to be grateful for his own life, or for the deeds which he had been able to do in that fight. And the only emotion that was left to him was sorrow for the brave men who lay dead on Bald Hill, and for Broken Arrow in the hands of his enemies.

And there was Clonmel, last of all, that eagle among horses, as he had stood up red and tall against the sky!

Now, out of that reappearance of the horse, and Melville, and the fate of Broken Arrow, and the battle's result, an odd feeling came to Cashel, that he was on the knees of the gods, and that they would dispose of him with or against his will. He felt as though running water had passed through and purified his soul. He raised his head. He could smile, and smilingly submit to fate.

CHAPTER XXIII

THE DEFEAT of Walking Dove, which was such a terrible calamity for the rest of the tribe, was a great thing for Young Thunder. It placed him in eminence as the one big, shining, outstanding, wise man of the entire tribe, and Jim Diver took it upon himself to do a little prophesying about Young Thunder's immediate activities.

"There's goin' to be," said Diver, "one of the most crackin' medicine dances that ever happened to the Cheyennes, and the young bucks know it. They're oilin' up their joints by doin' a little dancin' on the side, right now."

"It's a funny time for dancing," commented Cashel, "with the squaws still yowling and keening for their dead men, and the whole tribe mourning for Broken Arrow. He was a man, Jim!"

"Sure he was a man," said Jim Diver. "But nothin' matters now except Young Thunder, and the way he'll use his big chance will be to start the dance. Not a dance for fun, mind you. He'll pick out a list of braves and start them dancin' and keep the thing up a sickenin' length of time, till the boys begin to drop. He'll have most of his personal enemies on that list of dancers, and he'll work them till they wish they were dead. I'd rather take a floggin' than a medicine dance, any day. Already the bucks are startin' to try to buy off Young Thunder, and you'd better think up what you can bribe him with."

"Why should I bribe him?" asked Cashel, astonished.

"Because otherwise he'll certainly pick you for one of the dancers. You're quite a big man around here, Cashel. They talk about the Muskrat in hushed voice, let me tell you, because you broke the line, and all that rot. Why the devil *did* you break the line, man? You tryin' to make a hero out of yourself?"

Cashel, absent-mindedly, was juggling a clasp knife with a long, heavy blade. Sometimes he flicked it into the air and snatched it again by the handle, and sometimes he allowed it to fall, so accurately that it dropped within the finger's breadth of space between his heels. There had been a great need for knifework, from time to time, in the days when he was a member of the "gang" in New York, and he had spent many a long hour practicing.

"I wasn't trying to make a hero out of myself," he said thoughtfully. "But I don't see what that job has to do with making me dance till I drop."

"You don't? Well, you're a great friend of Walking Dove, which is one reason that Young Thunder will want to make you prance. And then again, you're an outstandin' warrior already. People are beginnin' to say that Walkin' Dove's medicine isn't worth a spoiled pair of moccasins and that you're the boy who managed everythin' in the raid for the two medicine mares. *Their* medicine, by the way, is better than ever because they carried you and Walkin' Dove through this hot job without a scratch. They'll want most of the best fightin' men to do honor to the Sky People at this dance, and you're sure to be selected."

"Suppose I buy my way out?" asked Cashel.

He pressed a spring in the handle of the knife, and the long blade slid back out of view.

"Hold on," said the squaw man. "Was that a trick?"

"Why, it's a spring knife, that's all."

"Give it to me," said Diver. "I'll try that on Young Thunder, and see if I can't get you off with it!"

He left immediately and came back in the course of an hour with the broadest of grins.

"The old devil," he said, "nearly laughed in my face when I told him that you wanted to look on at that dance. He certainly wanted to see the great Muskrat faint and fall on his nose in the course of that medicine dance. But when I showed him the knife, he swallowed three times and looked as though he saw the light. He had just been sayin' that the Sky People certainly would want to see the Muskrat dancin' for his new people and in their honor, but when he saw the knife he stopped himself so short that he bit his tongue. He said that he would have another conversation with the spirit that sits on his left shoulder and that carried his prayers up to the sky. I told him to go along and have that conversation, and in the meantime I would leave that knife with him on deposit for one day. After that, I would certainly come back for it, red hot.

"So I left him, and you can bet that he'll have the right kind of a report tomorrow."

This report raised the spirits of the boy greatly, and as the squaw man had promised, so it turned out. The "spirit" that was familiar with Young Thunder had gone to the sky and returned with notice that the services of the Muskrat could be dispensed with. In the meantime the preparations went forward at a great rate for the lustration which was to purify the tribe and make up for the sins of Walking Dove and his companions.

Furthermore, an absolute ban was placed upon all departures from the camp, except for the purpose of guarding the horses, and bringing them in at night. For the rest, not an arrow was to be drawn and not a gun discharged even if a deer walked into the very midst of the tepee. There was a sole exception, which was that if an enemy attacked the village, the warriors might defend themselves and their possessions; but for no other purpose might a hand strike, or finger pull a trigger, or bowstring be drawn to the shoulder. And if any man disobeyed this edict he would be covered with shame, blasted with dishonor, and immediately would lose all credit among men and all fortune in the chase and in battle. His senses would grow blunted. He would become a fool, pitiable among men and worse than dead. His best friends would fall from him, and shortly he would sink into a terrible death, probably with his scalp dangling from the bridle reins of some Sioux or Pawnee warrior.

Young Thunder was so exact and explicit regarding the penalties because he was perfectly sure, said Jim Diver, that no one among the Cheyennes would venture to break his orders, since the late fulfillment of his prophecy. Young Thunder was engaging to steer his blasted people through the eleven or so days that remained of this moon. He guaranteed to do it without causing the loss of a hair of their heads, but they were required to live on the provisions they

101

had at hand, live close, and pay strict attention to what further commands the chosen "spirit" might communicate to Young Thunder from above.

At the same time, he announced the dance.

Diver pointed out that a good fortune had already passed into the hands of the great medicine man from the warriors, young and old, who wished to escape from this terrible ordeal.

Forty braves were picked out, all men in the prime of life, from twenty to forty years old. First they had to have strong steam baths, and after that they were purified en masse by Young Thunder, who gave a little public dancing exhibition of his own. With burning sweet grass and other compounds he smoked and purified the celebrants, until they had reached a well-nigh perdurable sanctity. All the while he pranced about the medicine tent chanting, calling on the Sky People, groaning, praying, and then beginning a fantastic series of leaps and plunges while he drove all evil out of that lodge with the kicks of his heels and the nails of his hands. He had disguised himself as a cross between a grizzly bear and an antelope, and his head was a special masterpiece, for he carried the huge mask of a grizzly surmounted by horns. He looked to young Cashel like a child's imagination of a devil, and he and Jim Diver managed to exchange some private smiles; but the rest of the Cheyennes seemed to take this nonsense in the most serious way, anxiously regarding the squatting circle of dancers, and the medicine man nodding approval when he howled like a beast or screaked like a bird.

When Young Thunder had worked himself into a good sweat, he ordered the dance to begin and himself led the first round, with the braves following him. Their sleek bodies still glistening from the sweat bath, they started out at varying paces. There were some tried old hands among the lot and these refused to give away a trick. They began with a step as easy and restful as could be, knowing that they had a great distance of hours before them. But most of the young braves could not resist trying to strike the eyes of the Sky People, and their fellow Cheyennes, by cutting capers, stooping low, bounding aloft, and occasionally working up such a head of steam that they had to let it off in prolonged screechings that made the roof of the big medicine lodge vibrate.

Most of those younger men had deadly serious faces, as though they realized that upon their strength, endurance, and the excellence of their dancing depended the chances of the entire Cheyenne people, and that if they could not win the favor of the Sky People by their capering, nothing could be done otherwise to reintegrate the glory of the race.

This thing had no religious interest to the white men, of

course, but it did have the fascination of a long-distance race, and they callously laid bets on their favorites.

It might go on into the fourth day, said Diver, for Broken Arrow once had lasted that long, and every other man in the dance actually had been worn to the ground before Young Thunder had to call a halt. He had wanted to see Broken Arrow beaten because he was jealous of that warrior's glory. Instead, he merely beheld the greatness of the youth redoubled because the whole crowd of Cheyennes were willing to swear that it was only the might of Broken Arrow, as he staggered around the ring, that had won the favor of the spirits.

The lodge was packed to suffocation at the commencement of the ceremony, and in the very first hour there was a thrill for everyone when one of the youngest dancers, Black Rock, danced himself into a state of hysteria, leaping and raging around the ring until he began to foam at the mouth, and finally dropped senseless in a dreadful state of exhaustion.

Even Young Thunder looked concerned as he took charge of the restoration of the youth, and Jim Diver pointed out that if the boy died, the dance was a failure. It was the purpose of the medicine man to torment these poor fellows to the point of utter exhaustion, but not to reduce them to the last extremity.

That day and that night the dance continued. The density of the crowd wore away. Men and women went home to their tepees, with the chief attendance during the night consisting of the relatives of the performers. These did everything they could to keep up the spirits of their kinsmen, sometimes dancing a few rounds beside them, and throwing in a few hearty war whoops and hair-raising chants for good measure.

The next morning the dancers were going round and round with persistent steadiness, their bodies already gaunt, and the sweat running from them, while Young Thunder presided, striking a ragged rhythm by pounding on a big lump of rock with the peen of a blacksmith's hammer. But the number of the celebrants was reduced for the moment to thirty. Some of the others who had staggered and fallen would be forced to re-enter the dance by the remorseless Young Thunder, but as for Black Rock, he discreetly announced that that very sick young man had made a very acceptable sacrifice of his strength to the Sky People and was exempt from any further effort. Cashel looked in on this performance, and found himself in a corner, blinking the smoke of the fumes that incessantly rose from burning sweet grass out of his eyes. And suddenly a voice spoke softly beside him, and he turned to face Chapa.

CHAPTER XXIV

SHE GLOWED with emotion, and one glance at her showed that the emotion was anger.

"You are more famous since I last saw you," said she.

"Not famous with you, Chapa," said he.

"My gods are not your gods," she answered, "and I am not happy when I see you come here and sneer at them!"

"I haven't sneered," said he.

"I've watched your face," she said, "while you looked at them, the poor simple men who would not try to buy themselves out of the dance!"

He could not help the flush of guilt that burned into his face. And he struck back rather blindly to justify himself.

"You sent me away to fight, not to dance, Chapa," said he. "I am no dancer, if that's what you want in a man. I can't leap and caper like those fellows out there. I'm not as strong and straight and fine looking as they are. Without clothes I look like a frog, and I imagine that you know it!"

Two things struck his eye then—the glistening of a high light on the muscular, sweating shoulder of a brave, the color of a polished sard, and on the other hand the bright gleam of her hair which had no place in the duskiness of that lodge.

And then she asked him the last question that he wanted to answer: "Are you honest?"

He was amazed. His eye wandered. He could have sworn that somehow she had learned about his past life, and for almost the first time he wished that life had been different from the fact.

"You won't look straight at me," she told him.

He managed to bring his glance fairly upon her, but he could not hold it there. He felt his eyes widening as if in fear of her. He blinked, and looked away.

"You broke the Pawnee line," she said. "They tell me that you counted coup on the great white chief who led the Pawnees into the fight. I thought it was because you wanted to do some great thing. But now I see it was only because even a cornered rat will fight—even a water rat!"

She went away. He was glad that she was gone for he was stung to the quick, and yet he had no way of answering her. For a time he watched vaguely the circling of the dancers, moving like automatic machines, with a short and hitching step, and he watched how the fire dwindled, leaving them all in shadow, and how it leaped again and endowed the bronze of their bodies with a glowing patina.

Twice he had been hurt by her rebuffs, and twice he had felt their injustice, but on this second time he had to admit that she had touched her finger to one burning truth. He was a thief, a dishonest man, and she suspected his dishonesty, no matter if her grounds for suspicion were not the true ones.

He felt himself falling into a state of confusion like that of the atmosphere in the lodge, where wreaths of smoke twisted here and there, and the feet of the dancers thumped in a broken rhythm. There was pain in their efforts and pain in his own heart such as he never had known before.

And glancing after her, he saw that she already was gone, and knew that he loved her. He had aspired to take a squaw and live as a savage. Now he wished to have her as a wife, in the holiest sense of that word, but he felt that she had left him and placed a gulf between them forever. It was strange to the boy that the two things for which he could feel an actual personal reverence, and look up to them as if they were far above him, he had encountered in this tribe of barbarians. Among the whites, he had told himself that those who pretended to goodness were church-going hypocrites, and those who had pretended to greatness were simply the lucky criminals; but in spite of himself he was looking up to Chapa and to Broken Arrow.

A clamor broke out in the open beyond the medicine lodge. There was a note of admiration, of wonder, and of anger in the sound of the voices, and young Cashel went out from the big tent curiously, willing to be diverted and forgetful of himself and his troubles.

So, as he came out from the great lodge, the first thing that he saw was the face of Chapa looking toward the center of a crowd, bright with interest and wonder. He would have given loads of gold to cause that look on her face on his own account.

But looking into the crowd in the same direction he saw what had stirred her, and did not wonder.

It was Captain Fitzroy Melville, complete in the finest of beaded deerskins, his rifle cased beneath his knee and little silver bells running along his bridle reins. It was Fitzroy Melville, mounted on the king of all horses, Clonmel!

He was changed from his appearance in the caravan. His hair had been growing long, then, but now it brushed his shoulders. And in place of his riding clothes, he wore the true frontiersman's outfit, except that it was more splendid than most. His own light saddle was replaced by one of the Pawnee model; he was in every respect the beau ideal of the half-wild plainsman. Around him the Cheyennes were gathered, the women and children nearest and the braves at a less curious distance. No wonder that the crowd was becoming denser every moment and drawing all the admirers away from the medicine dance in the lodge. No wonder that they groaned with anger and sorrow as they looked at this man, and yet admired him at the same time. For they knew that this was the chief who had crushed them at Bald Hill and taken so many of their best warriors' lives.

Young Cashel himself was amazed by the effrontery of the man in riding into the Cheyenne camp. Then the captain spotted him in the distance and instantly waved to him.

Cashel went forward.

The Cheyennes gave way, and yet he approached the brilliant captain unwillingly. It was partly because of a guilty man's unwillingness to face one he has wronged, and it was partly that he hated to allow Chapa, the Beaver, to see him stand at the side of a man who was white like himself but who so far outshone him. Handsome and lofty sat Melville on the back of glorious Clonmel, the wind stirring softly in his shining hair. He might have stood for a hero out of a picture book.

But at last Cashel was before him, and saw Melville looking down at him half in interest and half in contempt.

"We're here again, Cashel," said he. "It was a long trail that you laid out for me. Or did you think that I'd let the horse go?"

Cashel flushed. He was astonished by the sense of shame that burned up in him. And yonder stood the girl, watching.

"I did you a wrong, captain," said he. "I've got to admit that I did you a wrong . . ."

"Tut!" said Melville. "I don't accuse you of that. And I haven't come here to punish you, my lad. I've ridden out into the jolliest game I ever played in my life. Do any of these staring fools understand English?"

"No, not one."

"I used to be the captain of a pitiful caravan, Cashel, but now I'm a chief and great medicine man among the free people of the Pawnees. Medicine man, d'you understand? Between a burning glass and a miscroscope, I've upset all of their chief priests and grabbed the job myself. It's the softest carpet that a man ever lay on. A train of presents arriving every day. If there isn't fresh venison, I raise my brows, and the whole infernal Pawnee nation trembles. Forgive you for stealing Clonmel? I bless you for it, my boy. But now tell me where chief what-not is, and come along to interpret for me. I mean old Two Sheep, Two Antelope, or whatever his name may be!"

Cashel looked at him with bewilderment.

He never had liked this man, even as captain of the caravan, in spite of apparent rectitude, and courage, and skill as a leader; but now that he had become a plainsman, he liked him less than ever. Something had snapped in Captain Melville. His eye was a shade too free and bold. His smile was too careless. He looked the picture of one who is sunning himself in lighthearted ease.

Why not?

It was the very ideal toward which the thief had aimed all the days of his life, but there was now a great difference in his attitude. Only by comparing himself with Melville could he vaguely guess that a great change had come over his spirit. For this thing was certain, that whereas he had hated the captain before, he no longer felt the slightest resentment toward him. Instead, he was cold with a true contempt.

They went slowly forward, surrounded so closely by the Cheyennes that their progress was necessarily slow.

And the captain talked at his ease, turning his head slowly as he observed every face. Certainly he had no mental or moral stop that prevented him from meeting the eyes of others.

"A fine lot of red grenadiers, these Cheyennes," said he. "The biggest pack of men on the prairies, I suppose, next to the Osages, and the Osages are too long-drawn-out and loose-coupled to make athletes. But still I prefer my tidy Pawnee wolves—less hair, and therefore harder to scalp. Though I must say that the women stop me a bit. How they stare at me, Cashel, my lad! How they stare!"

"They know who you are," said Cashel slowly, "even if they don't know *what* you are."

"Ay," said the captain. "I trimmed them to the quick the other night at the Bald Hill. I left the Pawnees still yelling and whooping calling me a Sky Spirit come to wipe the other red men off the plains. Well, Cashel, it's not a bad thing to be king, even of a pack of red wolves. But the women are a drawback, I must say. How's a man to pick out a lodge-keeper, cook, and all-around, free-of-charge servant when the lot he has to pick from are so bad? The chiefs are almost forcing their daughters into my hands. Old Snake-that-Jumps had a fourteen-year-old daughter that looks as though a horse had stepped in her face. And Bend-the-Bow has another that looks like mumps on both sides. One has to have some delicacy in these matters, Cashel. What have you done about it?"

"Nothing!" said Cashel, shortly.

"Hai!" cried the captain, turning a little in the saddle. "You aren't in such a quandary here. They have their own beauties, but by the eternal, Cashel, that girl yonder is white, isn't she?"

"What girl?" asked Cashel, with a sinking heart.

"That one. The one with the golden hair. Real gold, by heaven, and blue eyes! White, Cashel! But Indian trained! That's a combination so perfect that it almost makes me laugh. Cashel, what would her father be asking for her? I mean, the red kidnapper that calls her his daughter? I'll buy her in a minute, if I can. What? Have I stepped on your toes? Well, my boy, you're in this tribe and I'm out of it, but I'll give you odds that I get the lady and a blessing along with her!"

He broke into a hearty, ringing laughter, but Cashel did not answer. He was looking away from the handsome rider, and toward the noble head of the stallion with an odd sense that it was a disgrace to saddle such an animal with such a man!

CHAPTER XXV

ALL that the captain had said might have been put down to sheer lightness and carelessness of spirits, but Cashel felt that he was not deceived.

What of the girl?

He glanced back toward her and saw that she, the most dignified of maidens among all the Cheyennes, actually was following the stranger as a boy feels free to follow a girl. She came unshamed, flushed with excitement, her head held high, as always, and joy in her face.

Have her before Cashel? Ay, it looked as though he could beckon her into his hand.

And Cashel turned and looked up into the face of the captain.

"You have a grudge against me, Cashel, I'm afraid," said Melville lightly. "Probably based on a foolish feeling that you've wronged me. But as a matter of fact, I don't feel that way about it, as I've explained. Is this the tepee of old Two Antelope then?"

"Ay," said Cashel, "and there's the chief in front of his lodge."

An old squaw, breaking suddenly through the crowd, rushed at Melville with a scream, as though she would tear him from his horse. She was the mother of some dead young warrior, no doubt. Cashel took her by the arms. Pity for her came up from him as from a deep well.

"Mother," said he, "the stranger is a messenger. You'll bring a curse on yourself!"

And he gave her into the hands of the other women.

The captain was dismounting.

"Thanks, my boy," said he. "You've kept her from breaking her nails, and my deerskins from being torn. She'd like to have the ripping out of my eyes, wouldn't she?"

Cashel made no answer, but glanced from the white man to the braves who were gathering about their chief. It seemed to him that their grave dignity and simplicity was infinitely preferable, but he could tell that they looked upon the white man with favor. How could they understand his spirit, even if they understood his words? He would have seemed to them simply high-spirited and jovial, qualities they loved in a very brave man, and they were greathearted enough to appreciate the virtues of an enemy.

Clonmel was nuzzling fondly at his sleeve, but he dared not look at the fine head of the stallion, for the very strings of his heart pulled and sang with yearning.

He looked up. A great cloud, white as samite and shot with gold, was unfolding across the center of the heavens, as if it gave a bright promise to this meeting, and Melville was keen enough to seize upon this sight as an omen.

He waited until he had been introduced, giving the war chief gravity for gravity, and grace for grace, and then pointed upward.

"Tell him," said he to Cashel, "that the Sky People have put a lucky sign above our heads before we start this conference."

Cashel obeyed, and saw a little glint of superstition appear in the eyes of the chief. Then they went into the lodge.

They had to have meat, first, and then the pipe was ceremoniously passed by Two Antelope, after which the captain broached his business.

He came, he said, not to gloat over the Cheyennes because of their recent misfortune. It was true that all things were in the hands of the Sky People, who sometimes took pleasure in giving victory to the humblest warrior and pulling down the pride of the great chiefs. For his own part, he and the rest of the Pawnees, whom he referred to as "my people," accepted the outcome of the battle merely as a sign that the Cheyennes had recently offended the spirits who watch over all Indians, and they took it for granted, also, that the offense lay in the stealing of the two white mares.

Here he took occasion to turn to Cashel with a grin and remark: "Practice makes perfect, and you finished up a grand little job that night, Cashel. I could have guessed that you had your hand in it, even before I knew."

The eyes of Cashel lowered in distaste. And yet he remembered a time when any compliment from the captain of the caravan would have been doubly valuable to him.

The chief, in the meantime, having heard the first of this discourse, agreed with everything that was said, except that he could not see what fault had been committed in the stealing of the two white mares. Even in the last battle their virtue had been proved, since both the riders had escaped without harm, "even," he said, "when one of them rushed against the famous chief who was leading the Pawnees, the great man who had planned the battle, the invincible hero—upon his very person one rider of a white mare had counted coup, and then ridden safely upon his way, yes, and as he rode, he had found the Pawnee horse herd, and had driven them before him, a hundred head of chosen horses, the war ponies of the bravest and the richest Pawnees, all gathered and swept home to make the herds of the Cheyennes fatter."

This series of remarks Cashel translated with the gravest of faces, and as he listened, the captain's face contorted with a sudden fury.

"The next time, Cashel," said he, "it will be a different story, if you dare to face me again!"

"Day or night, captain," said the thief. "Day or night I'm ready to meet you. And if there's ever another battle, I'll promise to ride out in front of the ranks and ask for you—and your gun—and your medicine!"

Now, as he said this, such a disgust for this man took hold of him, and such a contempt for all that he represented in his new character as an Indian warrior, that Cashel raised his eyes and looked steadily, straightly into the eyes of the other. He thought nothing of it at the moment. He was not aware of using any power of the will, as he had used it before, in order to meet the glance of others, but suddenly his heart leaped wildly—for the eyes of the captain had swerved from his, and Melville was saying rapidly:

"Let the time come for boasting after the meeting, Cashel. In the meantime, tell this triple-plated jackass that I'm here to offer him a bargain that ought to warm the cockles of his heart."

"What is it?" asked Cashel.

"We had a warm time on our hands after the little fight was over. When the Cheyennes had finished running like a pack of wild goats—you can put it in pretty words, if you please—my boys spent a time ripping off scalps and passing their knives into the poor devils who were dying but not yet dead. A special group of them made a rush for that fellow who was pinned down under his horse. They wanted his hair so badly that I was interested. Besides, I'd seen you make a pass to save him right in front of me, and that made me think that he was worth something extra. I couldn't imagine

110

Cashel bothering his head about a chief that wasn't silver trimmed and gold lined!"

He broke off, cluckling, and still Cashel looked down to the ground to master and conceal his disgust and his contempt.

"So I ran out myself, Cashel, my lad, and kicked the boys away from the fellow who was down. He had a knife in his hand, still, and looked ready to die fighting. We had to slip a noose over his arms, and roll his horse off him, and then we found that he was quite unhurt—a wonder that he didn't have both his legs smashed like a pair of pipe stems. However, he could walk almost at once, and as I got him propped up, hair intact and all, I learned who he was, and was mighty glad I hadn't let them slice his throat for the sake of a scalp and three coups counted. Or would they have counted nine on a great man like Broken Arrow? At any rate, he's gone back to the Pawnee village and has a tepee to himself in the center of the town. Now, this is the point of all the talk. Tell this sour-faced old rat, Two Antelope, that I'm willing to exchange Broken Arrow, unhurt, intact, hair-on-head, eyes-in-head, hands-on-arms, and feet-on-legs, for the sake of the two infernal white mares!"

"Are you?" asked Cashel, astonished in spite of himself into a show of interest.

"I am," said the captain yawning a little, "and I rode all this distance to make the exchange. The point is that these people of mine are medicine mad. They'd rather have those two mares than a dozen warriors on hoof, I believe. The mares give them a magic standing, as you might say. I never heard such fool talk, but I'm here to make the offer. I have to please my idiotic people, and not myself."

Hastily, with eager eyes, Cashel repeated the offer, without all comments, merely saying to Two Antelope:

"He has come to bring us very great news, Two Antelope. He has come to tell us that the Pawnees will trade the great warrior for the sake of the two white mares!"

Two Antelope did not change a muscle of his face.

"Do you hear me?" said Cashel. "It isn't a joke. It's seriously meant. For the sake of the medicine of those two mares, the Pawnees will give us back Broken Arrow, Two Antelope! Answer him quickly."

"A quick answer is easily made," said Two Antelope, "when a foolish offer has been suggested. If it is horses that the Pawnees want, I myself will pay ten down for the ransom of my great friend, that good man, Broken Arrow. And other chiefs will pay nearly as much. We will fit up ten horses with rifles and saddles, tell him. Yes, or perhaps twenty, if he insists, though I would not offer as much right away. But as for giving up the two white mares, of course I am not as foolish as that!"

"How under the sky could you be foolish," asked Cashel, "in buying back Broken Arrow at the price of any two horses in the world?"

"My young friend," said the war chief, "this may not appear to you, but it is clear to me. In a battle, what difference does the strength of the greatest warrior make, when it is true that we have two horses upon the back of which any man is safe. Let the Pawnees choose their bravest men and send them out against the least of ours. We shall mount our warriors on the two white mares, and let them send six against us. I don't care. Neither will the two warriors, even though it may be their first battle! They will ride down toward the enemy, whose bullets will fly away from the medicine mares. The battle will be ours! And," he went on, with a sudden darkening of face, "at the battle of the Bald Hill, if the riders of the two white mares had thought of turning their horses straight at the enemy, who knows what might have happened, or how many of the Pawnees would have fallen, until they turned and ran like wolves from the field?"

He grew hot with excitement as he spoke, and when he was silent, he left Cashel staring helplessly.

"Is he still recalcitrant?" asked the captain.

"He'd rather give up his own head than the two mares," said Cashel. "But I tell you what. You can take back to the Pawnees half the horses of the Cheyennes, if you'll let us have Broken Arrow back in exchange!"

"They'd scalp *me*," answered Melville, scowling, "if I turned Broken Arrow loose for anything but the mares. These infernal idiots match my own lot of fools!"

"There is a feast in my lodge tonight," said Two Antelope, "and many Cheyenne warriors will be here. Stay with us, brother. We shall be glad to look in the face of a brave enemy."

Cashel translated.

"Glad to stay. It's a lark, my lad," said the captain. "And besides, it gives me a chance to hunt up Goldilocks. Where shall I find her, Cashel, my boy?"

CHAPTER XXVI

Go TALK to Rain-By-Night," said Cashel, and gave him the Cheyenne original of that name. "Or you can go with me. I'm heading there myself."

He led his tall, white companion to the lodge of Rain-by-Night, who was taking the air in front of his tepee, sucking at a long-stemmed pipe and watching with fascination the efforts of a dog to scratch its back properly against the top of a tent pin. Rain-by-Night, as Jim Diver had well said, was one of the sourest and ugliest braves in the Cheyenne nation, and also one of the least polite on all occasions. He hardly lifted his brows at his two distinguished visitors.

"It'll only be a matter of price," said the captain, as he clapped eyes on the warrior.

"Bid high, then," said the boy, "for I shall bid against you!"

"Hai!" cried Melville. "I guessed it. You remember that I asked you if you were running on that trail, my lad?"

"I am," answered Cashel. "I'm running with all my might on that trail."

He approached Rain-by-Night, and the latter nodded stiffly. Cashel was so angered that his fury stripped the last vestige of consideration or courtesy away from him.

"We've come buying," said he.

"The new three-year-old bay colt?" asked the chief, taking the pipe an instant from his lips, and looking at them with his wrinkled eyes.

"We come buying your daughter," said Cashel.

The warrior seemed not in the least offended. He merely nodded.

"In a wise man's house," said he, "every dog is for sale—also all of the women. But the man who shows his mind has to pay higher, and a rude buyer pays the most of all."

He delivered these dicta without so much as raising his voice; and restoring his pipe to his mouth, he sucked lazily at it again, still watching them out of his time-wearied, half-shut eyes.

"Very well," said Cashel, "we'll bid against one another."

"That is the best way for me," said the frank old cynic, "and the worst way for both of you. But in this fashion we shall get at the root of the matter most quickly."

He waved a hand, as much as to ask them to begin. He had not risen to greet them, or acknowledged the introduction to the captain with more than a shrug of his shoulders. Cashel translated faithfully to the captain all that had been said.

And he saw a flare of satisfaction appear upon the face of the other.

"You're bidding against more than an Indian trader," said he.

"Your money back East won't help you," Cashel warned

him. "They don't understand dollars out here. It's the knives and guns and horses you have that will count the most."

The captain frowned, nodded, and squared his shoulders.

"This is the coldest-blooded old devil I ever saw," he remarked. "I thought they did things with more grace, even among the Cheyennes."

"They do," answered Cashel, "but Rain-by-Night is the exception."

"Very well," said the captain, "even in Indian wealth I'll outbid you."

Cashel smiled sourly.

"I have something that will top everything you can offer," he said, "but you may as well try."

"I begin then," said the captain. "I'll pay him ten good horses, you can say."

"He offers you ten horses," said Cashel.

"That would be a bargain for him," replied the Cheyenne. "And you, Muskrat?"

"I'll offer fifteen."

He translated.

"Twenty, then," said the captain.

"Twenty-one," said Cashel.

"Have you that many horses?" asked Rain-by-Night.

"I have one in five of all the horses captured from the Pawnees the other night. The warriors have voted them as my share, because I started the stampede."

"That is true," nodded the brave. "It pays to be courageous. That is why I still keep a large tepee, though I have only a daughter, and not a squaw."

"I've offered twenty-one," said Cashel. "What about you?"

"I lay this rifle on top of the pile," said the captain, with a triumphant smile.

He slipped from the rifle case on the flank of Clonmel a fine Colts repeating-rifle, and the eyes of the chief flashed for the first time.

"I match you with the same thing," said Cashel, showing the stolen rifle which he carried, "and I'm still a horse up on you."

The captain bit his lip.

"I forgot I was dealing with a thief," said he. "But we're playing the parts of fools, here. We buck up the price of one another. We might as well be questing dogs, for all the effect that our howling has upon that old moon!"

"You haven't matched my price," said Cashel calmly.

As they delayed, it seemed that Rain-by-Night mistook their hesitation.

"It is time," said he, "that you should see what you are about to buy. Come into my lodge."

He led the way in and took a seat, allowing the others to accommodate themselves as they pleased. Young Chapa had started up, crimson of face, showing clearly enough that she had everheard their conversation when they were outside of the tepee. She offered to leave, but a gruff word from the brave stopped her.

"Stand still, Chapa," said Rain-by-Night. "I have been a kind father to you for this long time. I have let you refuse many braves, partly because I was used to having you about me, and partly because it enhanced your price to refuse everyone for a certain time. But now you are fully eighteen or nineteen years old, and before long you will begin to have wrinkles. Even so, you are at an age that cheapens you among the Indians. But here are two white men to buy you as a wife, and the white men marry women at an age when they are already grandmothers among the Cheyennes. Now, then, I want you to show them everything that will raise your price."

"Father," said the girl, "how can I tell that I wish to marry one of these warriors?"

"I can tell for you," replied Rain-by-Night quietly. "If they offer a good price and I give you to one of them, then if you refuse to live with the buyer and return to me, so that I have to give up what has been paid for you, you will wish that you were living in a badger's hole. I will make this lodge harder for you to bear than the center of a fire. I will have you work the skin off your hands, and starve you until your cheekbones crack the skin that overlays them. I will make you a thing that no warrior will look at without a shudder. I will give you the name of a bad daughter, and sweeten your work with a whip, or a blow from my fist. No, no, Chapa, you had better anger the bad spirits than to anger me! Now I have put up with your doings long enough. I will never find two men to pay me a higher price than these white men. Money and good things run through their hands like water through the bony hands of an old man."

Whatever answer came up to the lips of the girl, she checked it at once. It was plain that she knew the character of her adopted father perfectly, and what she knew snatched the color out of her face, and left her white and trembling.

One imploring look she cast at him, and then drew back to the side and watched the white men steadfastly.

"Bring them that last beaded moccasin," said the old Tartar.

She brought it submissively, and as Cashel and the captain bent over the fine beadwork, done with a cunning hand and a close eye, Cashel saw her glance lift timidly—and rest upon Melville. He knew then that all he feared was true. She was

115

more than taken by the splendid appearance of Melville. That robbed him of his awe of her. If she were such a child as to have to judge a man entirely by his exterior, there was no doubt that she would prefer the captain. Indeed, he himself, a day earlier, would have laughed at the idea of comparing himself with Melville. But since his meeting with that man on this day, he had revised his opinion. Either the captain had sunk in the scale, or he himself had risen, for he felt at least the equal of Fitzroy Melville. He was thankful that he had to please Rain-by-Night, rather than Chapa herself. He could thank all the powers of the sky that it was not her caprice that he had to satisfy.

"Now the quilled war shirt," said the foster father. "And then the two robes you have last cured."

Obediently, almost anxiously she brought them; and always, as before, her glance searched the face of the captain to find approbation.

Suddenly Melville laughed.

"It's enough," said he. "Listen to me, Cashel, and tell him honestly—I know enough of the lingo to follow you—that I have two rolls of lead and a whole barrel of powder left in my lodge among the Pawnees, and all of this I will deliver to him faithfully, together with six common rifles!"

Cashel, with a pinch at heart, faithfully translated, and the eyes of the warrior glistened.

"I offer in my turn," said Cashel, "all of the gifts that the tribe gave me when I was taken in among them."

"So?" said Rain-by-Night. "They would make a balance, very nearly. And if there is anything in favor of the lead and powder and rifles, it is matched by the fact that he comes from the Pawnees, I suppose, and you are a Cheyenne."

Cashel translated again, and the angry, half-desperate roll of the captain's eye showed that he was at the end of his roll call of Indian wealth.

"If the great chief, Rain-by-Night," said he, "will wait for three months, I shall bring in a whole mule train loaded down with treasures to pay for his daughter."

Rain-by-Night listened to this with the broadest of grins.

"Then great chief, Rain-by-Night," he mocked, "knows very well that your scalp is not fitted onto a skull of iron. That same scalp may be smoking above a Cheyenne lodge fire before the end of a month!"

Fiercely the glance of the captain flashed at the girl and then back toward the flap of the tepee.

"My horse!" said he. "Do you hear me, Cashel? I'll pay down my horse for the girl."

"You'll pay down Clonmel?" gasped Cashel.

"I will, if the old jackass knows enough to put a right value on him!"

Cashel was fairly staggered. But, honestly, he made the translation and glued his eyes to the face of Rain-by-Night.

All doubt about that wily old Indian's ability to judge the value of the chestnut departed at once, for the eyes of the Cheyenne burned in his head.

"And you? You?" he asked impatiently of Cashel.

The latter played his one remaining card.

"I offer you, father," said he, "a greater thing than the stallion. I offer you a medicine horse which will turn the bullets of the enemy."

He glanced at the girl, and saw her bite her lip with a frown of anxiety as she stared at Rain-by-Night.

The latter nodded and shrugged his shoulders.

"That is a great price," he said dryly. "There are chiefs among the Cheyennes who would offer a great price for the magic mare. But look at me, Muskrat. I am an old man. When the fight comes, I am left at home to guard the lodges. I show the young boys how to shoot and scalp. But I am not called out on the warpath like the youngsters of the tribe. The place of the old men is to be wise."

He grinned as he spoke the last word. The old cynic was plainly willing to let the white men see that he understood the truth.

"Medicine is very good," said he, "until the day when it is weakened. But all medicine grows weak. The fine white mare once in my herd, I would have to ride her into the battle. The tribe would demand it of me. One fight, two fights, she turns the bullets away from me—or my wrinkled body is too thin for the enemy to hit with their arrows and bullets. The third battle, I am shot through the head. The medicine is gone from the white mare. I am dead. My ghost goes off howling in the dark without a scalp. The wind blows me up and down the prairies for ten thousand thousand years. But if I have the red stallion, then I know that I can ride away faster than any enemy can overtake me, and that is the kind of magic that pleases the heart of Rain-by-Night!"

CHAPTER XXVII

As HE said this, old Rain-by-Night got up hastily, and striking open the flap of the tent, he stared out at the stallion again, with his eyes still on fire. Ay, it was plain that he understood the value of a horse. Though even a child could have given one glance at the fine head and the magnificent shoulders of the stallion and told something of his quality.

But the lad stared, in his turn, straight into the face of the girl, and saw her glance soften, and cling to the noble captain, and then sink embarrassed toward the ground.

It was plain that she was delighted with the result of the sale. He felt like crying to her: "I've been a thief. I've been a low rat, lower than the name the Cheyennes gave me. But now I'm a better man than this fellow. You're a fool, Chapa!"

He could not say that. This quasi-perfect man, the captain, had too thoroughly captured her fancy.

Still the old fellow turned back to young Cashel, and his greed remained with him. Perhaps he still could extract something extraordinary from the smaller of the two white men.

"The Muskrat," he said, "has offered a great price for a young girl. Perhaps he still has some great thing to give. And Rain-by-Night remembers that he has done a great many things for the Cheyennes. He has made himself, in two battles, one of the chief of their warriors. Since Broken Arrow is gone, who is there among the Cheyennes as famous as the Muskrat? Perhaps you can offer something else. It would not have to be as valuable as the red stallion, perhaps?"

"I live among the Cheyennes, father," said Cashel desperately. "You know that I have gathered a great deal of wealth since I came, which was not long ago. I still shall gather more. In another short time I shall have many more horses, and robes, and guns, and ammunition, which I would give to you. Wait for another year, then, and all that I make in the meantime I shall offer to you!"

The old fellow watched the boy with his greedy, hungry eyes, but at last he shook his head.

"I see that you are a young brave who loves battle," he said. "And in spite of the white mare, a bullet may strike you. If the great Young Thunder were to cover you with charms and lay both his hands on your head to bless you, still I should fear to wager a small bet on your life. Glorious warriors live short lives. I am old and withered. But I have counted only one coup in all my days and taken only one scalp. Therefore I still have a well-filled tepee, and smoke my pipe in peace. When my daughter is gone, I shall buy a good, cheap, faithful woman whom the foolish young braves have overlooked, and still my comfort shall continue. No, no, my son. I cannot wait for you to steal more horses or win more robes and guns. Here is my other son standing with both his hands filled with wealth to give to me. My heart is filled with sorrow for the Muskrat, but I cannot wait! Tomorrow or tomorrow the terrible Pawnees may drop on us like a rain cloud out of the sky, and then I shall need such a horse as the red stallion to save me with his speed."

He turned to the captain.

"It is for you to bring to me the price you have promised," said he. "The way is long, brother. But your horse is very fast. In ten days I shall expect you. Farewell, a happy journey, and a quick return. In the meantime, you are safe to come and go, for the knives and the guns of the Cheyennes are made harmless by Young Thunder. He has put his hand on the wrist of every warrior!"

The captain turned toward the girl. It seemed clear that he might have stipulated then and there for more time to make sure of her mind, but the attitude of the girl would have been transparently clear to a duller wit than that of the captain.

She stood by the wall of the lodge with her hands clasped before her and her head hanging.

"Like a silly young fool!" said Cashel to himself.

He himself left the lodge in haste; and outside, he paused for a moment to touch the bright, sleek neck of the stallion.

He could have felt himself comparatively rich in possibilities a few hours before, but he knew now that the two things he most had prized were lost to him—the horse that he had followed into the wilderness, and the girl who had held him there. And as he talked to the stallion, and Clonmel turned his big, speaking eyes toward Cashel, it seemed to the thief that a mysterious power had been lodged in the great animal: a power great enough to snatch Fitzroy Melville out of the ranks of respected citizens and turn him into a wild squaw man with brain and soul deteriorating hand over fist; a power that had sent a New York thief out into the wilderness, glad of a horse for a companion. And at last the big stallion was to gallop with a red Indian seated in the saddle, and cruel Indian heels digging at his flanks, and the cutting Indian whip flaying him!

However that might be, his own career was ended. The prairies held nothing more for him, and his mind turned strongly and suddenly back to his own kind.

What kind should he call his own? Slippery thieves by night, like Walking Dove? Such were the gangsmen he had associated with, and his soul revolted at the thought of them. Or brazen thieves by day, like Rain-by-Night? He scorned them also. But there were other men to be found, who went with their heads high in all societies and lived for the best that they could know. They were like Broken Arrow, and he knew which of the classes he would strive to enter when he returned to the cities of the white man.

The voices of the captain, talking his broken Pawnee dialect, and the Cheyenne brave, still continued in the lodge; but looking up from the stallion, he saw Chapa standing by the half-drawn entrance flap glancing curiously from the white man to the stallion, and back again at Cashel as though something about that pair amazed and distressed her.

He turned from her, at that, and went slowly toward the lodge of Jim Diver, feeling more hollow of heart than ever he could remember being in his young life before. He had not yet gone far when the red stallion whinnied strongly after him. He looked back to see the big horse with head high, staring after him, asking him in every feature to return.

Chapa, too, had taken a few steps from the entrance of the lodge and was watching him as if she never had seen him before and wished desperately to read him quickly and deeply now.

Whatever bewildered her, he could not go back to speak to her now, for he felt as though she were already embarked and an ocean opening between them.

In the lodge of Diver he found that the squaw man was gone; but Lucky Buffalo Bird was there, pouring more dried buffalo meat into the stew pot that hung above the fire.

She gave him one glance.

"Your stomach is empty," said she.

"No," said Cashel.

"Your heart, then," said she.

He was amazed by the remark and the human understanding behind it.

"Sit down," she commanded.

He obeyed.

She actually filled a pipe for him and brought him a coal from the fire, juggling it dexterously in her hands so that it could not burn the tough skin, finally placing it on the middle of the tobacco.

While the pipe was drawn upon, she stood over the youth, and then waved the rising smoke aside.

"Hai!" sighed the squaw. "Who would be young? Who would be growing? The child is never happy. His day is longer than my year. He cannot have enough games to fill his hands for a single day. He is always yawning and trying to look around the corner. He expects to fill his belly at the meat pot ten times a day. And the young man is worse. His heart is always hollow."

"Why should it be?" asked Cashel.

"Because what he wants today he hates tomorrow. There is a young brave I could tell you about. He came to the Cheyennes with his hands empty. They were filled in a day! Honors were heaped upon him. He could be a chief, if he cared to ask the young men to ride out with him. But he will not ask them. He is sad. What does he wish for? Does he want to pull out all the tail feathers of the Thunder Bird? He has more guns than he can shoot and more horses than he can ride. He can have a wife from any chief. The chief's daughters would gladly come to his tepee for no price at all. But he prefers to buy trouble in a white skin!"

He stared at her again, and saw her nodding and smiling.

"Ay, well," said she, "but tomorrow will be better. A slow horse takes only one more day in a year."

"What do you mean?" asked Cashel.

"And a crooked gun is like a crooked eye. It is no use till it is straightened."

He knew suddenly what she meant. He had been looking deep and straight into her eyes until her own glance wavered aside.

"Eat, my son, and sleep," said she, "and do the thing that lies before you. The Sky People will take care of tomorrow. Or," she added, "you could talk the poison out of your heart!"

CHAPTER XXVIII

Now, as he listened to the squaw, it seemed to him that there was some peculiar knowledge and understanding emanating from her. Certainly she seemed to hint a complete familiarity with all of his troubles.

Suddenly he said bluntly:

"I wanted three things. Tell me what they were, if you can?"

"A horse, a wife, and a friend," said she, instantly.

It staggered the boy to hear her.

"Do you see the inside of a man's mind?" he asked her.

"I use my eyes and ears," said she, "and I think that the medicine men don't do any more, except that they shake rattles and make a smoke through which they talk. Besides, all people are the same."

"I never have found them so," said Cashel, beginning to look on her as a tremendous seer.

"They are all born, they live, they die," said the squaw. "So they are just the same. And they want the same things. A woman wants a husband and children; a husband to take care of and be proud of; and children to love. Men want glory. But you have found enough glory, of course. What makes you unhappy, then? Because you have missed the other things—a fast horse, and good weapons, and a friend, and a wife. Well, you have the guns and the knives and the rest. But you haven't the remaining three. Even a medicine horse is not enough for you."

"Tell me then what horse I want," asked the boy.

"I don't need to make medicine in order to answer that. I've heard you tell my husband. You want the red stallion which the white chief of the Skidi is riding."

"Very well, then. And what wife, tell me?"

"The one with the white skin."

"How do you guess that?"

"We like what we're used to," said she. "The Pawnees prefer to eat the things they grow out of the ground because they're used to them. They Cheyennes prefer to eat what they kill in the hunts. After a while, we can learn to like new things. But it takes time. So after a while you may be able to see women with red skins, but it is still too soon for that. All you can find is Chapa."

He was amazed by the simplicity and truth of this reasoning.

"Very well, then," said he. "And for friends I have Walking Dove and Jim Diver, your husband. They both have been kind to me."

"No," said the squaw. "For men with strong hearts want friends who are greater than themselves. And honest men, too. Walking Dove is an Indian, but he is too like a white man to please you. He has red skin, but he thinks around a corner, like a white man. My husband is a great warrior. He has taken many scalps. But still, he is a white man who is thinking like an Indian. Therefore he is not the friend for you. He laughs at everything, including the things that you admire most."

Cashel rubbed his knuckles across his chin and puffed earnestly at his pipe. He began to respect this woman more every moment.

"Who, then, *do* I want as a friend?" he asked her.

"Who does every man among the Cheyennes want as a friend?" asked the squaw. "Why, of course they want the bravest heart and the strongest hand and the truest mind. They want Broken Arrow for a friend, and so do you. Otherwise, would you have tried to save him in the battle of the Bald Hill?"

He sighed.

"You have looked into my mind and seen everything," said he. "Nothing can be hidden from you."

"Yes," said she. "I am hidden from myself, and that is the great trouble, always! We make our sorrows by thinking wrong."

"But my sorrows are real," said he.

122

"Are they, my son?" she said, and smiled a little, which made a wonderful change in her usually dour face.

"You have named what I want, and I lack all the three things," said he.

"Ah?" she grunted, her eyes glimmering at him as though she could convince him to the contrary.

"Consider the horse. It is gone. Another man rides it, and he is a great chief."

"The white Pawnee? Ay, but dead men do not ride horses, my son."

"I understand you. But he is here in the camp. He is protected by the laws of the Cheyennes. I could not touch him."

"If you did, you would be tortured to death and made a sacrifice to turn away the anger of the Sky People," said she, calmly. "But on the other hand, when he leaves the village and is one hour's ride away, you are free to follow him."

"The white mare never could catch him."

"Patience carries a heavy load," said she.

He sat up straight and put the pipe aside. Clasping his hands about his knees, he stared at her as at the fountainhead of all wisdom.

"It might be," said Cashel.

"It can be," said she. "And that would be a great battle!"

She grew fierce at the thought of it, and then the fierceness faded out of her face.

"And the wife?" said Cashel.

But he answered himself, sternly, "A dead man cannot take a wife, either."

The squaw nodded.

"So a little word grows into a great action," said she.

"But the friend!" said Cashel. "Broken Arrow is in the village of the Pawnees!"

"He is still alive," said the squaw, "and therefore you should be happy."

"Aye, but how long before the messenger returns to the Pawnees and tells them that the Cheyennes will not trade the two white medicine mares for the warrior?"

"He has not yet returned," answered she, as stern as before.

"I shall meet him, I shall overtake him, I must!" said Cashel through his teeth. "But even if he is killed, still word will some other way come to the Pawnees and they will then torture Broken Arrow to death."

"He is still alive," said the squaw, "and the Muskrat is a great thief!"

"Ah?" muttered Cashel, not understanding her purpose.

"He is still alive, and a great thief like the Muskrat might steal him away!"

Sweat started out on the face of the boy.

"He is kept in a lodge in the middle of their town," said he.

"Only the Sky People know tomorrow," answered the squaw, and suddenly walked from him out of the tepee.

It left Cashel to brood with fear and excitement on what she had said.

Certainly she had showed him how to cut the Gordian knot, but it was no simple matter to apply the remedy, no matter how clearly she had shown the way.

He could wait until Captain Melville was gone an hour from the village, and then follow the spoor of his horse. But this meant, also, that the white mare must run like a sailing bird, and that the red stallion should be kept back to less than his full pace, whereas it was likely that, once under weight, the captain would well understand the danger he was in of pursuit, and keep Clonmel at full speed until he was safe in the Pawnee village.

The chances, he felt, were largely against his overtaking the captain, but if that could be done, he felt a fierce confidence that he could conquer the leader of the caravan.

What had become of that caravan, now? How had they proceeded after they were deserted by their leader, the man sworn to stay with them until they had been conducted out of danger to the far-off Pacific Coast? How were they wandering? What other captain had they chosen?

And suddenly a greater scorn than ever for Melville came over him. It was understandable that he should have been tempted away from his duty to reclaim the lost stallion, but it was beyond belief that, once having recovered the horse, he should leave his caravan to wander helplessly on its way. Certainly if he met Melville, he would hesitate no more to fight the battle out to the death with him than would a Cheyenne hesitate to kill and scalp a thieving Pawnee.

But even supposing that he should overtake and dispose of Melville, even supposing that he should again have beneath him the splendid speed and strength of the stallion, he was still as far as ever from saving Broken Arrow from the fiendish cruelty of the Pawnee women.

Grimly he pondered.

It was impossible, he told himself. No man could enter the village and escape again safely, to say nothing of taking with him a prisoner sure to be so strictly guarded as the famous Cheyenne prisoner would be.

And yet, as he shook his head and vowed the thing could not be done, he felt the rising and surge of the great temptation, and the more he argued, the more firmly was he decided to make the great effort!

His mind wandered rapidly toward possible helpers.

There was Walking Dove—but instantly he knew that

Walking Dove was far too hardheaded to risk his scalp in order to save that of a future rival for the headship of the tribe. Walking Dove would never embark on such a task as this.

Jim Diver, then?

But Jim Diver was interested in only one thing—the collection of Pawnee scalps to avenge the old wrong he had received so long before.

Certainly Diver would never commit himself to an action so dangerous. Besides, though it was conceivable that one man might insert himself into the Pawnee camp, it was far more impossible for two to do the same thing.

The breath of the boy failed him in sheer terror. He rose and walked from the tepee, shaking his head, actually shuddering with the greatness of his determination not to be tempted in this manner.

There he saw the squaw returning, carrying a load of water for the lodge, and as she came up, she said quietly:

"Breathe deep, my son. The good, sweet air will give you courage."

She passed him, and he knew that she was sure he would attempt the impossible.

As she entered the tepee she said in the same matter-of-fact voice:

"The white Pawnee already has ridden to the west!"

CHAPTER XXIX

THE moment he was left alone, with Diver's squaw gone into the lodge and the white mare shining like milk not three steps from him, where she munched at some dried grass that had been brought in for the sacred animal by one of the herd boys, young Cashel was perfectly clear of mind.

The sun stood almost overhead, but a little westward of the zenith. And he told himself that by the time he had completed his preparations, he would be within the hour's limit for leaving the camp. Bitterly he grudged that head start to the rider of the red stallion.

He re-entered the tent without a word to the squaw and began to get togther the essentials for the journey. He took one good knife, the Colt's revolver and the repeating rifle, a good stock of ammunition, some jerked venison, a light robe made of a hide of a buffalo calf, a saddle, bridle, and a saddle pad made of Spanish moss, which never mats or grows soggy with perspiration so as to cause saddle sores.

He gathered these things together in silence, carried them

out, and equipped the white mare for the journey. Then he went back into the lodge. The squaw held out to him a little, pale, rubbery twist of the intestines of a deer, filled with a reddish-brown powder. Another twist of the same sort contained grease. And she pointed out that by combining the two he could change his color to that of a sun-stained red man. There was still a more important matter of disguise, if he were to enter a Pawnee camp, and this was to be effected by barbering alone.

As if to a prophet he listened to her, and presently was sitting cross-legged on the ground, while she stooped above him, and with a pair of shears that Jim Diver possessed, clipped his hair close to the scalp, leaving only a ridge, like the clipped mane of a horse, in the center of his head.

Young Cashel, in a little hand mirror, watched the transformation, and wondered at himself. In a few moments he was given the look of a savage wild man. The squaw helped the transformation by taking a red stain and turning the scalp lock and the whole top of his head, down to the center of his forehead, vermilion. That was the Pawnee way. Finally, she mixed the body stain and rubbed his head and neck with it until it was the proper color to suit her taste. By this time Cashel did not know himself. There was brutality about his features which he never would have guessed before that moment.

Even when this work had finished, and she had pointed out that he could similarly stain the rest of his body, she was not finished with him. She picked up a handful of dust and pebbles from beside the fire in the center of the lodge and blew upon it three times, sending out showers of smoke-white dust, and a few of the little pebbles. Those that remained she scrutinized carefully, first for their position and reaction one to the other, and then counting them precisely, twice over. As last she dropped the remnant and dusted her hands violently, one against the other.

Cashel had been long enough among the Indians to know that she had made medicine and could guess that it was for his benefit.

"What is the answer?" he asked.

"You will have part of the things that you ask," said she. "Ride out, my son. Unless," she added with a faint sneer, "you are afraid of the medicine of Young Thunder, who has frightened the rest of our tribe!"

As she said this, there was something so malevolent in her expression that he hardly knew whether to thank her for her ministrations or to suspect her of merely sending him out to his destruction. He finally made a curt gesture of farewell and left the lodge.

Cutting back among the lodges, he would have a good chance to leave the camp seen by almost no eyes at all, but just as he swung up into the saddle, just as the mare willingly stepped forward against the bridle, he was stopped by a harsh voice that barked at him from the side, like the bark of a dog.

He looked across fairly into the face of Young Thunder.

Apparently that great magician had just left the medicine tent to go for a moment to his own lodge, perhaps to freshen the paint that made his face hideous. It was made still more ugly by the expression with which he now stared at Cashel, and asked curtly what his white brother meant by riding out from the camp while the embargo was laid expressly by himself upon all such movements.

"You are bound out toward the land of the Pawnees," said the medicine man, "as if the wolves will not know the difference between themselves and a muskrat! You are riding out secretly to try to do some great thing. Young man, you have been at Bald Hill and seen the strength of my medicine and my prophecy!"

Cashel looked calmly upon him.

"Young Thunder," said he, "it is true that you have spoken against war parties during the rest of this moon, but there are ways of persuading the Sky People. Suppose that I drove ten good horses into your herd. . . ."

The medicine man actually blinked with covetousness and answered hastily, "I shall ask the spirit who sits invisible on my shoulder, until he gives me an answer, and while you are collecting your horses, I shall make medicine to learn . . ."

"You've made enough already," broke in Cashel, "to show me that you're a fraud and scamp, Young Thunder. D'you think that I'd pay you for your medicine? I'd as soon pay a whirlwind of dust for hiding the sun. Things happen as they will, brother, and you can neither make them come nor stop them from going."

Young Thunder's smile stopped only by degrees, partly because he could not understand this white man's imperfect Cheyenne, and partly because he could not understand how any mortal might be rash enough to incur his displeasure— to actually invite it with insults. But when he slowly comprehended, his old face puckered like paper in the fire. He lifted up a skinny arm, with the fist turned into claws, like the talons of a bird stooping at prey. His thin chest heaved with a deep breath of hatred.

Cashel swerved the white mare toward him—she was a gentle thing that answered the least touch upon her guiding rein—and with the butt of his heavy rifle he tapped the exploding breast of the medicine man.

"Listen to me, Young Thunder," said he. "I am going out to make war on the Pawnees. If you have any friends, send them out to warn the Pawnees that I am coming. Because if I count a coup before your precious eleven days are ended, every man in the Cheyenne nation will know that you're a faker and pretender. They will strip off your medicine tools and your rattles and your stolen bear claws. They'll drive you out of the village, whipping you with unstrung war bows. The children will pelt you with handfuls of dirt and mud. The women will scratch your eyes out if they can. And everyone will say that the only good your medicine is, is to bring on trouble like that of Bald Hill, and never to do the Cheyennes any real service. Do you hear me, Young Thunder? Go back to your big lodge, and tell your squaws to start making medicine and praying, not for the rest of the Cheyennes, but for your own mangy hide! Because I'm going to show the people what a scoundrel you are, Young Thunder!"

The medicine man had the breath expelled from his body. His fury grew greater than ever and all sorts of denunciations flamed in his eyes and quivered on his lips. However, he couldn't get the breath back, and presently he was taken with a real convulsion of impotent anger that made him twist and gasp, and begin words and break them off in the middle, though his shaken fist and then the movements of his naked knife showed that he would like to break every bone in Cashel's body and to wind up by cutting his throat.

When Cashel started off, the medicine man ran after him a number of paces, still gasping and choking, and turning up a face made hideous by its hatred. But still he could only gibber out his wrath, and Cashel, putting his heels to the mare, bounded her away from the reach of the ugly old specter.

The last of the lodges were whirling past him when a pony darted swiftly up to his side and he saw beside him the athletic form of Two Antelope, the buffalo robe blown sheer back from his shoulders by the wind of his gallop.

He pointed ahead with a questioning hand to which Cashel answered with a decided nod.

"Brother, brother," said the chief, in great emotion, "you go to destroy yourself, and all of the tribe with you! Young Thunder has spoken and . . ."

Cashel leaned a little to the side and shouted, "Young Thunder is a fool, and the Sky People have sent me to prove it!"

He rushed the white mare on. The last of the lodges winked past him, as if carried to the rear on a stream of wind, and suddenly he saw that Two Antelope no longer was beside him. He looked back and observed that the chief had reined in his horse just outside the line of the lodges. There he sat on the back of his pony, with one brawny arm raised, waving the hand back and forth. And, in his heart, the boy knew that the chief wished him well. After all, it was to his benefit more than any other if the new and tyrannical power of the medicine man was broken and the faces of the warriors were turned back toward their war leader.

The broad arms of the prairies stretched wide on either side of him. The flashing green and silver pale, where the wind riffles ran upon it, glanced away on either hand. He looked back once more. The mere tops of the lodges appeared, like ships hull-down on the horizon. And a little later, when he turned for a final glance, he saw merely the smudge of smoke that forever hangs above an Indian village. This, too, thinned away in the heat haze of the midday, and he was alone in the wilderness once more.

He brought the white mare down to a trot. She stepped out well at this gait. And instead of racking his body to bits, her grass-cutting stride floated him smoothly along. He was tempted constantly to fling her forward into a full gallop, but he dared not do this. It was not by mere speed but by patience, as the squaw had said, that he could manage to come up to the captain.

And it seemed strange to the boy that he should be again committed to the uncharted sea of the plains with nothing to lead him but the trail of the red stallion.

It lay fair before him, sometimes lost in a region where hard gravel came to the surface, but appearing again instantly in the grass beyond. It showed that the rider of the great horse was disdainful of being trailed. He knew what was striding beneath him, and he scorned all pursuit.

Yet Cashel knew that he was gaining ground.

When he stopped to breathe the mare, he could see the grass curling up right again, where the long-striding hoofs of the stallion had beaten it down not long before. And then pushing forward again at the same steady gait, only resting her on the upslopes of the prairie undulations, at last he saw a blink before him like the shine of a rock, and a little later his glasses picked out clearly a horseman jogging across the treeless grass.

CHAPTER XXX

HE GREW frantic with eagerness and pushed the mare more than he should have done, but though she worked along bravely, and sometimes gained a little on the other, still she could not appreciably diminish the distance between them. What could have been a greater tribute to the power of the stallion than that of his own free will, unurged, he kept up such a gait as this?

Night came slowly down on Cashel, and still the captain was beyond him.

He determined to strike straight ahead, slowly. It was not probable that Melville would be such a fool as to make his camp on the direct line he had been passing over in the day, but nevertheless there was a great chance that he might make a small fire of some sort for his evening meal, if he camped.

Or would he ride straight on through the night?

Cashel decided against this. He must take the chance. So he kept the white mare traveling steadily forward through the dust, with her head falling with fatigue.

For five miles or more he kept her at her work. But still there was no sign of a fire on either hand.

There was no means of finding the actual trail, now, unless he risked making a light, which would be fatal folly. Therefore, he determined to camp. He selected a little hollow between two comparatively high swales of ground. The hollow would keep the mare out of the sky line. On one of the high places he rolled down his blankets and prepared for the night. His hope was that he had overridden the halting point of the captain, and that therefore he would be able to spot the latter when he resumed his course in the morning. But rest was necessary for the mare—rest and good grazing.

He could hear her feeding, tearing off the grass with quick, ripping noises, like the tearing of cloth, and this sound put the boy to sleep.

He wakened a dozen times, sitting bolt upright, with a feeling that the bright stars were falling about his ears and his head thrust up into the heart of heaven. Then, as his senses cleared, he was aware of the vast, quiet prairie. And once or twice he was awake so long that the silence was broken, and he was aware of the thin embroidery of sound which forever floated on that wide horizon of danger.

The howl of a buffalo wolf and the impudent barking of a coyote near at hand wakened him in the first chilly gray of the dawn, at last, and he quickly prepared for the day's business. He saddled the mare, and looking anxiously around, he strove for two things—to find the silhouette of a horseman either behind him or ahead, and to discover, also, the glitter of water.

The water he saw almost at once. But there was no sign of the horseman. He determined, therefore, to get to the water, and then to cut for sign, though his heart already was falling. But when he had finished preparing the horse and rode it to the top of the nearest swale, there, far off in the northeast, he saw the form of a rider.

He bore down on it with the field glass, and the silhouette grew clearer. No Indian pony was that which stepped so proudly in this depressing start of the day. Clonmel, Clonmel for a thousand!

He laid his plans at once.

A casual spotting of trees, which the glass showed him far in the west, probably outlined the course of one of those prairie draws which run dry in the summer, but are apt to carry a plunging, bank-full torrent during the rest of the year. He decided that he would make for this faraway point, letting his horse have a mere taste of water on the way at the silvery glint of light that seemed to indicate a tank or pool in between.

Then, by running rapidly down the valley of the stream, if one were there, he stood a good chance of cutting off the rider.

This plan he executed. He forced the mare to a round pace and kept her at it constantly until they had reached what proved to be a mere small tank, the margin of the greenish water surrounded by a wide stretch of sun-cracked mud, with the slime burned gray as ashes on its surface. However, Indian ponies know how to use all sorts of fuel for travel, and the white mare made no objection to this, though the boy could not endure filling his canteen from its surface.

Then he rode on, faster and faster, as he felt the good animal warm to her work.

He reached the line of the trees and found there a better thing than he had hoped for. It had once been a stream bed, but in some manner the waters had been diverted much higher up so that there was a broad, smooth grassy bottom for him to ride along, with banks high enough to hide him from sight, if he stooped a little in the saddle. And, far away, against the pink of the east he saw the rider going leisurely forward.

He took full speed from the white mare, then, urging her on frantically.

The banks increased on either side. The trees grew thicker above. And still the good mare flew onward, though the grass had disappeared from the bottom, and the going was treacherously rough with rolling stones.

So he came down the draw, until he judged that he had cut the line of the rider's approach. And there dismounting, he crawled up the right-hand bank of the draw, rifle in hand, and pushed his way through the tall grass of the verge.

Cautiously he raised his head until his eyes were clear of the wind-flickered heads of the grass, and then looking forth he saw—nothing but the bright green of the prairie, pale and shining under the rays of the new-risen sun!

Amazed at this, but thinking that the captain, if it were he, might have increased his speed and crossed the draw before him, he swung his glass about and stared toward the west.

But still the prairie was empty to his eye.

It was only when he swung the glasses southwest that he found what he was looking for. Two miles away a rider on a free-striding galloper crossed a swale and disappeared beyond, and reappeared still going rapidly.

It was Clonmel, beyond a question. He thought that the red glint of the horse showed its chestnut color, and even at that distance, through the glass, he thought he could be sure of the captain's erect figure in the saddle. Indians rode humped well forward, their legs hunched up by the very short stirrups.

He could see now what had happened to his well-laid plan.

The captain, undoubtedly not at all aware that he was being pursued, had simply laid out an irregular course across the prairie so that his actual route could not be forecast by trailers. He had borne north on the first day, in order to swing south on the second. And crossing the draw well behind Cashel, and after the latter had crossed the point of intersection of their ways, he had struck cheerfully forward across the plains.

Sadly, Cashel went back to the mare. She was thoroughly blown. There was not a chance of her matching even the easy gallop of the stallion as the latter now went forward, and Cashel decided to rest her for a few minutes before he so much as took her up the western bank of the draw. When he did so, she stumbled and grunted like a spent horse, and he took her forward for a time with loosened girths, trotting before her with the lariat in his hand.

Half an hour of this had him sweating, the sun climbing higher and hotter, but the mare seemed to have regained some of her strength. He mounted her again, and set forward at a dog trot, watching the fresh spoor of the horse he was following.

Twice that day he saw the other. Once it was nearly at noon, and again there was a dim silhouette far before him on the western horizon. But though he hunted again that evening for sign of a fire, there was no token of any camper. Apparently the captain had decided to do with uncooked food on this journey, and reluctantly, grudgingly, the thief admitted the other's foresight.

The third day came. Again he launched forward, but he

needed half an hour to cut for sign before he regained the proper trail, and found that already old, for the other had made an early start.

All day he struggled forward. And it was not until late afternoon that he saw the haunting, illusory silhouette against the sunset sky.

And again he missed it in the evening hunt, and again in the next dawn he had to cut for spoor, and finally to trail again across the weary plains.

Four days he had ridden, and for four days he had seen no living thing, not an evening owl hunting field mice, not a wolf on a hill, nothing but the appearing and disappearing form of the captain and Clonmel, and two or three buzzards, sailing so high that they were merest specks in the sky.

In the mid-afternoon of the fourth day, he knew that the white mare had done her best and could do no more. She had made three tremendous marches and shown her great mettle every step of the way. She simply was matched against a superhorse, and had been worn down to a ghost. Now, sadly gaunted in the belly, her back arching with starvation and weakness, sweat starting out on her at every sudden effort, her head hanging, it was clear that the least and most common Indian pony could sight her in the distance and catch her in an hour's run. How, then, could she be expected to bring him up with Clonmel?

That creature of fire and whalebone seemed unexhausted in any way. Cashel could tell by his spoor that when the captain gave him the rein he bounded forward with the same matchless stride, and the deep marks of his hoofs showed how he spurned the turf with the excess of his chained-up vigor.

There was no other horse but Clonmel. He stood alone, a king of his kind! And the heart of the thief burned feverishly for him.

Toward evening of this day, as he still lingered forward along the trail, not in hope, but still unwilling to turn back from a work to which he had put his hand for so long, he began to see on his right hand a green glimmer of a mist which, as they drew closer, turned into a heavy fringing of willows along a stream; and when they drew still nearer, he was aware of the broad sheen of a big river beyond the trees.

He found that the ground was scored and rescored by the sign of many horses, and finally, among these he completely lost the spoor of Clonmel.

But still he kept on until he saw before him a silver haze above the willows and above the stream, hanging like a spring mist in the air. He knew that it was smoke. He could guess that this was the Pawnee town.

And as he came up on a bit of higher land, he saw at last that what he feared was true.

Beneath him lay a broad sweep of green prairie, and over this, riders were herding horses toward a village composed of big earthen huts, above which the smoke gathered, and then floated up into the upper atmosphere.

He had failed to catch the fox; he had merely run him to earth, and to what an earth, and how guarded!

CHAPTER XXXI

THIS TOWN of the Skidi Pawnees was laid out with a good deal of regularity, but what made it seem so much like a white man's town was that the lodges themselves were built of thick sod, and these particular ones either had just been resodded with green grass turned to the outside, or else the grass had grown out on the huts with the spring rains; at any rate, they appeared like square houses painted green, in the distance, though when Cashel turned his glass upon the place, he could actually see the wavering of the grass, and the bright wind riffles in it.

Altogether, it made a wonderful scene of barbarous plenty and strength, especially considering the multitude of the horses that loitered over the plain, shaking their heads angrily as the herd boys rode up to start them toward the village, sorting them on the way. Here was a little group of a dozen for the successful warrior, and there were one or two animals going to the lodge where slept the man recently impoverished by marriage, or by an illness that had forced him to give all to the medicine man, or by sheer carelessness in this matter of accumulating worldly goods.

But all of those horses were sleek and looked strong, and the youngsters who acted as herdsmen whirled here and there like birds on the wing. Never was there such deft herding. These boys carried bows and arrows, the bows being little under the size of the regular war bows, and while Cashel lay watching, he had a chance to see how well the youngsters could perform, for when a big black crow rose with lazily flopping wings out of the meadow, one of the boys stopped his mount, whipped an arrow onto the string, and shot it upward. The arrow seemed to raise no more than a dripping of feathers, but a moment later it toppled and swung toward the earth in crazy circles. The successful marksman, with a yell that echoed thin and sharp as a knife to the ear of

Cashel, shot his horse toward the spot and snatched the bird out of the air.

Even the boys of this tribe had teeth like this. How, then, about the grown warriors?

He looked at the white mare in the dell behind him. She was plainly exhausted, and needed at least a twelve-hour rest with good grazing before she would be capable of a great effort, such as stretching away toward the distant Pawnees at any rate of speed. And if he went on toward the village on foot, he would need a fairly safe place for caching her.

He went through the willows toward the river, leading the mare behind him. He found near the water's edge exactly what he wanted. It was a flat, marshy stretch where the grass grew thick, the finest sort of fodder, and where she could get water every ten steps, if she chose. Then he hobbled her very short, so that she could only get about inches at a time, unless she made a great effort. The saddle, bridle and pack he cached separately, finding a thick little grove and tying them into the branches where the foliage was the thickest.

He left the rifle with the rest of his belongings, because in case of danger, he knew that he was little likely to be able to defend himself for more than a few seconds. He was embarked on a task where secrecy would be far more important than accurate shooting.

He carried with him only his revolver. He was dressed in a loinstrap, moccasins, and the light robe of a buffalo calf, which was wonderfully thin.

Before he donned these clothes, he mixed the stain as Jim Diver's wife had showed him how to do, and with this he rubbed himself from head to foot. It had a peculiar, pungent, disgusting odor, but he trusted that this would pass away before he had been long in the air.

Then, throwing the robe over his shoulders, he advanced again along the edge of the woods and took up his former station for viewing the Pawnee town.

Dusk was now flooding the willows like the rising of a dark water that stretched far out in pools that filled the hollows of the prairie land, though still the low knolls were rosy with the last of the western light, and Cashel decided that he still must wait.

He was glad of the delay, if only all heart for the adventure did not pass from him before the night came.

At least he could shift closer to the edge of the town, and this he did, shifting back to the willows and working his way up among them until he came to their verge. For they had been cleared away to a considerable distance on each side of the village, no doubt partly for the sake of the firewood, but essentially to prevent any foe like himself from creeping in such cover to the edge of a sleeping town.

From this point, in the fast-fading twilight, he crept out, snake-like to the brow of a little eminence immediately over the town, and lay stretched flat in the grass.

He could feel it turning cold and wet with dew about him; the ground seemed to sweat out a chilly moisture also and Cashel felt weakened by nakedness and exposure. How could he help being aware of his knee caps that dug into the ground, far different from the big-muscled legs of the Indians! And if it came to a time when he was at grips with them, he knew that he would not last long.

This thought made him fairly dizzy with fear, and a moment later he received a shock that nearly made him spring to his feet and bolt, for a wild screech rose up out of the Pawnees. It was composed, so far as he could judge, of the voices of women, and it seemed at first to burst forth from the very ground, just before him.

Even after he had located its source properly, he still was very ill at ease. And finally he knew that the only thing that would force him to complete his attempt was the distance he had covered and the greatness of the effort he already had made.

As the night settled, he was glad that there was no moon, but the stars alone cast far too bright a light to satisfy him. Moreover, now there were various bars and gildings of firelight that slid out from opened doors and apertures in the huts and passed far out onto the prairie, and no matter how he moved, two or three bright beams seemed to be following him and searching him out with accusing fingers.

He wrapped himself closer in the robe and watched the full night gather, keeping his eyes from the lights in the town, and often covering them with his hands, for he knew from of old that the eyes need some time after the fall of the day to acclimate themsleves to the requirements of the night.

When he was sure that he had given his eyes time enough to pierce the shadows as well as possible, he still told himself that he must wait until the village grew quiet; but there seemed little chance of this. For some reason or other, the Pawnee town was given over to a wave of sound that washed from one side of it to the other, with the continual screeching of the women, like so many devils, rising above everything else.

He would have to go in while there were still many people about. That seemed clear. But the final blow to his hopes was the appearance of watchmen for the night!

He thought at first that they were simply delayed riders

returning to the town, but presently he was sure that the same "paint horse" had passed before him twice, and then he was able to make sure that a regular procession of four or five riders continually circled the town. Perhaps it was the forethought of Melville who had caused this guard to be set, since it was certainly not the practice of the Indians, except in time of close contact with the enemy. But it might well have been that the captain had noticed the rider who clung to his trail so persistently during the four days of his flight from the Cheyenne encampment.

Now, with the bright stars to show him, and keen-eyed watchers to follow his movements by that light, he told himself that the limit to his possibilities had been reached and passed.

Another cause came into his mind to stop him. Which was the continued yelling and screeching of the Pawnee women. They might be even now tormenting Broken Arrow to death!

These considerations were enough to turn Cashel back, but still he could not go, obstinately staying in his place, as though an external force held him there.

At last he rose to hands and knees and finally erect on both feet and went straight toward the town for a hundred yards. At the first sign of a sentinel, he sank into the grass and remained there flat on the ground. But he found that the grass was not half as long as it had been at a little distance from the village. No doubt the horses had eaten it down on their way to and from more distant pastures.

He had hardly sunk down to the ground when he saw the sentinel—it was he of the vivid pinto—turn straight toward him. With shield and rifle prepared, the warrior came on, and poor Cashel knew beyond doubt that he had been spotted.

To lie still was to fall like a helpless woman into the Pawnee hands, and their cruel joy in getting him would hardly be less than that they felt in capturing Broken Arrow. To rise and run was simply to be speared as he fled.

He stood up, at once, and walked straight toward the brave.

The latter raised his rifle and made a motion with it, which Cashel answered with a gesture with both hands, a confused gesture. He knew that these plainsmen could talk perfectly well by signs, but he also guessed that the confusion of this sign he had returned might occupy the mind of the Pawnee for an instant.

A moment later he was straight in front of the brave. The latter reigned his horse back a step and barked a harsh question which of course was unintelligible to Cashel.

He, however, went forward with his left hand extended,

the gesture of amity all the world over, and going still closer, he caught suddenly at the rifle.

He heard the gasp of the startled Pawnee's breath. Then, pulling himself up and forward by his grip on the rifle, Cashel drove the heel of his revolver into the face of the warrior.

He dropped, but the head of that Pawnee was made of tough stuff. He lurched down from the horse as though he were shot through the brain, but he still had enough strength and wind power to let out a terrific screech. The sound of it seared the brain of Cashel like a flare of terrible fire. The head of that fallen Pawnee rang hollow with the second impact of the pistol butt, and this time he slumped like a dead man to the ground.

But the yell had done its work.

Glancing back, Cashel saw a guard galloping toward him from either side, at full speed, rushing out from the verge of the town as fast as they could drive their mounts.

All thought of Broken Arrow he cast behind him. Cat-like he climbed into the saddle of the fallen Pawnee's horse and sent it bolting off over the swelling and falling prairie ground, while a loud shout of fury announced behind him that the two pursuers had passed the spot where their companion lay stretched on the ground as though dead.

CHAPTER XXXII

WHATEVER the possibilities of their horses, it was certain that the Pawnees would wring the last shred of effort from them to overtake the fugitive. And Cashel told himself, with cold lips, that he would use five bullets on the enemy, and surely save the last one for himself.

He banged the horse's ribs with his heels, and the pony shook its ugly, long-haired head, but could not go faster.

He was not holding his own. Looking sharply back, he saw them looming blacker and bigger behind him, while from the direction of the town he saw in the background a confused multitude pouring out, men on foot and horseback, as though to repulse the attack of a large host, while the heads and shoulders of the riders showed in dim silhouette against the stars as they sailed off in the pursuit.

He was still looking back when the horse seemed to fall away beneath him.

It was merely that they had dipped into a shallow draw, and any other rider on the whole of the wide plains probably would not have been discommoded by the downshoot.

But Cashel was no natural horseman. He was unsteadied in the saddle, and that was enough for the pony.

At the bottom of the slope it jerked to the right like the snap of a whiplash.

To the right he ran, but Cashel landed flat on his back upon the turf!

All the stars in the heavens bunched above him in a single, glowing, dancing mass, and when these cleared back to their proper places, and he could draw a gasping breath, he pushed himself up on his hands to look about him, wondering why Pawnee lance heads were not already in his throat.

With a roar like the surf, they were shooting all to the right, leaning far forward to jockey their mounts to a great effort, and in front of them, but still at an angle, poured the pursuers, full tilt.

Young Cashel wondered if they had lost their brains, but looking more closely, he could see that from their angle they might think a rider was still in the saddle on the fugitive pony.

One riding on the side of the brute, Indian fashion, might still be concealed from the eyes of the pursuers.

He got to his knees and shook the dizziness out of his head.

Continual new supplies of horsemen were streaming out of the village, footmen, boys, even women were running out also. And even such an amateur general as Cashel would have been glad of this opportunity to rush the town from the opposite side at this moment when it was stripped of the greater part of its defenders—and all by the ruse of a single man—while the Pawnees now rushed headlong in pursuit of an empty saddle!

That sickening fear which had made him weak now left him, in large part. Even the ghastly whooping and yelling of the braves did not oppress him, but picking his robe up about his shoulders, he walked straight back across the plain and toward the town! For he began to feel, like a half-blind fatalist, that either high good fortune was with him, or else he had come to the last night of his life.

He could see several men picking up a limp form from the ground and carrying it in toward the lodges. That was his Pawnee of the "paint" horse, no doubt.

But leaving these people on his left, with the mass of curious observers before them, he kept a little toward the right and headed straight on.

A wild yelling in the distance made him look back. The Pawnees no longer pursued, and he could guess that they had captured the runaway horse, at the last. What would they do now? At least, he could guess, they were not likely

139

likely to comb the prairie far and wide in search of him, unless they, like owls, could see his spoor in the dark of to search for him immediately in the town. They were more the night.

So, still more confident, he marched forward, keeping himself erect, and wishing for a few extra inches to make him more like the stature of the usual Pawnee brave. He passed the thick mass of people on the side, and though he dared not turn his head toward them, still it appeared to him that two or three heads turned toward him, and that two or three arms were pointed in his direction. Perhaps they wondered how it happened that one of their people had been so far ahead of the rest, though on foot?

Cashel gained the shadow beside the wall of the first lodge and paused there. Looking back across the prairie, he could distinctly make out, in the starlight, the low-flying, shadowy horsemen who swept here and there across the plain. They were scattering wide. They looked like a pack of great hounds that have lost a burning scent suddenly, and yearn to recover it.

This glance was all that he dared allow himself. Then he turned his head resolutely forward.

He had no absolute plan, from this moment, for he was only reasonably certain that such a prisoner as Broken Arrow would be held somewhere near the center of the village, and for that reason he wanted to get to the heart of things at once, though he realized that he might be wrong in this assumption. Also, and above all, the nearer he came to the midst of the town, the more he multiplied the danger in which he stood.

It was wonderful to see how thoroughly this alarm had swept the town clean of inhabitants. However wary the Indians might be, certainly it was not hard to throw them off their guard in such a manner as this. He kept his robe well muffled about his face, with one hand pressed against the outside of his jaw. So he had seen a brave pass by him in the Cheyenne encampment, apparently tormented by toothache. That might be his own excuse to answer any question with a stifled, mumbling sound. His voice and his accent at all costs must be concealed if he were confronted by a questioner.

Going on cautiously, he was aware that at least a large part of the hunters had poured back into the town, because he could hear the echoes set up by their voices as they entered among the houses, and the barking of the dogs rang hollowly, as though already they were at the heels of the white man.

And then, as he hesitated at the corner of a hut, looking

wildly about him, more and more aware that he never could find the right place in this wilderness of unknown earthen shacks, he was astonished to hear a voice speaking in English without much trace of an accent.

"I would have brought the white mare, but I thought that I would not have a great chance of doing it. They watch her like a great bright moon, as if they would die if she disappeared. So I took six good horses and left the town. I changed horses every few hours. I came fast across the plain. I thought that I would overtake you, but it seems that you traveled slower than me, because you had only one horse."

It was Walking Dove, the Cheyenne! And now he moved into view, walking down the alley between the houses, a tall man dressed in complete deerskins beside him, with long, flowing hair brushing his broad shoulders.

"I came only fast enough to lead the Muskrat into the village, Walking Dove."

The 'Muskrat' leaned against the corner of the lodge, which shadowed him even from the dull light of the stars, and he trembled from head to foot, not with fear, but as a bull terrier trembles when it sees battle and yearns to be in the midst of it, tooth clashing on tooth and striking for the soft, warm life in the throat.

So trembled Cashel.

He had learned to hate the captain before this. He loathed the Cheyenne suddenly with a still more profound scorn and hatred, because it was plain that the rascal had deserted his people and come to their enemies.

"They'll be glad to see you," said the captain.

"They will," answered Walking Dove complacently. "They know what I am worth. They have paid with their own scalps for the privilege of knowing!"

"Here is my lodge," said the captain. "Come in with me. There is room for you here, and you shall share the place with me, Walking Dove."

"Good!" grunted the Cheyenne, and passed in with the captain to the indicated lodge.

Cashel, soft as a shadow, was instantly beside the earthen wall of that shelter.

A dog came toward him, snarling, but when he whispered and held out his hand, it moved to him with violent puppy wagglings of tail and body. It licked his hand and then rubbed against his knees—a great, gaunt, wolfish thing in appearance, but man-made into the companion of a man. Six months more and it would have been able to distinguish well enough between the scent of friend and foe, but now it merely kissed the hand of the enemy. It even let Cashel go back to where the pride of the village stood, the king of horses—Clonmel—glimmering even by starlight, and eating with a good appetite a ration of dried grass, while a little coterie of Indian boys, apparently not drawn from this bright attraction even by the battle alarm outside the village, squatted on their haunches and from a respectful distance admired the tall stallion. They might be red snakes in the making, but the heart of Cashel was warmed as he looked at them.

He drew back into the shadows again, for the murmur of voices inside the hut attracted him, and as he stepped deeper into the shadows, again, so that merely the dimmest outline of the stallion and the crouching lads appeared to him, he could hear the conversation distinctly within the hut.

The viewpoint of Walking Dove was perfectly understandable from a Machiavellian attitude. He had twice worked himself to a position of great eminence among the Cheyennes, and twice with power in his hands, he had failed under the eyes of the entire tribe.

Therefore, he had come to the greatest enemy of the Cheyennes because he could be sure that no further fame or advancment waited for him among the ranks of his own warriors. He never again would be trusted on the warpath.

"For the taking of the two mares," he said, "they give all of the praise to the Muskrat. They say that if the Muskrat commanded at the Bald Hill, we would not have had a disaster. Well, that is in their minds and it never will be out again."

"I would have been twice as glad to see you," confessed the captain, "if you had found a chance of slipping a knife between the ribs of that same thief before you left the camp."

"I would rather go into a panther's cave to take a panther's scalp," said the Indian frankly, as usual. "I have seen him stand up and walk through a Pawnee camp, where the ground was littered with fighting men. I have seen him walk among them by magic and kill a waking man, armed, and standing on his feet! No, brother, I shall not go alone into the tepee of the Muskrat. And you had him behind you for four days across the plains? Why did you not turn and end his ride for him?"

The captain laughed, for with this man he seemed willing to be frank.

"Because I've seen him shoot, Walking Dove," said he. "And now what is this great scheme of yours?"

"To take the Broken Arrow with us, and make three chiefs who will soon rule the plains!" said the Cheyenne.

CHAPTER XXXIII

SOMETHING rustled above the very head of Cashel, and he almost leaped back with an exclamation. It was only an owl, swinging low across the roofs. His heart had jumped into his throat, but still he was able to hear what was said within the house:

"Broken Arrow is a Cheyenne," said the white man.

"He is a Cheyenne who will die tomorrow," said the other. "And if we make a bargain with him, he will keep his end of it. He's an honest man!"

"What use would he be to us?"

"There are three things needed," said Walking Dove. "A white man, because the whites have money and guns, and guns and ammunition win battles; an Indian who understands the people of the plains and knows how to make schemes of war and schemes of peace that will keep growing like a rush in spring; and another Indian to lead the fighters. You are the white man, brother. I shall do the planning. I like honor, but I am no lover of knife edges and bullets. I shall get some rattles, and drums, and sweet grass, and grizzly bear claws, and terrible masks, and turn myself into a medicine man to talk to Tirawa like an uncle in no time. But the battle chief, that is Broken Arrow, he cannot be beaten. You can ride out with him and be the chief, but he will do the headlong charging and win the battles."

"Walking Dove, you are ambitious."

"I have lived among the whites and learned ambition," said Walking Dove. "The whites find it hard to beat the Indians. They have bellies that are too big. They grow tired too soon. They cannot march. The Indians run away when they please and fight when they please. And only Indians can beat Indians. Very well. You bring the guns. We lead out the Pawnees. They are good fighters. They are as good as the Cheyennes, nearly! First we beat the Cheyennes. Then we attack the Crows and the Blackfeet to the northwest, and afterward we move against the Sioux. We can make a kingdom. You will be the great chief. I will be the medicine man, and so we both grow rich and famous. Other men have thought of this, but we, brother, would be able to do it."

The other was silent for a moment, but then he added: "How can we save Broken Arrow from the Pawnees, Walking Dove? They hate him more than they hate poison."

"Because it never occurred to them that he could be made to join them."

"And can we?"

"We have one chance in two. Death is a sour root for any man to chew. Let us go and talk to him. Are you permitted to enter his tepee?"

"I enter wherever I please," said the captain. "Come with me now!"

They left the lodge, and Cashel slipped after them. Still their voices, carelessly raised because they felt secure in the language they used, floated back to the ear of the thief.

"Could it have been the Muskrat whom the Pawnees nearly caught, just now, Walking Dove?"

"Nearly caught? They were far from catching him! He has counted a coup and nearly brained one Pawnee. I saw the man. His face is smashed and spouting blood. If he lives, he will not see again, I think. It was the Muskrat, of course. He knows how to steal up on a village."

The captain halted and turned. Cashel slipped to the dark of the ground and lay still.

"He has come to steal the stallion, Walking Dove! The rascal may be in the village now!"

Walking Dove laughed softly.

"Well," said he, "I should not like to have a horse which the Muskrat wanted. I would expect to lose that horse and have my throat cut, all on one night. But not even the Muskrat would come in here. Are you afraid of that, brother?"

What answer the captain returned, Cashel could not hear, but the two went on together, shoulder to shoulder. They did not go far, but passed straight through a considerable group of braves, all of whom paused and stepped back a little to stare at the pair. Undoubtedly the arrival of the Cheyenne had made a sensation in the camp, and Cashel felt that he could well understand, now, the shrieks of the rejoicing women in the town. They were glad to see this formidable champion added to their list of warriors.

The two went on and Cashel, feeling that he was certain to lose sight of this pair if he now turned aside, went straight forward, huddled in his robe, one hand pressed on the outside against his jaw. A harsh, jocular voice addressed him. A towering Pawnee brave was moving past him, another on each side.

Cashel merely groaned. Another voice spoke. A hand shot out and caught his shoulder, and the heart of the thief died in him. But he turned and with the hard edge of his palm struck the hand away.

He saw that hand jump back to the handle of a knife, but the weapon was not drawn. As though he disdained the

144

comparatively small stature of Cashel, the big Pawnee went striding on, his head turned over his shoulder, his harsh voice pouring out what Cashel could well guess to be insults.

He went on, thanking heaven for this escape, and perfectly willing to let sleeping dogs lie, while he saw the two whom he followed turn in at the door of a small lodge which stood a little out of the regular rank of the houses. A fire, kindled near the face of it, bathed it and its vicinity with a fairly strong light; but Cashel turned immediately to the rear of the house, and stepped close to the wall.

He did not need to depend upon ears alone, in this instance. For a chink had opened, through the falling away of a couple of sods—overdried, perhaps, and crumbling—and through this chink he could both see and hear what occurred in the interior.

There was only one great danger, that if he applied his face to the aperture, he would be seen by the keen, restless eyes within the hut. The other, that the light issuing forth would show him to any chance passer-by.

He tried to counter both evils by keeping well to the side, and only peering askance into the interior of the shack.

There were now five men inside it. One was Melville, as handsome as ever, or more so on account of the flush in his face. Another was Walking Dove, garbed in his most splendid apparel, with a great headdress of eagle feathers sweeping behind his shoulders clear to the ground. Two more were apparently the guards. For they were armed to the teeth, with knives in the belts, pistols of the old-fashioned make, and in addition, they had a handy array of clubs, several rifles, and a pair of short throwspears, also useful to meet any sudden charging attack. They were well armed, and furthermore they looked hardy warriors of middle age. Men not quite so agile as the younger braves, but very apt to keep their wits about them and not fall a prey to sleepiness in the middle of the night.

The fifth man was of course Broken Arrow.

He was securely bound, but not as strictly as Cashel would have expected. Two turns of rawhide around his wrists were tied firmly together. It was green hide, in narrow strips, looking hardly strong enough to hold the muscular arms of such a warrior, but Cashel knew the ironlike power of even the green hide, and was not deceived.

His feet were secured together in exactly the same fashion, but there was a greater length of hide between the legs, so that it was plain he would be able to rise and move, if need be, something as a hobbled horse may do. It was not

145

upon bonds that the Pawnees depended, but upon the keen eyes of their guards who watched over the prisoner.

The bearing of the warrior was perfectly easy. His handsome face, unmarred by any of the ferocity or grossness which usually appeared in a red man's features, wore what was almost a smile. He sat erect, as though he did not need the support of the backrest which rose behind him, and he nodded pleasantly and spoke a few gentle words in answer to the greeting of the white man.

Of the presence of Walking Dove he seemed totally oblivious!

But to Cashel, as he stood at the aperture, staring hungrily in, it seemed that desperate as his adventure had been and still remained, the effort was worth while. He lost his regrets as he stared at the famous warrior. And, at the same time, he noticed with surprise the very apparent youth of the brave, which he never had noticed when the man was erect upon his feet, with his weapons about him.

"Tell my Pawnee friends," said the captain, "that I'll be answerable for the security of Broken Arrow. They can go off and get a snatch of sleep. We'll be here for an hour, I take it."

Walking Dove nodded.

He appeared to be a good deal of a linguist, for he turned and translated into Pawnee at once the request of the white man. The two Pawnee braves hesitated for a moment, speaking quickly and softly together. Then they moved readily out of the hut.

Young Cashel left his place of observation at the same moment, and passing to the corner of the house, he saw both of the former guards retire to a little distance, where they paused and discussed something with great earnestness, again. Then they went slowly on. One of them, at least, was not entirely pleased or satisfied with the manner in which the guard had been changed in the guard hut. And, as Cashel knew, the objector was very well right. However, he apparently allowed himself to be persuaded.

Still Cashel lingered there at the corner of the hut, for he did not hear the murmur of voices coming from the hut again. In the meantime, he looked toward the open space in front of the building.

The fire there lighted a limited space, to be sure, but beyond the brilliant circle over which its direct rays fell, there was an obscurity in the distance through which he could see the flashing of a dog's teeth, and the dull gleam of a boy's body, racing at play, or the glitter of a lance head, or wicked flash of a hatchet blade. Men, women, children, dogs, Indian ponies were passing to and fro

146

through this entanglement of shadow and half-light, and he felt that he was in the midst of a populous city of enemies. More than that, it was a city where every foeman had teeth. The very children could launch a straight arrow, as he had seen that day; the very women could use a murderous knife.

Suddenly it seemed to him that, no matter what happened, he was surely lost, and almost the easiest way was to remain where he was in the center of the danger rather than striving to break away at once through the heart of the Pawnee town.

For no matter what peril lay before him, it would be more than halved by having with him that silken-smooth fighting machine, and good-natured destroyer of men, the Broken Arrow. Only the not too thick skin of the sod wall of the house separated him from that hero, and Cashel, hearing the murmur of voices, hurried back to the hole in the wall from which he was maintaining his surveillance. He wondered, as he took up his position again, that he had not been seen before this. For he could see from the corner of his eyes, from time to time, the passage of dim figures through the darkness. If they noticed him, they took no heed of him at all!

CHAPTER XXXIV

HE SAW that the three had adopted characteristic attitudes, the moment that they were left alone. The captain stood posed against the fire, for which the spy on the outside was grateful, since it threw a great column of shadow washing up against the spy hole and enabled him to look in more freely, without danger of the firelight sparkling on his face like a red gilding. Fitzroy Melville's legs were spread, his arms folded, and with his handsome head thrown a little back he smiled down upon the conversation between the other two in a quite godlike fashion. Walking Dove, on the other hand, sat on his heels close to the prisoner in the manner of one who wishes to argue a question closely, while Broken Arrow maintained always an air of utter detachment and courtesy mingled.

Said Walking Dove, speaking Cheyenne, of course, to the captive: "I was very troubled when I heard about your capture, Broken Arrow. I thought that people would blame me, in a way, because I led the party that lost the battle at the Bald Hill. And finally I could stand it no longer, and I decided to ride out and hunt for you, and see if I could set you free from the Pawnees."

147

"My brother," said the captive in his pleasant voice, "has a great heart, then. And he has come freely into the camp of the Pawnees? Then he has been able to cover their eyes with his hand as he passed by."

The irony did not escape from Walking Dove, who replied: "A second thought is usually the best thought. When I came close to the Pawnee town, I hid in the grass, and I watched the men herding the horses, and I watched the young braves riding and maneuvering their horses in front of the town, and then it seemed to me, suddenly, that although they wear their hair in a different manner, there is little difference between the Cheyennes and these people!"

"No," said the prisoner. "There is little difference to a man with two tongues."

It was a very neat hit, Cashel thought, for he understood enough of the finesse of Indian parlance to understand that a double meaning was conveyed. A man with two tongues possessed two languages, of course, but also he was a natural liar.

Walking Dove saw fit to glide smoothly over this implication. He merely accepted the pleasant part of it, and went on: "And as I thought of this, I wondered at a new idea that came to me. All of the Indians of the open country are closely akin. They speak with one sign language, for instance. What a pity that they never have been gathered under one head! What a pity that they never should learn to obey one set of chiefs, and march in one great army! Then they would be able to do as they please. The Ojibways lie north. Far south there is a Mexican moon by which the Apaches ride over the long river. Do you see, brother? All of the country between could be made into one great happy hunting ground. There would be no more wars. Perhaps the robber Crows and the Blackfeet would be wiped off the earth, unless they changed their ways. But all the others would live together like brothers!"

For the first time the prisoner turned his eyes and looked directly at the speaker.

"That is a great thought, or a great dream," said he.

"The Sky People sent it to me!" said Walking Dove with enthusiasm. "And I was about to rush home to my people and ask them to attempt the task, when I remembered Young Thunder, who stands like a snarling dog in front of every man's lodge, and threatens with his teeth and his old-woman's spells, in case a warrior attempts to do some great thing for himself and for his people."

"Young Thunder," admitted the brave quietly, "is a bad man."

"He is!" said the other enthusiastically. "But there were

148

the Pawnees just before me, a people as good as the Cheyennes—riding as well, striking as hard, and accustomed to living and working together. They know how to bring other people into their ways. See how they have handled the Skidi! And inside that town which I was looking at I knew that two great men were living. One was the white chief of the Pawnees who struck us so hard at the Bald Hill. Am I not a man to learn at the feet of my enemies? You see, Broken Arrow, that the great chief now stands by my side!"

"That I have seen," said the captive dryly.

"And besides the white man, who holds the Pawnees in the hollow of his hand, there is the greatest warrior who ever took scalps for the Cheyennes! There is a man who never would call himself a chief. Why? Because he saw that our wars were too small and too petty. He saw that they were waged against our own kinsfolk, the other Plains Indians! And when I thought of this, I made sure that I must show him the great truth in a way that would open his eyes. A war to make the red man *free* from war! A glorious fight to end scalp-taking except from the heads of those who are not our true people! I said to myself that I would try to come to Broken Arrow and show him a way to do this great service. Then he would be glad to lead out the Indians on the warpath. What difference would it make to him whether they were Cheyennes or Pawnees? Then I remembered, also, that the Pawnees were about to destroy him—not pleasantly, with a swift knife point splitting the heart, and no pain, or with a bullet like a sword through the brain, but with terrible tortures, the women tearing his flesh, and burning him little by little, like a bird before a roasting fire.

"When I thought of that, I knew that the Sky People truly had sent the great inspiration to me. They had spoken through my mind. They sent me on a mission for my people, not for my own fame, but for the fame of a chief whom all the young men would gladly follow. I came immediately down. The Pawnees saw me. I spoke to them as to brothers, and they listened. I spoke to the white chief and he understood. He is rich. He can get us hundreds of good rifles. He can turn our robes and our spare horses and pemmican into rifles and powder and lead. He sees the great idea. He, also, would like to be one of the chiefs of the prairie people. So I came with him, at last, to you. I stand before you, brother, offering you the leadership of a mighty war party on the greatest war trail that Indians ever rode along, and the Sky People tell me that you will think, and agree that I have spoken the truth!"

He ended on this point, and Cashel, carried off his feet by the picture which Walking Dove painted, held his breath.

It was hardly doubtful that the plan was possible. Well organized, headed by a capable chief, and backed by the forethought and deep intelligence of a white organizer, it was hardly doubtful that any one of the great plains tribes could readily bring its neighbors under its leadership, and then advance to a great conquest of the entire sweep of the plains, from Canada on the far north, to the northern plains of Mexico on the south,. And well had Walking Dove painted the picture of the future.

When he had seen the truth for himself, he still hung breathless on the response of the Broken Arrow.

And that warrior, after communing with himself for a moment, answered: "Suppose that we should all join, and that the Pawnees under us should ride out on the trail, whom would they first wish to strike?"

"The Crows, perhaps, or the Blackfeet, or the cutthroat Sioux, or the Comanches."

"Walking Dove, they hate the Cheyennes above all other people. If I go to the Pawnees and say that I am willing to become one of them if they will spare my life, I can tell you the first question that they will ask me."

"What question, Broken Arrow?"

"Will you lead us even against your own tribesmen, the Cheyennes?"

Walking Dove exclaimed: "They are not wicked enough to wish to make you . . ."

Broken Arrow lifted his head.

"Brother," he said softly, "they asked the same question of you when you came in among their lodges, and their spears and their guns swarmed around you!"

Walking Dove threw out both hands in a vigorous effort at denial, but his voice stuck in his throat for an instant, and the captive went on: "You told them that it was necessary, and therefore you would do it, but only for the good of the whole red people of the plains!"

"That is true!" exclaimed Walking Dove. "You see exactly as I wish to have you see, Broken Arrow."

He had fallen into a patent trap, and Broken Arrow went on calmly: "You are a man with such a great mind, Walking Dove, that it may be true that the Sky People have spoken to you, and that through you they are speaking to me. But if you have an invisible bird sitting on your right shoulder or your left, as Young Thunder says he has, tell that bird to fly up to the Sky People and tell them that Broken Arrow is only a young man. He does not know very much. He still has to sit at the feet of the wise men of the Cheyennes. And that these wise men say that no man knows enough to talk until he first has lost his ability to ride a wild horse, fling a spear, take a scalp, and count a coup. But I still can do these things, Walking Dove, and therefore I am not able to talk and think for myself. I can only repeat what the wise men have told me, and they have said that the Cheyennes are my people! They are my mother and my father. They are my ancestors; their spirits hang in the air above me; they are my hands in battle, and my brain on the war trail; they are my blood; they are my bone and strength; and rather than lift my hand against them, I will far rather let the Pawnees cut me into small pieces and burn the pieces before my eyes. And, unless they cut out my tongue first of all, I shall be able to sing a war song, and despise them, and taunt them to the end, because they are wolves. They are worse than wolves. They are dogs that follow where men go first. They have run from me in battle and they shall run again if the Sky People set my hands free to deal with them."

He had worked himself up to a high pitch of excitement as he delivered this speech, and yet his voice had not risen, nor had the words become more rapid. Only his breast heaved more rapidly, and the sweat polished his big, arching forehead.

Walking Dove closed both his fists.

He shrilled harshly at the other:

"Broken Arrow, I've given you a chance for your life, and a chance to grow famous! Do you hear me? You are throwing away your life! You will die horribly. And instead of that, I offer to make you a great chief among these brave people. To give you a great name and a great fame among the Pawnees!"

Broken Arrow smiled faintly.

"Brother," said he, "fame and name are words that I never have heard among the Cheyennes, therefore I would not know them if all the Pawnees came and sang them in my ear!"

"Broken Arrow!" shouted Walking Dove. "You have been . . ."

"Hush!" said Broken Arrow. "When you speak, I hear the wolves howling and wish for a gun!"

CHAPTER XXXV

IT WAS LIKE a fist stroke to end the conversation.

Walking Dove, whose reflexes were a shade ahead of his thought, had a knife in his hand instantly, and the point of the knife at the throat of the captive, but he was jerked backward by the shoulders by the tall white man.

Such was his fury that Cashel thought for a moment—and wished it!—that the Cheyenne would bury the same knife in

151

the breast of the captain. But whatever might be the weaknesses of the captain in a moral sense, physically and in courage he was able to impose upon greater braves than Walking Dove. The latter dropped the knife back into its sheath and muttered between his tight-drawn teeth something that Cashel could not hear, for Walking Dove hissed the words.

"I don't know what's been happening," said the captain, "but I do gather that Broken Arrow has warded off your spear point, Walking Dove, and that he's managed to put his own through your gizzard, in spite of the fact that his hands are tied. Did you tell the fool that he's going to be tortured to death?"

"I told him that, of course."

"And still he would do nothing?"

"He told me that he would not."

"Although if he joins the Pawnees they're willing to trust his life to his own hands?"

"He told me," quoted the Cheyenne savagely, "that he wanted me to be silent, because when I spoke, he could hear the howling of the wolves, and wished for a gun!"

The captain grinned broadly.

"He's what the schoolbooks would have called a noble man and a martyr," he confessed, "and by the Lord, I admire the chap. Look at him now, seeing nothing but his own thoughts and forgetting us like a thin mist!"

"If I were alone with him," said Walking Dove furiously, "I would soon teach him to see his own blood more than his own thoughts!"

The captain looked down at him, half amused, and half serious.

"I don't think you would, though, friend. You might have your knife sharp and your muscles all set for the job, but I think that something in that rascal of a Broken Arrow would stop you hard like a stone wall before you struck the blow. I actually think that you're afraid of him even as he sits there with bound hands, Walking Dove!"

This implied insult, and not very distantly implied at that, made Walking Dove fairly tremble with rage.

But the captain went on in the same easy manner that used to infuriate the Bandon Cashel of the caravan days:

"I'm going to give you a fair chance to knife him, Walking Dove. I'm going to go and call the guards who had charge of the unlucky devil, and I'll lay you a revolver against a hunting knife that you won't turn the trick while I'm away!"

He stood for a moment with the firelight in his face, bigger and handsomer than ever, Cashel thought, but with a devil glittering in his eyes. There was no doubt that he thought the Cheyenne would not have the spiritual courage to murder his old companion in arms, but that the captain would be rather pleased than otherwise if the mischief happened.

After that one backward glance in which he surveyed and measured the pair, Melville went out of the hut with his long, sweeping, graceful stride, and flickering once against the light of the fire outside, he was gone into the night.

Then Cashel knew that his chance had come. But knowing it, his fear ran back on him, like the cold afterwash of a wave whose head already has passed. He trembled and felt giddy. And for one moment he glanced around him through the fire-stained darkness of the village at the half-lost forms moving here and there. It seemed to Cashel as though he had wakened into a dream, a nightmare. Everything was unreal —the smells of cooking meat, the scent of the acrid smoke, the sounds of a dogfight on a large scale in a distant corner of the place, sweeping closer, and somewhere also far off, an Indian youth bursting forth into the caterwauling of a Pawnee love song.

Cashel mildly hoped that the devil would take both lover and beloved, for the sake of that so-called melody.

Then his wits and his nerves came back to him, and with them an odd certainty that Broken Arrow was a man worth dying with, or for.

He went straight down the side of the lodge, turned the corner into the full flare of the fire outside, on which some boys were heaping more fuel, and as the flames caught and tossed upward with a loud crackling, he entered the hut.

The noise of the rekindling flames outside covered any sound made by his own soft-shod feet, and yet he cursed the increase in that fire, for the screen at the door of the lodge was drawn aside, and purposely kept so, in order that the random observation of any passer-by might at any time fall into the lodge. It was true that the sense of personal pride and dignity in the Pawnees kept the warriors from lingering around that door, and made them whip the boys away from the same post of vantage, but it was also true that people constantly were passing by and able to view, from one vantage point or another, most of the interior except the corners. The captive was not in one of these corners, but posted almost opposite the door, through which the rising fire now threw a strong glow, almost equal to that of the fire in the center of the hut.

If the Pawnees were called wolves by the rest of the Plains Indians, then Cashel felt exactly like a stray village dog that had wandered in among a thousand long-toothed devils.

Before him stood Walking Dove, with back turned. And Walking Dove had a naked knife in his hand and was leaning a little forward, over the prisoner, and it looked to Cashel as though the renegade Cheyenne were going to win that revolver, which had been bet, by slipping the glistening, curved blade of that knife into the hollow of the prisoner's throat. It looked so much so that the Colt came out into Cashel's hand by magic from beneath his buffalo robe. But he did not shoot. They were talking, and Walking Dove's voice was so blurred with hate and with passion that Cashel could not make out the words, at first, but he did hear the prisoner say, as he calmly looked up: "You will not kill me, Walking Dove. Even the Pawnees know that you were once my friend, and they would despise you. Besides, they would hate you for giving me a quick, sweet death instead of slow fire, about which you were talking to me. No, no, Walking Dove. Keep yourself from murder! Afterward, you would have to leave other people and go live by yourself, with the underground people burrowing under your feet."

He said this actually with warmth, as if to a friend, and Cashel was staggered both by the words and the tone of the captive.

Said Walking Dove:

"You have made me a fool and a weakling in the eyes of the white chief, Broken Arrow. He will come back and find you alive and never stop smiling at me!"

"It is better to have people smile when they look at you than it is to have them turn their backs," said the prisoner in the same gentle voice. "You are a Cheyenne, Walking Dove, and you are a chief, and you captured the white mares and became glorious in the eyes of the tribe when you did that thing. You will not throw away all of your glory like dust, I think!"

Cashel saw the other draw back a little, and as he drew back, the glance of Broken Arrow flicked past the chief and lighted on Cashel.

It was a mere touch of the eyes, and yet Cashel knew that he had been seen, recognized, and still the prisoner could control his expression perfectly! Never had he seen such control in any man.

"You are a dead man," said Walking Dove slowly. "You are carrion. The Pawnee dogs will eat the last of you."

"No," said the captive sternly. "But the greatest braves will fight to have my heart and eat courage with it. Men will not fight over your body in that fashion, Walking Dove."

The knife jerked up instinctively in the hand of the latter. Yet he held the stroke.

"They will remember," went on the captive quietly, "that you have two tongues!"

Certainly that last taunt would have launched the chief's

154

knife at the breast of Broken Arrow, but as he swayed for the stroke, Walking Dove's eye caught at the form standing behind him, and he whirled around with wonderful speed, and a low grunt of effort.

Once more he stood above Cashel as he had stood on that other day in the prairie, gaunt, his muscles on the strain for a death stroke.

But the blow was already on the way from Cashel's hand, and he was stepping in to give it force. He had intended it for the back of the chief's head, gripping the handles of the gun hard, for it was sticky with the blood of the man he had beaten down in front of the village. Now he struck the Cheyenne exactly as he had struck the Pawnee, except that here he used the long, heavy barrel of the weapon, instead of the butt.

It had plenty of weight for the purpose. There was a sharp, distinct ringing, as of metal on metal, when the gun barrel clanged on the forehead of Walking Dove, and that hero dropped sideways—straight into the low-built fire!

Cashel could not help following that fall with both hands and dragging the Cheyenne out of the glow. He saw one shoulder badly scorched. An ugly smell of singed flesh filled the air. But he plainly saw that the breast of Walking Dove was working, and he was glad the fellow lived.

After all, they once had worked together to enter a Pawnee camp and do a wild bit of work!

"The knife, brother, the knife!" said the captive rapidly, but not loudly.

Cashel scooped up the fallen knife of Walking Dove and with it sliced the bonds of the other.

He expected that Broken Arrow would rise up like a flame. Instead, the other remained for a moment kneading his ankles, where the rawhide had sunk a deep impress. Then he accepted Cashel's arm and rose to his feet.

One breath he took, as if he drank all the sweetness of liberty in a second. Then he stopped and gathered up not a knife or a pistol or a rifle from among the weapons that were freely placed about, but a good club with a head of knotted, hard wood, with a red string attached to the handle, and an eagle feather fluttering from the end of the string. The loop of this he passed over his wrist.

"I am ready, brother!" said he, and smiled at Cashel in a way that lifted the heart of the boy in his breast.

They turned, and as Cashel faced the door, he saw two forms move through the darkness outside like shadows through water, red lighted, and then in the doorway appeared the same two burly guards who had charge of the distinguished prisoner a few moments before!

155

CHAPTER XXXVI

IT WAS STAGGERING, because it seemed impossible that Melville could have found the two guards so quickly and returned with them, but beyond a question there they were, and the lofty form of Melville himself behind them!

Straight into the ugly, mumpish face of the first man, Cashel fired. It was as though he had pulled a leash that let a spring loose. The stricken warrior bounded into the air in a horrible and foolish manner, like a jack-in-the-box, and flung backward, dead in the air. His body stopped the bullet his companion had already fired, and the shock carried living and dead to the earth.

Straight over them the two ran, and Cashel saw the Cheyenne warrior, even in that terrible moment of suspense, dip down quickly as a bird catching up a grain of corn and touch the living one of the two guards.

He had counted coup—doubly valuable, a coup counted on a living enemy!

Big Melville, when he saw the running forms of the two, did not hesitate. He whirled and ran for his life, with a loud yell for help. Yet he was not really a coward. It was that the suddenness, the total unexpectedness of this thing had toppled over his stronger self. He had not made six steps before he whirled about and opened fire with an accurate six-shooter. The first bullet kissed the very ear of Cashel. The second darted by him like a hornet flying down a strong wind. But then, at the heels of Broken Arrow, he dodged around the corner of the next lodge.

He saw the Cheyenne glance over his shoulder and reduce his pace at once, and it seemed to Cashel one of the bravest things that he ever had witnessed. For the warrior ran like the wind, and Cashel was only a mere blunderer in comparison. Yet Broken Arrow fell back almost to the side of his companion, running a half-step in front to lead the way.

It was like running a gauntlet through an entire army. Ramiform daggers spread more and more thickly about them as the yelling of Melville and the uninjured guard from the hut behind them roused the warriors. And above all the shouting, Cashel could hear Broken Arrow's name being yelled through the night. That name turned out the Pawnees like a swarm of angered, startled bees, each with a deadly sting!

And, the instant the fugitives were seen, they were recognized simply and swiftly by the first glance at the long, flowing hair of Broken Arrow, as the wind of his running blew it out behind his shoulders. They were saved for a moment by only one thing—the suddenness with which they appeared around the corner of one lodge and the quickness with which they could get past the corner of the next one before a Pawnee brave would have a chance to aim a shot.

Bullets and arrows were dangerous to their own people, so thick grew the swarm, but the fastest runners of the tribe were bounding after the pair. Broken Arrow they never could catch in a fair test. But Cashel knew that he was a dead man unless the Cheyenne could work a miracle in his behalf.

He felt a breathing behind him. Something like a shadow stretched across his heart; then Broken Arrow whirled like a bird on the wing, and struck with his club.

Cashel heard it thud heavily. Then he was fleeing onward, straining for speed, and the tall Cheyenne running lightly beside him like a mother wolf beside her cub.

It was useless, this way. He could not save himself. He could only drag Broken Arrow back to death.

So he gasped, "Go on, Broken Arrow! Save yourself! I'm able to manage for myself!"

"There!" said Broken Arrow, and turned, as though he had gone mad, straight toward a swarm of people who had burst out through the door of a lodge.

The Cheyenne was in the lead. The club swung and landed as he reached the crowd, and the yell as he counted coup stabbed at the ears of Cashel. It meant something to those Pawnees, too. Startled out of their first sweet sleep by the alarm, they no sooner staggered outside than a charge of devils was upon them, and the terrible war cry of the Cheyennes!

Pandemic fear seized them, and they scattered, so that Cashel saw beyond them the dim forms of horses.

He leaped on, half hoping, now. They had covered such a vital distance on foot that it seemed possible they might draw clear, with swift horses underneath them.

So he rushed forward, and heard the barking voice of the Cheyenne calling to him. "Shoot, brother! Turn and shoot!"

He turned, blindly obedient—blind with the effort of the race, also—and four strides behind him saw the leaders of the Pawnees running.

In their faces he emptied the revolver, shooting without aim, merely working the hammer with his thumb and flinging bullets toward the shadowy, writhing mass.

They flung backward. They dodged to either side, yelling. In the distance, he heard a woman's screech of pain, and knew that one of his bullets had flown wide indeed!

157

"Here!" called the singing voice of the Cheyenne.

He turned, bolted for the nearest horse, seeing Broken Arrow on the back of another. As he leaped upon the back of the animal, the brave, challenging danger, deliberately rode back around Cashel's mount, and the latter, from the tail of his eye, saw the club swinging.

It was all madness. It was all impossible. It was a luxus of terror and confusion.

But the terrible Cheyenne war cry still was ringing behind him as Cashel turned the head of the Indian pony and buried his heels in its flank.

It could run. Luck had put him on the back of a capable little war horse, he knew by the first bound of it—if only he could keep in his place upon the bare back! He gripped hard with his knees. One hand he wound in the flying mane, and then ventured to look back.

Broken Arrow, having made the last rear-guard stand, was coming after him faster than belief, leaning low along one side of his horse, and still swinging the burly club in readiness for a last stroke.

He saw this dimly, not so much on account of the darkness, as because of the pandemonium that had burst up in the camp, for the yelling of women and children and the furious shouts of the Pawnee braves affected all his senses and turned him numb.

They swerved in and out among the huts. It was perilous work. Not only were other mounted men now taking up the trail, but Cashel felt as though he were mounted on a greased tiger, so active, so bounding, so catlike in suddenness were the movements of the pony beneath him.

For all his speed, Broken Arrow, riding as only he could ride, ranged along side, and would have passed, but deliberately reined back his pony in order to keep the rear guard.

Cashel did not challenge that dangerous honor. He could not even recharge his weapon, for he dared not loose his grip on the mane of the horse. He was helpless to do anything except cling to the slippery back of the little racer.

Looking to the right, he saw that they were near the outside of the village, but also, in that direction, he saw a number of horsemen between the gaps of the lodges, paralleling the course of the fugitives, and one of them with the panache of a war chief.

Cashel's heart sank again, but still he would not let the feathered head of a Pawnee upset him now. They had done too much. Liberty was too close to be walled away from them, he felt. So much luck and blind good fortune would not have come to them, only to be snatched away again a moment later.

"Hai!" called Broken Arrow.

He looked back, and saw his companion making a sign to turn about.

Cashel, half fearing that the brave was mad, but knowing that he, at least, could never get out of the town alive, prepared desperately to obey.

At the second cry, he pulled hard on the lariat.

The pony spun like a wheel beneath him, swinging him with a jerk far over to the left side of the horse. The next instant it was off at full speed, leaping away so quickly that Cashel literally streamed level along its back, holding by his hands to the mane.

Then, by degrees, he managed to reseat himself.

Before him was the great ringing, unending battle cry of Broken Arrow. He saw the club swinging, dim through the darkness, and flashing like steel in the firelight that occasionally rolled out through some open door.

Right and left the hero struck. Cashel could understand why he had chosen that heavy weapon for a fight through a melee.

Knives reached up at them. It was like the snapping of dogs on either side of Cashel.

Still they rode on.

He saw a brave Pawnee leap tiger-like out of the crowd and aim a stroke at the Cheyenne in mid-air. He was met by the terrible downward beat of the club and crumpled back on the heads of others.

Some struggled to get closer for a blow, but those in the direct path of the riders flung to either side, frightened by the mad rush of the horses.

It is hard to stand to a charge of horses in the day, even when mounted. But at night, in the crowded dark, and on foot, the sight of the racing ponies seemed to terrify the bravest.

They gave back. They split away like water and left a bright gleam of faces on either side of the flying animals.

It seemed minutes to Cashel that they rode through this press. It was only a few seconds. They had doubled back through their immediate pursuers like hares between the legs of the hunters, and they had the same success that nearly always attends that maneuver. The very overforce of the crowd stultified its efforts.

Then Cashel saw his leader, who had broken the way with his great club, swerving to the side. They broke away from the clinging torrent of people. In an instant they were dodging away among the outermost lodges of the town. The yelling of the Pawnees grew farther back, suddenly, as though walled away from them. Yet he thought the ferocity of it was still more horrible than it had been before. He needed some loan word from another language to describe it.

But now the open night lay like a blessing before them, bright with stars. The cool, dark air rushed upon their faces. They were almost free.

CHAPTER XXXVII

IT WAS not altogether as near to freedom as they could have wished, however. The uproar of the Pawnees was comparatively stilled, with only single voices breaking out behind them with a special violence as the warriors darted out to the edge of the town. However, there was a more ominous sound than the mere yelling, and that was a beating upon the ground, muffled by the thickness of the covering carpet of turf.

Cashel looked back, and he saw behind him a luniform crescent of riders breaking away from the lodges of the town. They were composed, he knew, of the cream of the tribe, who had seen him flash past at the heels of Broken Arrow, and who had taken time and used forethought enough to get into the saddle before they launched their pursuit. Now they came in a huge rush, those furthest away being the ones who first had guessed his purpose and had swept out into the grasslands, and the last of the line curving in close to the verge of the lodges where the latest riders were now darting out, constantly reinforced by new ones.

He gripped the lissom body of the pony more firmly still, and as if responding to the force of the pressure, the hardy little warrior of the plains tossed his head higher still, and bounded off at a greater speed.

Yet still it did not make the speed of Broken Arrow's mount—although Broken Arrow made a burden a good deal greater than the white man, and though his horse was no larger than that of Cashel. It was a sheer proof of the superior excellency of the Indian's horsemanship!

What was of even more interest than the running of the two ponies, however, was the performance of the moon-shaped line of the pursuers, and Cashel had hardly ventured two looks to the rear before he was willing to swear that they were at least holding even the swiftest of the enemy. Only that terrible tremor of the beaten earth was beneath them, and the throb of many different hoofs, pulsating with a singular rhythm, like the fluttering of one great, frightened heart. He was surprised when Broken Arrow wasted enough of the strength of his horse to swing it close beside that of

160

Cashel, losing a few lengths of precious distance as he did so.

Broken Arrow stretched an arm toward the rear.

"Brother," he called in his quiet, cheerful voice, unstrained or hoarsened by the terrible war whoops with which he had startled the Pawnees as they broke out of the village, "look behind you!"

Cashel obediently looked back.

Some of the first edge of the pony's running had been taken from him by that great burst of sprinting, and it was more easily in hand. He turned, and behind him he saw the dim line of the enemy, straightening, and now bulging out in the center, as though a peculiar attraction were lending force to all of the enemy immediately behind them. They had struck a patch of ling, or short heather—at least, the ground was covered with a very low shrubbery in which the hoofs of the horses slipped a little, though it was not high enough to brush against their knees. And before the enemy struck this same obstacle, Cashel saw a rider break out from the center of their line as though he had been driven by an explosion—a man on a tall horse, which bounded forward away from the rest as though they were tethered, and it in full frolic.

And when Cashel saw this, he was amazed, because he had forgotten that such a horse could exist outside of a dream. Onward came the horse, flying, and presently he was overtaking the fugitives so fast that Cashel could see the shadowy sweep of the hair that blew over its shoulders.

Then he knew that this was either the white man or Walking Dove, and a moment later he was sure that it was Fitzroy Melville in person. There was no other man who would sit so straight, disdainfully straight, in the saddle. There was no other horse that could have leaped over the intervening ground so easily.

It was Melville, coming down upon them like thunder, with a glimmering ray of light balanced upon the pommel of his saddle, Melville, with one of his fine Colt's rifles balanced before him—and well he knew how to use such a weapon to the best advantage! As one light struck, Cashel continued to stare.

He heard his companion calling in the same easy, cheerful voice, "You carry a gun, brother. There is only one way to stop that rider!"

There was only one way, of course, and Cashel cursed his folly for not acting at once.

His seat was steady enough, now, as he grew familiar with the gait of the pony. He jerked out the Colt's revolver and hastily he reloaded its six chambers. Now he turned again, and saw that the big stallion was sweeping momently nearer, coming like a stormwind across the prairie.

Twisting still farther around, he waited, raising his gun and letting his hand grow accustomed to the undulations of the prairie. And at last the body and the thrusting head of Clonmel came into the sights.

He fired. But he knew that he had missed even as the finger pressed the trigger. His eyes had closed, and in spite of himself, he had pulled to the right.

He looked again, fiercely, cursing himself again, and this time he told himself that, Clonmel or no Clonmel, for his own life and that of his friend, he must shoot straight, with open eyes, and this he strove to do.

He made believe, like a child. He played that game, telling himself that the horse at which he fired was no more than a ragged Indian pony, thick legged and humpbacked. So, with forehead knitted, and with jaw set hard, he drew his bead again, and caught the fine, lean head of the big stallion surely, and firmly within the sights. Clonmel was dead. He had the life of the great horse under the very touch of his finger, and still he could not fire. He lowered his hand, gasped for breath, and tried to draw bead again.

He could not fire.

Then he heard the voice of the Cheyenne calling beside him:

"What is it, brother? What is it?"

"Take the gun!" called Cashel in response. "*I* cannot shoot at him."

He felt the hand of Broken Arrow touch his upon the Colt.

"Is it the man, brother, or the horse?" he asked.

"The horse, the horse!" cried Cashel, with a groan. "I can't draw a bead on him. My finger won't work to shoot at him. But the man—I wish he were done for now!"

The Cheyenne withdrew his hand from the gun.

"I am no great marksman," said he. "I might hit the horse and not the man!"

"What if you do?" cried Cashel. "Take the gun, Broken Arrow. It is your turn with it. Your own life and mine depend on it, for otherwise he'll surely ride us down, and nothing will keep *him* from potting us like pigs in a pen!"

Said the Indian:

"A knife, an old blanket, a pair of moccasins, a headdress, may be big medicine that a man will die for. Why not a horse, then, my brother? And what is your medicine is my medicine, and if you will die happily, I shall die, also!"

"Broken Arrow!" insisted Cashel, desperately. "Take the gun. Try for the white chief of the Pawnees, and if you miss him and strike the horse, at least our own lives are safe!"

The Cheyenne waved his hand, and as he waved it, there was the clang of a rifle behind them, and Cashel felt a shock, and then a burning pain along his side. It was followed instantly by a weak desire to roll from the saddle. Anything to stop the wrenching of the galloping rhythm at his body.

Broken Arrow had swerved sharply in, and galloped toe to toe with him. The willows, toward the left, streamed by them in a blur, against the stars.

Again the rifle clanged, and this time Cashel's pony stumbled violently.

He saved himself from falling from its back, but only at the cost of such a pain that he seemed to divide in two, as though white lightning had cloven him. He remained dizzy, only aware that the gallant little horse was laboring violently, and losing speed. Still it struggled, its ugly head pushed forward, its ears back, defying death and pain in silence. His heart went out to that brute exhibition of courage, and the onefold devotion of the wild pony.

"Your horse is dying, brother!" he heard the voice of Broken Arrow calling.

"Take the gun!" he answered. "I am done for. The horse and I are dying, Broken Arrow. Ride on. Take the gun. Ride with all your might. If you can get to the willows on your left, just there you will find the white mare that I rode, pastured by the edge of the river, and I shall turn back and try to stop them. . . ."

He told himself this in other words, as he fought against the pain in his body in order to speak, and held out the gun a second time to Broken Arrow. If he turned, knife in hand, no doubt Melville would drive at least one bullet through his body as he charged, and no doubt the tall stallion would be swung wide. And yet he trusted with a strange surety that he would be able to reach the big man and send his knife into the heart of the other, before he died!

The Colt's revolver was taken hastily from his hand, but as he pulled on the pony's head to swing it around toward the enemy behind them, Broken Arrow closed in on him. An arm of iron gripped him about the body. He felt the hand of the Indian slip as it closed over the spot on his side which was wet with running blood, but then he was wrenched from his place and found himself dangling across the withers of the other pony, while the green of the willows, muffled with the shadow of the night loomed close before them.

It was the death way, the lich road, he felt, and on the damp earth beneath the willows he would be able to stretch himself, and dig his fingers into the cool ground, and die.

That was like a promise of heaven to Cashel, at that moment!

Behind them he heard the beating of hoofs, nearer and nearer. Again a rifle clanged behind him, again, again, again.

163

And far spent though he was with agony, he was able to count and tell himself that now the deadly rifle of Melville was empty. Empty without further damage done, it seemed. And what a marksman the big fellow was to drive two bullets true to the mark in such a light as this, and from the back of a galloping horse.

Farther back, still, a wild wailing of battle yells arose triumphant, as the Pawnees saw their enemies turn into the covert.

Then the green of the woods closed over them, joining above their heads in green Gothic vaults, crossed with lierne and ogive faintly open to the sprinkling of bright stars above them.

The gallop ended. Behind them, horses were crashing through the dusk. But Cashel was allowed to slip to the ground.

CHAPTER XXXVIII

CASHEL slipped to his knees. He slumped weakly down upon his side. The ground was cool, as he had hoped to find it. The touch of it seemed to ease the pain of his wound, as though mother earth were taking up the burden of his agony out of her great pity for her son.

But then a crushing, painful grip fell upon his shoulder.

"Brother, brother! This is the time to fight for your life!" said the voice of the Cheyenne above him.

"I am tired of my life, Broken Arrow," he replied. "I cannot live. I am ready to die. I leave you to live after me, and to fight. Find the white Pawnee if you can. Find him and kill him. He is not worthy to have Chapa for his wife. . . ."

His voice ended in a groan, a loud and womanish groan, which he had barely enough manhood to suppress and control toward the end.

"Chapa! Chapa!" he heard the Cheyenne murmur. "What does she have to answer for here, also? Chapa, Chapa! Bad luck come to you, a short life, and a naked tepee, and no children to weep for you!"

His grip wrung the shoulder of Cashel again.

"Do you hear me?"

There was a distinct crashing of the outer brush of the willows.

"I hear the Pawnees coming, brother!" said the white man. "Let me stay here! I am ready to die. I have done enough, seeing that I have brought you away from them alive!"

"The greatest cowards," said the Cheyenne, his voice lowered but fierce, "is the man who give away his own life. You lie down like a child when it feels pain!"

"I am dying," said Cashel earnestly. "It is not the lack of courage, Broken Arrow."

"Stand up!" said the Cheyenne. "You know that I shall not leave you. You give me back to the Pawnees if you lie here!"

That grip persisted on the shoulder of Cashel, but he did not feel the other lifting him. By his own power he managed it, and yet he felt no sense of effort. It was a magic levitation that transported him now as they passed forward under the trees, the horse panting behind them. The warrior's hand was still on him, binding the lips of the wound from which the blood ebbed, and the arm of Broken Arrow gripped him hard.

"Which way is the white mare?"

"Ahead and to the right, a little."

He had recognized a dead stump just ahead of them.

And as he spoke, he grew dizzy. He was not so much aware of pain. This seemed to have left him in great part, but he was conscious of a terrible effort, and the trees crawled past him at a snail's pace. He wondered, vaguely, why men should struggle so for their lives, when death was a mere sweet closing of his eyes!

And then he was reminded of a grim night in his boyhood. He was barely past fifteen when three of an enemy clan had cornered him at the foot of a blind alley. He had managed to climb the wall, but they reached him with their knives as he dragged himself up, and he was almost dead when he crawled into his boarding house. He remembered how he had closed and locked the door behind him, just as the enemy came running up and threw their weight against it, and how he had passed the newel at the foot of the staircase, and how he had dragged himself on hands and knees upward to the hall above, and writhed across the threshold into his own room, and fainted there.

He had lived through that frightful ordeal. And now he had to repeat to himself automatically that though the pain had been frightful and the effort beyond count at that moment, still life had been sweeter than ever afterward. Yes, that had been a great turning point, and from that night he could date the beginning of his manhood. All his companions had turned new faces toward him. He was from thence forward the hero who had faced three of the enemy, barehanded, and brought his life away. They had to consider him in their innermost counsels. Men who were years his senior looked up to him. It was the accolade for the thief. So he told himself, mechanically, lifelessly now, like some weary old clergyman at the lectern. He might live past this, and life might be sweet again to his taste!

Far behind him was the noise of the hunting Pawnees.

"They will come slowly," said the Cheyenne, reassuringly, and added: "They know that they are not hunting children this night!"

Then a dim white shape rose from the ground before him, and he heard the soft whinny of the white mare!

He reached her soft, moist muzzle. He laughed, weakly, foolishly. And yet he felt for the first time a real reassurance, and a hope that he might escape with his life.

The iron arms of the Cheyenne lowered him to the ground.

A fierce, soft, insistent voice was asking him where he had cached his saddle pack, and at last he was able to remember and to speak. Then drowsy fever overcame him, and he was almost asleep when the same hands of iron began to draw a bandage around him.

He looked up. The dreadful pain made the stars swim and swirl together, with a delicate leaf mosaic drawn against them overhead.

"Broken Arrow!" he gasped. "I cannot breathe. You smother me with the pain!"

"Hush!" said the warrior. "The Pawnee devils are near us. Hush! All will be well."

He groaned.

The hard hand was crushed down over his lips. Not like a hand. Like the heel of a heavily shod boot, bruising his mouth until he tasted his own blood.

But he did not feel the pain of that. He merely grew vaguely thankful that he, at least, did not need to meet that terrible hand in battle. If it crushed him now, it struck for his own welfare. Loosely, weakly, he surrendered to that strength and to that overmastering will power.

The bandaging went on. In fact, he could hardly draw a breath.

"Now, stand up."

He rose.

"They will search to the rim of the water!" he heard the other murmuring. "Where can we hide? Where can we cover ourselves?"

"In the water!" said Cashel.

He added, "Look, Broken Arrow. There we can hide ourselves. It is cold. We can drink, and lie there, and float down with the stream lightly—there is no more weight in me than in a bubble. . . ."

His mouth was closed rudely once more, and yet he found that he was being supported forward once more toward the

166

river, and then his feet were entering it, and his naked body.

He looked back, shuddering.

Above him, he saw the white mare, with a saddle cinched upon her back, faltering, nosing the stream, and then coming down into it with cheerfully cocked ears. Beside her walked the Indian pony which they had stolen from the Pawnees. And it, also, came into the stream with little misgiving.

How could they do so, he wondered.

As for himself, the cold froze the little breath that remained in his body. It was driven up into his throat. No oxygen remained. In his helplessness he turned toward the Cheyenne, but he could not speak, and only saw by the starlight that the face of the warrior was grinning. He looked like some cruel oaf, enjoying a practical joke at the expense of a friend.

The next step, he entered into deep, soft mud and sank suddenly, so that the water closed above his head.

He was dragged up by the hair, swayed forward through the stream, and now they came to a place where the bottom shelved upward a little, and then Cashel found himself hidden behind a little bush that floated on the surface, a bush recently washed afloat, no doubt, and now anchored by some long, tenuous root that stretched out from the bank of the stream.

It spread out, wide and low. And behind it Cashel saw just the heads of the horses, raised high, and the brightness of their eyes, taking a reflection of the stars, and the shoulders of the tall Cheyenne, bowed close to the stream.

The arm of the warrior supported Cashel beneath the armpits. The whisper of the Cheyenne was at his ear.

"Now a little patience, brother, brother! Death seems a good thing by night. But when the morning comes up, you will be still alive, and not among those who rot, their brains ended, their thoughts gone, their hands stiff, their fingers useless. You will live. Draw breath carefully! They are close, they are close above us—they are here!"

They were there indeed.

As Cashel struggled a breath inward, at last, and felt some relief from the sensation of strangling, he heard a crunching under foot among the leaves and the twigs on the bank of the stream.

Then voices sounded, carefully low pitched.

He heard the voice of the captain himself saying:

"They have taken to the water, Walking Dove!"

And that hero answered savagely: "Look for yourself. The stars are shining on the river's face. Do you see any shadow of a head breaking it? Or perhaps," he added ironically, "they are walking on the bottom of the stream?"

167

Said the captain calmly: "That wouldn't surprise me a great deal, either. After tonight, I think that devil of a boy can do anything he puts his hand to. He's a magician!"

"I shall cut the magic out of his heart with my own knife!" said Walking Dove fiercely. "Hai! He stood straight behind me. The cur of a Broken Arrow sat and smiled up in my face. He pretended to act like a very noble man. He all the time knew that the Muskrat was behind me. Ay, like a sneaking thief of a water rat, creeping up behind me! I turned —he smashed his gun into my face!"

"He might have killed you," said the captain quietly. "You ought to be grateful for that."

"I'll cut out his heart with my knife," repeated the chief savagely. "Was he sent down out of the sky to make a fool of me? Now I have no people! The Pawnees will never let me come back. They will say that I set Broken Arrow free.

I have lost the Cheyennes. I have no people. Every tribe will suspect me and call me a traitor! Look sharply. Somewhere along this bank they must be hiding!"

"I've given enough time to this hunt," said the captain, "and I have to leave the last hand to the Pawnees. They have better night eyes than I. And yet I tell you, Walking Dove, I would pay more to see that boy dead than you would pay to have the captaincy of a tribe. And I know how hungry you are for that. See the shadow along the edges of the river, like kohl on the eyelids of those Egyptian girls—but never mind trying to understand that. What about that shrub in the water, my friend? Suppose the pair of them are behind that?"

CHAPTER XXXIX

CASHEL, no matter how careless he had been about life before this, could feel the horrible finger tip of fear running up his spinal column, and he sank down until only his nostrils and eyes were above the face of the water. He saw the Cheyenne shrink down a little, also, but still with his muscular arms extended toward the heads of the horses.

They, with bright, fearless eyes, kept their ears cocked, and seemed to enjoy the strangeness of their position heartily.

"There is nothing behind the brush," said Walking Dove. "That's only a little sandbank. You often find them here where the still water stands. The bush is growing in that, and you can see that there's nothing behind."

"Well," said the captain, "here's for it, anyway, and may

God send the bullet home through the brain of that sneak thief Cashel!"

A rifle clanged with wonderful loudness. The vibration seemed to burst the eardrums of Cashel, and he heard a heavy impact close to him, and saw the head of the Indian pony drop down suddenly into the water.

A twig, cut from the bush before his face, fell into the water and floated gently down toward him. And as he straightened again, slowly, he saw the image of a star in the water close by—such a beauty as no lapidarist ever held in his hand.

"You see?" said the Cheyenne on the bank. "You have called all the Pawnees near by for nothing. And it was a sandbank. I heard the bullet strike."

"It struck the water, of course," said the captain. "A bullet often makes a heavy sound of impact like that. It depends on the angle from which it strikes the water."

"You shot too low and hit the sandbank under the bush," said the Cheyenne tersely.

"I did not," said the other. "I know where the bullet went. I saw it clip a twig from the bush."

"Every man's best companion is himself," said the Cheyenne.

"You have an ugly tongue," answered the captain. "What ever you may feel about this night's business, my friend, I want you to know that I feel no better toward you. I half wish that Cashel had broken your skull, instead of simply smashing your nose. If it hadn't been for your foolishness, Broken Arrow would still be back there in the camp, and Cashel would now be toasting slowly over a good Pawnee fire!"

"You . . ." cried the Cheyenne.

And then he checked himself, his voice lowering to a snarl. And Cashel saw his companion, Broken Arrow, moved by some odd impulse, lift from his belt to the surface of the water a knife broad at the hilt, straight bladed, looking like one of those ancient daggers called a "beef tongue."

He could understand the impulse. The very fingers of the warrior itched to send that blade hard home into the throat of his fellow tribesman.

"Good!" said Walking Dove. "I understand. And after this . . ."

"Keep off from me," said the captain coolly. "This revolver is loaded, and you ought to know that it shoots straight. I'll blow your head open, Walking Dove, as surely as I'd put my heel on a chestnut, if you sneak up closer to me. Here come your friends the Pawnees, besides, and you'd better clear out."

169

Walking Dove, seeing himself reduced to the position of a mere make-game, groaned aloud in the anguish of his resentment. But now there was a rapid and noisy stirring through the brush, and several men seemed to come out onto the bank of the stream. Cashel heard the captain explaining in very broken Pawnee what he had been about, and the harsh, rapid, dissatisfied answer of the Pawnees.

No matter how they valued the captain, it was clear that they were as angry as hornets. And, after all, it had been at his directions concerning the change of guards that Broken Arrow had been enabled to escape.

They tramped off, again, calling sharply to one another.

"They are very angry!" said Broken Arrow, in the faintest of whispers. "But they are nothing, compared to the man above us. The white man thinks, and his thoughts are too sweet to please me, brother!"

There on the bank above them, Melville began to whistle softly to himself.

Then he spoke to the stallion, which apparently stood behind him on the shore.

"Good boy, good old Clonnie," said the captain. "I've taken you out of his hands, at least, even if he has robbed me of everything else. I've given up my old good name, I've given up my reputation and everything that mattered to me on account of that one sneak thief. But at least I have you, old Pegasus—ay, and more will come—more will come!"

At the thought of what more *would* come to him, the captain laughed a little, and then Cashel could hear him withdrawing down the bank, and then pushing back into the brush.

It was high time that he left, for the current had flowed the body of the dead Pawnee pony around. Broken Arrow could prevent it from drifting down the stream, and thereby betraying that they were above. But he could not keep it from sagging out in the current close to the surface, for the body of the little animal was heavy and round with fat and therefore very buoyant. If the captain had remained another moment on the bank, he hardly could have avoided seeing the shadowy form in the current beneath his position.

Then a great Jovian voice thundered down the stream, and looking in that direction, Cashel saw half a dozen Pawnees ride down naked into the stream and, slipping from the saddle, start swimming at the tails of their horses across the stream.

It seemed that all hope was destroyed, if the other bank was thus patrolled, himself weakened by his wound, and with only one horse between them.

But all the noise of the search began to fade into the distance on either side of the stream, and at last his companion said, "Now, brother, Heammawihio has taken them away from us. We are free to move, and if you will keep a great heart and a strong courage, we may cross the stream."

"It is watched," protested Cashel.

"It is watched, but only by six men. We must start at once, before the cold of the water enters your wound and chills you to the heart. But look! The stream is very quiet. The only wind blows from this bank and will help us. I shall be at your side. The white mare is strong and will not fear the water. Let us start!"

He talked gently, like a woman to a child, and the last of Cashel's strength rose to meet this final call.

The dead pony, at last, was beginning to drift away, its head sinking beneath the surface, but the whole body distinctly outlined under the surface and refusing to sink.

They struck out into the stream. Cashel's hands had first been fastened to the down-stream side of the white mare, lashed to the saddle thongs that hung beside the pommel. The rifle was raised, so that its muzzle appeared above the surface of the water.

And as the mare struck out for the far side with a good courage, Broken Arrow took to the water near her, swimming very powerfully, and himself giving a hand to draw on the latent weight of Cashel. The latter, as long as he was able, kicked to help the progress through the current, but there was very little power in him, and soon his body trailed straight on in the stream. His very head dropped, and once the strong, rude hand of Broken Arrow jerked his nostrils above the surface by yanking heavily on the hair of his head.

Anger and resentment gave him warmth and strength enough to keep that position for a time longer, but the cold ache of pain seemed to be penetrating his body from the water, soaking deeper and deeper into his vitals. It was a sick pain. It made him close his eyes. And when he opened them, he swore that he had been half his life immersed in that water, struggling with death.

Sudden blackness rose before him. He thought that he was fainting, but it was merely the shadow under the opposite bank.

Then his trailing feet struck bottom.

They mounted the other side. He felt the body of the mare trembling with the effort she made; Broken Arrow supported him near by.

The thongs that held his wrists to the saddle were cut. His fingers were numb and would not respond to his efforts to work them. The whole of his arms, indeed, was numbed to the shoulder, and the shoulder joints seemed rusted, and out of place.

Like a limp rag he bent over the Cheyenne's arms, and the latter carried him lightly up into the shelter of the willows.

He was laid on the ground, and darkness swam quickly, mercifully over his eyes.

He was sure that he was dying. He tried to speak to Broken Arrow, to give him some last message, but his breath died in his throat. He hd a feeling that there was no more air in his lungs. And so, rapidly, unconsciousness came over him.

When he opened his eyes again, he was lying in exactly the same position. He could hear a light sound of dripping water, and saw that Broken Arrow, still faithfully with him, was wringing a thin buffalo robe dry. An end of it was tied around a small branch. The other end he held and twisted until the moisture gushed and dripped from the skin.

There was the dim, milky outline of the white mare. But beside her was a more dim and shadowy form of a second horse. He was amazed.

Astonishment gave him the force necessary to lift his head. Not one extra horse, but another, and another, and another! They had a little herd of five animals gathered about them. Had they been round up on the plain, these latter four? No, for a saddle was on the back of one.

Then he knew that he must have lain there senseless for a long time, while the Cheyenne wandered off to hunt down better means of transportation. He lay back, weakly, with a ridiculous desire to laugh again. Laugh at what?

At the strange destiny that stretched him here, too feeble, almost, to feel his own pain, but at the mercy of a red man, and more sure of the virtue of that Indian than ever he had been of the honesty of any man of his own race.

So he looked up, wondering why the stars no longer twinkled so brightly over his head, but gleamed with a pale and uncertain light.

The trees, too, seemed less misty, more green. And gradually he knew that he had lived through this night, and that the dawn was stealing across the sky.

There was a fluttering in his breast. He told himself that it was the last flame of life in him, wavering like the flame of a lamp that lacks oil and is about to flicker out.

CHAPTER XL

STILL the Cheyenne worked with a feverish haste. He had cut two long, limber poles, at least twenty feet in length, perhaps more, and these he tied to the saddles of two horses, so that they appeared between them as a pair of shafts. Across the space between the head of the rear horse and the tail of the leader, he tied on the buffalo robe, and when this was done, he laid Cashel upon this improvised litter and started north from the river over the open prairie land.

The pink of the dawn was about them. The horses trotted steadily forward, and the long poles, giving beneath the weight of Cashel, supplied him with an easy pair of springs, breaking every shock. His eyes closed, weighted down. He slept, no longer shuddering, but at ease, with hope to warm him and the promise of a bright day coming.

It was much later when he wakened. The sun was well up. When he lifted his head, he saw no sign of the river trees to the rear, but discovered that they had voyaged deep into the green plains and nothing lifted around him against the horizon except the low, dull crests of the waving ground in the near distance.

He looked straight up, and to the right. There was a shadow that broke the rays of the sun and kept him in the shade, and it was the silhouette of Broken Arrow, riding barebacked upon one of the ponies. He smiled down at his companion.

"All is well?" asked Cashel.

"All is well, brother."

At this assurance, Cashel fell asleep again.

The day grew hot. He wakened as they halted at a runlet of water, where the horses drank deep. Here Cashel was laid on the ground and the bandage removed. The wound was bathed with great care, and burning some sprigs and seeds of grass that he had gathered along the way, the Cheyenne applied a coating of their ashes to his friend's wound. Over this the bandage was drawn once more, but Cashel found infinitely greater ease than he had experienced before.

That place saw their first meal, supplied from the old pack of Cashel's saddle, but the hurt man could eat but little. In the afternoon, fever came to him, and made him drowsy and fretful. Besides, the pain recommenced at three or four in the afternoon, with the sun pouring down its fiercest strength. Broken Arrow's naked body and his horse were constantly interposed to make a shadow for Cashel, but now and again his horse slipped back or worked ahead and for an instant the sun glared down, casting a wave of heat like hot water over the invalid's body.

And Cashel, looking up with wonder at the red man, saw the fierce sunlight coruscating from his shoulders and burning around his head. Sometimes, when he fell into a half delirious sleep, he thought that Broken Arrow was on fire and would waken with the name of the warrior on his lips, and the reassuring voice of the brave in his ear.

The rest of that day was nightmare to him, and even the gentle motion of the litter became a wild torture against which he had to shut his teeth to keep from groaning. But when he wakened from a brief doze, he always could tell by the ache in his throat that he had been moaning heavily in his slumber.

He was glad when they made a dry camp for that evening.

He lay on the ground, with the blanket beneath him, his head slightly raised on the saddle pad, and felt the slow, irregular beating of his heart. But it no longer fluttered, and he was able to eat a little of the jerked venison.

"No more Pawnees?" said he.

"None under the sky, brother," said the brave.

He slept, and from his sleep wakening a dozen times, he found always that the Cheyenne sat cross-legged beside him, ever ready with a hand upon his and an undying patience in his voice of reassurance. Or, at most, Broken Arrow was leaning upon one elbow, yet never allowing weariness to creep into his manner or into his speaking tone.

And Cashel came at last to the morning, wonderfully refreshed.

He had an appetite that morning. His strength had returned in a great degree, as the hard, clean living in the open for such a length of time had put him in excellent condition to recuperate from a great shock, and the drain of the lost blood. Only, when he strove to move, he found that his muscles along the side were horribly stiff and each effort left him weak and sweating with pain.

They began the journey again. The litter received him like kindly arms, the pleasant, cool sky of the morning arched over their heads, and Cashel, forgetful of his pain—for it was as nothing compared with the first day—found himself smiling up toward the zenith.

He was so much more alert that he could note the manner in which the head of the Cheyenne was evermore turning toward the distant horizon, and gradually he realized that Broken Arrow was by no means sure that they were freed from danger. Always the pale circle of that horizon, like a blue belt of danger, surrounded them, retreating, following, now seeming to shrink smaller as they came to hilly country, and now sliding back again to its usual limitless dimensions. He could hear, near at hand, only the noise of the saddle leather creaking from the weight of the litter, and the whispering and rushing of the wind through the grass, as it ran in a bright wave that began at one horizon edge and galloped swiftly across to the other, like the flash of a great scythe sweeping the prairie.

Then, too, as he lay in the litter, half dreaming, he could hear from time to time the thin, small sound that floats always on the verge of the prairie sky, the wolves, the eagle screams, or the deep, dull vibration of a stampeding herd of buffalo, a vast distance off. They passed for half a day over the great roadway that one of those herds had left, the grass beaten into the ground so that dust puffed under the hoofs of the horses. Millions upon millions must have flowed like raging water across that soil.

Once the voice of the Cheyenne called his attention, and lifting his head a little, with his left hand behind it, he saw half a dozen buffalo wolves feeding on the dead that lay scattered behind the stampede. Above them hung the buzzards, and he thought, as he had once before, that life might disappear from the face of the plains, but death always is visible in the air or on the ground.

He suggested to Broken Arrow, that afternoon, that he might try to sit in a saddle, so they could make better speed, but the Cheyenne smiled and shook his head.

That day he asked how Broken Arrow had managed to get the four horses, and the Cheyenne told the story with his usual modesty.

"When we came to the far shore," said he, "I saw that my brother the Muskrat was very tired and sick. I knew that he could neither ride nor walk. I thought first of making a travois, and leading the horse, but this would be very slow travel, and besides, the travois makes such a trail that even a little child could follow it through the middle of the night.

"Then luckily I remembered the six men and the six horses that had swum across the stream beneath us. So I took the medicine mare, and I rode down the stream to the east for several leagues until I saw a horse come out of the trees and go down to the water to drink, and then come back, moving with trouble, because it was hobbled.

"I was very glad to see this horse, and therefore I slipped from the mare, tied her in the trees, and went forward to find out what I could. I came to a sound of voices. I found that there were four or five braves sitting in a circle under the stars. They had many horses behind them in the woods.

They had several saddled horses, and there were others, to serve as remounts.

"I crept so close that I could hear everything they were saying, and they were talking about the Muskrat, and saying that it was useless to follow him because he would be sure to melt away against the edge of the sky. For this was the second time that he had walked through a strong Pawnee camp, surrounded by hundreds of warriors. They said that the medicine of the Muskrat was so strong that he threw a magic dust into the air, and after that no man could use his eyes to see the Muskrat. So they would not ride any farther.

"But as for the white chief who swore that he had hurt the Muskrat with his rifle bullet, the chief was simply boasting, and of course he had not hurt the new Cheyenne at all, but merely the horse he had stolen. Now, beyond a doubt, the Muskrat was riding the wonderful white mare, and no bullets could touch him, and not even the red stallion, perhaps, could overtake him!

"I listened to this talk for a while, and then I stole back to where the horses were. It was hard to select them, but I tried to pick out the best. I got four of those horses, and one of them had a saddle on. I led them off as softly as I could to the place where the white mare was waiting. As I was going along, I heard them begin to shout and yell behind me, so that I knew they had found that some of their horses were stolen. However, I knew that if I went fast they would hear the horses running, and know what direction I had gone in. I untied the white mare and led all five along quietly. After a while, I heard a rush of gallopers coming after me. I thought that they would run right on top of me and my horses, and I was about to jump on the back of the white mare and go off with her.

"However, they did not see me, though I could see their heads bobbing between the tree trunks and against the stars. I was closer to the ground, and therefore they did not see me. I kept pulling at the leads a little so as to keep the horses busy and not give them a chance to think about their friends and whinny and call to them through the darkness.

"In this way, I let the hunting wolves go by me. After that, I kept on walking, and went up the stream until I came to the place where I had left you. You woke up while I was making the litter, and therefore you know everything else that has happened."

This story was told so simply that Cashel for a moment almost missed the danger point—the rush of the Pawnee horses behind the single warrior, and the sublime nerve with which he had kept on walking and failed to bolt in order to save himself.

It was a simple thing that he had done, but only by simplicity of action had it been made possible. And only through that action had it been made possible for Cashel to travel at such a good rate across the plains for two whole days!

He made no comment for a long time on this story. But at last he said:

"I suppose that the Sky People had their hand in that, Broken Arrow?"

The Cheyenne looked him full in the face with the gentlest of smiles.

"They love my brother the Muskrat," said he, "and therefore they would not let his friend Broken Arrow die in the Pawnee camp, nor on the riverbank under the Pawnee knives."

CHAPTER XLI

FOUR more days they journeyed across the plains, and during all of that time the buzzards in the air and the wolves they had seen feeding on the buffalo carcasses were the only living things that broke the round horizon of danger that traveled with them.

In the evening of that day, they saw the mist of smoke rising against the yellow of the afternoon sunlight, and then the winding of the little river through the plain.

Here Broken Arrow made a halt, and asked Cashel if he could ride. The latter felt strong enough. Only when he tried his legs, he grew dizzy and staggered so that the white mare came and nuzzled him, curiously. He was as uncertain on his feet as a newborn colt, and Broken Arrow smiled like a father, watching him.

"You cannot walk very well," said he, "but you can ride. See the white mare. She will go with you as gently as running water. She loves you, and she will step as though the ground were the breaking surface of a marsh. Try her back, my friend!"

He arranged the saddle on her back while Cashel sat on the ground, wondering at the feebleness of his knees. And a vague excitement grew up in him. They were about to enter the village, and he guessed the fine purpose of Broken Arrow. If he returned with Cashel lying stretched in the litter, it would be almost as though *he*, Broken Arrow, were the deliverer, and Cashel the delivered. He wished to have the white man on horseback. Then his weakness from the wound would make his feat all the more commendable.

He found himself saying, "It is not fair to you, Broken Arrow. And if I pretend that I can ride a horse, I am saying the thing which is not so. . . ."

As that Indian phrase for the word "lie," which does not exist in any Plains dialect, came on his lips, Cashel stopped speaking, abruptly. He was stopped by his own wonder at himself and the words that he was using.

In the old days—surely it had been in another world—he would never have hesitated. The greater the sham and the greater the show, the more contented he would have been. The more others were deceived by him the greater his personal triumph.

That was not his feeling now. The old life lay far away from him, and all of the ideas that he had gained from it.

"Perhaps," said Broken Arrow seriously, "this is not altogether the thing which is so, but also remember that there is another thing the Cheyennes cannot see, and that is how Broken Arrow sat in the Pawnee lodge with his hands bound and his feet bound, and enemy before him, and all the Pawnee braves between him and freedom. They cannot see the Muskrat coming without fear into that lodge. They cannot see him strike down one enemy, and set me free, and shoot down another Pawnee brave at the door of the lodge. But at least let them see the Muskrat bringing me safely home to my people! Otherwise *I* shall be pretending the thing which is not so, and they will think that I have done everything, and saved my friend, besides!"

Cashel allowed himself to be persuaded, and yet still with a small, guilty feeling in his heart that baffled him.

He allowed himself to be lifted into the saddle, and took the guiding rein of the white mare into his hand. Then they set forward, with the warrior in the saddle on another horse, and the three remounts led behind him.

They went slowly onward, until they came to the verge of the stream. The swimming pool was deserted. There was only an old woman, filling a deer paunch with water at the edge of the river on the farther side.

As they came out on the bank, with the Cheyenne village spread before them on the farther side, Cashel saw his companion lift both muscular arms to the sky, and heard him say:

"You spirits who see me, if my hands are not clean and if my heart is not clean, take away from Broken Arrow his return to his people. If my hands are clean and my heart is clean, let no warrior among my people envy me because you have sent a strong friend to take me out of danger and give me back to life!"

This ended, he rode down the bank, keeping closely beside the white man, lest Cashel should slip from the saddle—for

178

there was no power in the legs of the Muskrat to grip the sides of the white mare.

She went, however, fully as daintily as Broken Arrow had prophesied, and entering the water, she made step by step with the greatest care, until they came out into the shallows of the farther side. They were near the old woman, as she finished filling the water bag and raised it.

"Mother," said Broken Arrow, "is all well with our people?"

She uttered a frightened cry, and turning toward them shaded her filmed and ancient eyes from the sun, staring, but not making them out more than forms of mist.

"Who are you?" said she. "Have you dared to leave the town while Young Thunder forbade it? Do you dare to come back to it now? The dog-soldiers will beat you until you cannot move for days, and the medicine man will make you dance in the next medicine dance in spite of your stiff legs!"

"Is there to be another dance?" asked Broken Arrow curiously, who had heard of this from Cashel.

"The first one was not enough. There is only one more day before the moon changes. And therefore of course the braves must dance at once."

"What spoiled the first dance?" asked Broken Arrow.

"The Muskrat ran away from us and went out into the prairie," said she. "Who are you, if you are friends, that you don't know that the Muskrat left us and went away, and therefore he undid all the work of the first dance? He defied the curse of Young Thunder, the fool!"

"I am Broken Arrow," said the warrior, "and this is the Muskrat, who took me away from the middle of the Pawnees. He struck them down, and cut the cords that tied me, and killed and slaughtered the Pawnees, and cut a way through them, and made me free. His medicine is stronger than that of Young Thunder, as you see. Young Thunder is only a fool!"

It seemed doubtful if the old creature heard the last part of this speech. She had only vaguely grasped the first part of it, but at least the name stuck in her ears and gradually conveyed some meaning to her feeble wits.

"Broken Arrow! Broken Arrow!" she screamed now. "Broken Arrow is now being burned by the Pawnees. They are tearing him to pieces. Broken Arrow . . ."

She came toward them with a hand extended, as though she were feeling her way through the night, but when she had almost run against the head of the Indian pony, and actually saw through the dark of her eyes the fine face of the warrior, then a wild cry of joy came shrilling up from her lips, and dropping the water paunch, so that its contents spilled unheeded down the bank and back into the stream, she turned her back and ran with an amazing lightness and speed up the slope toward the village.

Broken Arrow looked after her with a smile.

"Is she your grandmother?" asked Cashel, amazed.

"No, no. She is one of the oldest women in the tribe, and one of the best, and one of the most foolish. She has mourned for a dead husband, and for three dead sons. But you see that she still is glad when a Cheyenne man returns to his people. I am glad that we found her!"

Cashel looked after her, bewildered. It was as though a vision from heaven had opened before the eyes of the old creature, and still she ran forward, shrilling out her good tidings. She reached the edge of the village, and they could see a pool of children gather suddenly around her.

Even Broken Arrow, it appeared, was not so modest that he could not enjoy a fine entrance into the village.

"This will be a black day for Young Thunder," said he. "This will be a day when he will wish that I had burned at the stake, and that you had been cut to pieces by the Pawnee squaws. Hai! Now his medicine is weak! He forbade all men to leave the village. He prophesied, and his prophecies are now proved worth nothing! He thought that he would be the head man of the tribe, and now he is going to be no more worth while than a barking dog!"

This was more venom than Cashel ever had heard the brave express before.

He could not help asking why the warrior hated the medicine man.

"Why should there be medicine men?" asked Broken Arrow simply. "Our heads are as close to the sky as the heads of the medicine men. Tell me, does the Muskrat ever make medicine?"

"No," said Cashel.

"Yet he rides out and conquers wherever he goes."

"And is hurt, and lies on his back like a weak woman for many days, and his friend Broken Arrow has to risk his life to get many horses and carry the woman home to the Cheyennes!"

Broken Arrow seized upon one word of that reply, only:

"True!" said he. "This is your home. May it always be so, my friend. And yet I am afraid. Blood draws to blood, and the white skin attracts the white skin. Will it be long before the eye of the Muskrat looks east where his people live?"

Then a great emotion of joy poured up into the breast of Cashel and made him throw out both his arms.

"Your people are my people, Broken Arrow," said he, with his hands held out toward the village. "Your ways are my ways. My hands and my heart were unclean when I came to you. I think that they are cleaner now. I shall live here. Always I . . ."

"Hush!" said the Cheyenne. "What a man promises to himself should be promised in secret. And I know that the thing that we wish to run away from is always the thing to which we have tied ourself with a vow!"

The wisdom of this remark could not but strike Cashel. Then they rode up the slope side by side and entered the village.

They did not get into it easily.

Before them, from among the lodges, they heard a great cry begin, rising rapidly toward a roar, and then a wave of people were seen in the gap between the tepees, with Young Thunder standing before them, holding out a wand in one hand and a war lance in the other.

No doubt he saw in the return of Broken Arrow and the successful exploit of the Muskrat the end of his brief regime as a man of great medicine and mystery, a man who read the future like the past.

So he tried, shouting shrill and small, to stem the tide, but it only swayed before him for an instant. Then, seeing the favorite warrior of the tribe returning, and his white-skinned deliverer beside him, hysterical joy overcame the crowd, and they rushed past Young Thunder in a single wave. He was upset. He sprawled on the ground, and stamping feet went cruelly over that old man as the Cheyennes poured out to greet their hero.

CHAPTER XLII

ANOTHER man of importance had ridden into the village on this morning. It was Captain Fitzroy Melville, bringing with him a long train of ponies, on the backs of several of which were imposing packs. He carried with him trinkets and toys of many kinds, and robes, rifles, ammunition, besides those twenty good ponies.

In addition to the regular string of ponies, he had one half-breed mare, which was apparently a cross between good Kentucky stock and the best type of the plains animal. He intended to use this animal when he rode away from the camp. For the red stallion, the famous Clonmel, was to remain behind him in the camp of the Cheyennes.

He could take the loss of the great horse with a good deal of equanimity, for he had learned, on the prairies and among the Indians, to regard a horse as a mere means of casual transportation. It was true that on the day of battle a swift horse might be a huge advantage— but chiefly if one wished to run away, and that was a course which the captain did not expect to follow very often. Otherwise, the fastest horse in the world did not make much difference for traveling across the plains. It was better to have half a dozen or more stout ponies, hand-picked. These would keep you galloping from dawn to dark, live on thistles and cactus if necessary, drink every other day, and wind up a ten-day journey in almost as good flesh as when they started. Or else, run down until they were simply skin and bones, they still could be made to gallop until they died, falling by the way to offer mean picking even to a buzzard. They were dirt-cheap. And the captain was rich in the sort of goods that cost little at home and sell high to Indians. He was reasonably willing, therefore, to part from the stallion. He had intended to use the famous horse, in the first place, for a breeding farm in the far west, but since he had given up that plan, what purpose would be served by diffusing that precious blood loosely through a whole herd of runty Indian ponies?

To be a great chief was not the captain's ambition. His lodge was built among the Pawnees. He wanted a wife to take her place in it. And the white skin and the beauty of Chapa had filled his eyes.

When he came into the camp of the Cheyennes, he was greeted, as usual, by a silent train of admirers and of those who whole-heartedly hated him for what he had already accomplished against the Cheyennes. However, since he came on a friendly errand, and since he was willing to leave such a great train of wealth behind him for the sake of a single squaw, the warriors and the women hardly knew whether to hate him most or deride him most.

He heard one old woman say:

"A high price makes a lazy wife!" And he understood enough of the language to catch her meaning.

But he only smiled at this, and went on until he reached the tepee of old Rain-by-Night.

The latter came out with a robe hunched about his narrow, skinny shoulders and could hardly forbear rubbing his hands with delight when he saw what was to him the wealth of Croesus standing before him. Chapa came out behind him, but when she saw who had come, she turned hastily on her heel and, drawing the robe over her head, re-entered the tent.

There was a ready interpreter standing by, and through him the captain asked what was wrong with the girl, that she had not spoken when she saw her spouse-to-be.

"A woman," said the old warrior, "is like a bird turning in the air and never able to decide to which hilltop it wishes to fly. She wanted to be the wife of the great white chief of the Pawnees. But then the Muskrat rode out from the Cheyennes, and broke the will of Young Thunder, and crossed his medicine, and is causing another long dance to be held to purify the people, and my daughter is so pleased by all this that now she wishes she were to marry the Muskrat and not the great Pawnee chief!"

He laughed as he spoke, showing two yellow fangs in front, giving him a half-witted expression when his mouth was open.

"When did she make up her mind to that?" asked the captain darkly.

"As soon as the squaw of Long Bull told her a great lie— that the Muskrat was going to try to take Broken Arrow away from the Pawnees. But she believed that!"

The captain winced a little when he heard this.

He knew very well that Cashel had accomplished the impossible task on which he had set out; for that very reason he had ridden posthaste across the prairies to close his bargain with Rain-by-Night before the new white hero of the Cheyennes returned to the village.

"Here," said her, "are all the things that I promised, and a little more, for a good measure. Let me have the girl, Rain-by-Night, and I shall start away at once, because I see that it doesn't please the young men of the Cheyennes to have me in their camp."

Rain-by-Night nodded.

"You still want my daughter?" said he.

"Yes," said the captain.

"Well, an unwilling wife makes a cold lodge. But let me look at what you have brought. That brown pony, there, is broken down in the knees! And this gray one has sore shoulders. See how he stands! Have you brought me the weeds and the cast-outs of the Pawnee horse herd, my son?"

There was not a thing wrong with either of the ponies which the captain had brought, and he pointed out this fact, offering to ride either of the horses up and down in front of Rain-by-Night and replace them with others at the will of the old tyrant. But Rain-by-Night was proceeding carefully through the entire group, mumbling and grumbling for the good reason that if he did not talk, he would have had to allow his pleasure to shine out from his face. As it was, he was able to make a hostile remark about every one of the animals which had been brought to him.

"You have cheated an old man!" he said at last to the captain.

"Look through the rest of the goods, however," said Melville, who guessed that the other was carping more by force of nature and habit than because he really found anything wrong in the outfit.

So the packs were opened, and the guns and the ammunition counted out, and the knives, the hatchets, and the blankets produced. But still Rain-by-Night managed to keep a sour face, though his heart was fluttering with delight.

It was not until he undid one bundle and found in it a flaring piece of calico that he was overcome with pleasure. It was a cheap print of red, yellow, and blue, in the most glaring possible combination, but the brightness of it so filled the fondest wishes of Rain-by-Night that he could not help crying out.

That let loose the flood of his content. He went grinning through the herd of horses, running his fingers down the fine, lean muscles, and then came back and patted the weapons and the lodge utensils. He was made, at a stroke, the richest man in that tribe, and he swelled with the burning importance of his new dignity.

"I shall bring her," said he. "If you were even the renegade Walking Dove, I would sell her to you for such a price as this! This is the value of twenty wives! May you find them all in Chapa!!"

He laughed scornfully as he said this, and was turning toward the tepee when the first great shout burst upward on the rim of the town. The jubilant outcry rose and rang through the air.

"Hurry!" said the captain, suddenly struck with chilly fear, as he guessed what this might be.

"Some great thing has happened," said Rain-by-Night, "and it must be that a warrior has returned. Only two went forth. Perhaps they have done some great deed? But what could be as great as to bring home the two white mares? What except the bringing of Broken Arrow himself?"

"Come, come," said the captain. "We have finished our bargain. Chapa is mine. Bring her out to me, father!"

The old warrior looked with his broken-toothed grin at the white man, glad to torment him by even this small delay.

"Why should we hurry?" said he. "You have enough glory among the Pawnees. Let my daughter stay here to see the last fine sight she will see while she is still a Cheyenne! Chapa! Chapa!"

He called, and the girl came slowly from the tent, looking toward Rain-by-Night steadily, but with her eyes very wide, so that the captain knew that she was vividly aware of him, but dared not turn her head in his direction. It hurt him. And yet he thought her all the more desirable in her reticence.

In the meantime, the wave of noise had grown like thunder with continual shouting.

A dust cloud pitched up above the tops of the lodges.

A host of dogs, half-mad with the excitement of their masters, came leaping, tumbling, snarling, fighting, racing through the camp, as heralds of the procession, and forerunners of the triumph. And behind these came hurrying children, still with their heads turned over their shoulders so that they would miss nothing of the show, and yet lead it on its way.

There was such a confused mass of loud shouting that it would have been hard for anyone to make out what was being said, but presently, the captain saw the girl run to Rain-by-Night, and catch his withered shoulders, and shake them as she cried up in his face.

Rain-by-Night started to become violent. His mouth opened like the mouth of a child. He looked more a half-wit than ever before.

And then the forefront of the women came milling among the lodges, whooping, screeching, gone mad.

After them appeared the warriors.

But where was the dignity of the lofty Cheyennes? These fellows yelled, tossed their arms, beat one another with fists, broke off into individual war dances of exultation on the outskirts of the crowd, brandished their lances, their deadly knives, their rifles and pistols, and terrible, narrow tomahawks.

Still, they preserved one inviolable circle in the center of their milling crowd. This open space was dim with a blowing fog of dust that rose continually, but through it the captain was able to make out that two mounted men were riding within the kernel of the crowd.

They were the focal point of all this wild enthusiasm, and he could guess who they were.

He gripped the shoulder of Rain-by-Night, and pointed toward the girl, but Rain-by-Night rolled his head toward the white man and showed a blank face in which there were only glimmerings of the commencement of hysterical excitement.

Nearer came that pandemonium.

It was literally impossible for mere thoughts to form in the mind, in the presence of that hideous din, but now the captain could look through the mist and there he saw first the gleaming form of a tall Cheyenne warrior with fine, strong features. Unforgettable features were there. And he recognized with a sinking heart the face of Broken Arrow.

All that he could have wished undone had been accomplished.

But as the Cheyennes danced and raged and went fairly

mad before Broken Arrow and his companion, it seemed to the captain that it was not the famous warrior who made them rejoice the most, but his companion—that much smaller man, lost in the dust cloud, that rather bent, frail form on the back of the shining white horse. Ay, a white face, and the man was the thief, Cashel, looking thin, and strangely grave, and waving his empty hand at the Cheyennes from time to time.

They were leading him toward his lodging with this triumph, and the man he had delivered from the Pawnees was a mere decoration in the central picture!

Broken Arrow had returned.

The captain grasped the shoulder of Rain-by-Night again and shouted in his ear. But the old man pointed toward the train of horses, and even toward Melville's stallion, with words that the captain could not understand, but with gestures that plainly meant that he refused the price. And then, pointing toward Broken Arrow, it seemed as though he asked if a train of horseflesh, no matter how fine, could be compared in value with such a gift as Cashel now made not to Rain-by-Night, but to the entire Cheyenne tribe!

It amazed the captain. He could not believe what he saw and heard. For he knew Rain-by-Night was an accomplished miser, and yet now the old man was swept off his feet by hysterical patriotism!

Yes, he had actually plunged forward into the crowd, and his daughter with him.

Their hands were thrown upward, as if in an all-hail to the conqueror. They, too, had lifted faces, and their lips were strained apart in the wild welcome to the outcast of the city, the outcast of the caravan, the sneak, the thief, the lawbreaker of the whites, now grown into a new self. For in the gravity and the modesty of that face the captain was aware of the birth of a new soul and thereby, as in a shadow, guessed at the corruption of his own!

CHAPTER XLIII

THROUGH that vast turmoil, Cashel went forward in the midst of a dream, dizzy, sick, and weak, but still seeing and hearing everything. He had seen Jim Diver leaping and flinging his long arms like any other half-mad Indian above his head. He had seen Jim's squaw laughing and reeling drunkenly in the completion of her joy—she who had inspired all of the boy's deeds.

186

He had turned to her and stretched out his hand. He had seen that mere gesture, that mute acknowledgment, bring the tears of joy running down her face.

And he had seen the great chiefs and the warriors swaying and pitching about him.

Behold! Two Antelope in person strode through the mob, and with his own hand grasped the lead rope, and with his own hand led the sacred white mare forward through the press, causing them to fall back slowly as he advanced.

"I have been a thief!" said the boy to his own heart. "But *this* I have not stolen, thank God! And after this, what is there worth stealing in the world."

Sometimes he looked toward Broken Arrow, smiling, because he loved the man, and the sight of him gave the boy strength. But always Broken Arrow was gesturing and waving toward his deliverer, as though calling the attention of the warriors again and yet again to the greatness of the deed that Cashel had done. Within the horizon of danger there was one burning moment of glory, and that moment he now tasted!

Through the dust, through the crowd, he saw a tall man break on a tall horse. He was aware of the fine head of Clonmel, and the stern face of the handsome captain.

Close beside him Melville reined his horse.

"Cashel," he seemed to say, "there's one more thing left for you to win. Come out on the prairie, near the river, this evening. I'll be there as the sun sets. Come out, and I'll finish the account with you!"

So, in the crimson and golden moment of the day, as the sun sank, Cashel walked from the village without the Colt's rifle under his arm, but a simple, heavy, old-fashioned rifle such as the mountain men had used long before. He could not carry the stolen gun to use against its owner. He wished that he could wash the guilt of that theft from his hands and from his mind.

It had been hard to rally his strength for the effort.

But first he had lain in the lodge of Jim Diver, his eyes closed, never speaking, while the squaw dressed the wound in his side, and applied wonderfully soothing dressings that drew out the inflammation, and let the knot in the middle of his forehead relax, at last. Then she applied a new bandage that gripped the lips of the wound more softly, and yet firmly enough. Men were fools, she declared, in the care of a wound. What did Broken Arrow know? He was a man in the giving of wounds, but a child in his care of them! Jim Diver himself sat by, smoking, grinning, speaking little because he knew that the effort of speech was too much, just then for the youngster.

And he said, merely, "I thought that I was takin' in a fellow to talk to and to listen to. I didn't know I was takin' in another one like Broken Arrow, hot as lightnin', by the Lord Harry. Lay quiet, son, and rest. Lucky'll fix you fine!"

So he rested through long, precious moments. But when he said he was walking out from the lodge, they neither argued nor resisted. They did not even comment when he took up Diver's best old-fashioned rifle, where it hung loaded on the rack.

He was a man, now, and his own master.

And now he had slipped quietly from the village. Inside, they still made high festival. The wood for the fire was heaped around the central space. The warriors were tuning up their throats for the great war dance by shouting wildly their favorite chants. The old men were freshening the memory of their greatest deeds. For Broken Arrow had consented, at last, to share in the dance! For the first time he would boast. And Cashel knew why; it was because Broken Arrow there in the firelighted circle would proclaim the deeds of his friend, the Muskrat! He would tell the story of that deliverance, making his own deeds small, and the glory of Cashel all the greater.

And so Cashel was able to walk through a section of the camp swept clean of even the old people and the dogs. He walked onto the prairie, and crossing the first swale, slowly, he finally saw before him the proud form of Clonmel, glimmering in the rich light of the end of the day. Clonmel, but no man near him? Perhaps the captain stood on the other side of the stallion?

He came within a hundred feet. But certainly the captain was not there. And suddenly Cashel realized that if this battle was to take place, Melville meant no ordinary duel, but an Indian fight. He would strike from behind, if he could!

It made Cashel's brain spin. He was prepared to stand on mark and fire at an agreed signal, as white men should.

But now he turned and snatched up the heavy rifle butt to his shoulder.

He saw the captain then.

Evidently Fitzroy Melville's last shred of honor had gone. He had lain flat in a bit of grass taller than usual, and now as the enemy went past him, he raised upon one knee and was drawing a sure bead!

Cashel should have leaped to the side.

He could not! His weakness was so great that he staggered as he turned, and that stagger saved his life; for as the rifle of the captain clanged, the boy heard the bullet whistle thin past his face.

He raised his own weapon, but he realized his terrible weakness now. The muzzle of it wavered terribly. He could not train it on a mark.

And he was so close that he could hear the hammer of the repeating Colt's rifle click on the next cartridge!

Yet there was no explosion.

Still with the gun butt at his shoulder, still with the muzzle wavering wildly, in his weak hands, he saw the captain struggle fiercely with his weapon.

Then Melville, hurling the jammed and useless gun from him, pitched to his feet and raced across the prairie with a wild cry that rang back like the cry of a loon. He dodged from side to side, and leaped high, now and again, in his running, to unsteady the aim of his enemy.

A rise of the prairie ground shut him from view.

Cashel was alone, and the rifle unfired, and Clonmel coming to whistle at a trot, with happily pricking ears.

He could not drag himself up to the saddle. But with one arm thrown around the neck of Clonmel, leaning heavily on it, he walked slowly back to the Cheyenne camp and to Jim Diver's lodge.

His senses did not leave him. There was only a dimness through which he heard the squaw scolding him in a barking, harsh voice as he was stretched on a bed. Men would never have done fighting! Never cease endangering themselves! All the glory in the world was not enough for any one of them!

But Chapa? he said to himself. And he wondered, for the squaw was a prophet.

He did not need to wonder long.

Before the wild chant of the scalp dance began, a voice sounded at the entrance to the lodge. He saw a shadowy form enter, and the grim voice of Rain-by-Night was speaking in the lodge.

"I have brought a thing that I never was able to sell at my price," said Rain-by-Night. "Now I see that the best thing I can do with it is to give it away. Take this young fool, and give it to the Muskrat, if he cares to have it."

Rain-by-Night departed, and Cashel heard the laughter of the squaw, low-pitched, and strangely softened. "Oh, my son!" said she. "I have told you!"

She left the lodge. But still there was another person within, standing by the flap of the entrance, still as a shadow, never stirring, waiting, waiting.

And Cashel, understanding, gathered his strength to raise his head and look toward her. But first he looked upward, letting his thoughts drift with the rising smoke, through the vent, and toward the Sky People who live in eternal blue peace forever.